Ghost Child

Caroline Overington is the author of two non-fiction books, *Only in New York* and *Kickback*, which won the Blake Dawson Prize for Business Literature. She has twice won a Walkley Award for Investigative Journalism, and has also won the Sir Keith Murdoch Award for Journalistic Excellence.

She lives in Bondi with her husband and their young twins. www.carolineoverington.com

Also by Caroline Overington

I Came to Say Goodbye

Ghost Child

Caroline Overington

arrow books

Published by Arrow Books, 2014

2 4 6 8 10 9 7 5 3 1

Arrow Books
The Random House Group Limited
20 Vauxhall Bridge Road, London, SW1V 2SA

www.randomhousebooks.co.uk

Addresses for companies within The Random House Group Limited can
be found at: www.randomhouse.co.uk/offices.htm

The Random House Group Limited Reg. No. 954009

A CIP catalogue record for this book
is available from the British Library

ISBN 9780099584759

The Ra~~~~~ ~~~~~ ~~~~~ Limited ~~~~~~'s the Forest St~~ ~rdship
Council®~~~~~~ ~nisation.
Our bo~~~~~~ paper.
FSC is~~~~~~ ~ading

Print~~~~~~4YY

For Katie

I see you in the sky above
In the tall grass
In the ones I love
Bob Dylan

Dear Reader,

Thank you for picking up this book.

I'm hoping that once you start reading it, you won't be able to put it down.

You may already know that I'm a journalist and an author, based in Bondi, Australia.

You might also know that my books are based on real events. I change people's names and move things around a bit, so I don't get into trouble, but the stories themselves are true.

This book, *Ghost Child*, is a good example: it's based on one of the real-life stories I had to cover as a reporter in Sydney.

The events, and some of the characters, may shock you, but then, maybe not. We have the same crimes here that you have in Britain: children disappear, and there's always a range of different suspects. The police don't always know what happened, and some crimes go unsolved for years.

I'm not sure that we ever did find out the truth about what happened in this case. People still talk about it and wonder if justice was done.

I've put down what I think happened. Maybe you won't agree, but that's okay. A good book should get a good conversation going. I hope you enjoy the story – and that it gets you thinking.

Yours,
Caroline Overington

Prologue

On 11 November 1982, Victorian police were called to a home on the Barrett housing estate, an hour west of Melbourne. In the lounge room of an otherwise ordinary brick-veneer home, they found a five-year-old boy lying still and silent on the carpet. His arms were by his sides, his palms flat.

There were no obvious signs of trauma. The boy was neither bruised nor bleeding, but when paramedics turned him gently onto his side they found an almost imperceptible indentation in his skull, as broad as a man's hand and as shallow as a soap dish.

The boy's mother told police her son had been walking through the schoolyard with one of his younger brothers when they were approached by a man who wanted the change in their pockets. The brothers refused to hand over the money so the man knocked the older boy to the ground and began to kick and punch him.

The younger boy ran home to raise the alarm. Their mother carried the injured boy home in her arms. She called an ambulance, but nothing could be done.

The story made the front page of *The Sun* newspaper in Melbourne and the TV news.

Police made a public appeal for witnesses but, in truth, nobody really believed the mother's version of events. The Barrett Estate was poor but no one was bashing children for loose change – not then. Ultimately, the mother and her boyfriend were called in for questioning. Police believed that one of them – possibly both – was involved in the boy's death.

There was a great deal of interest in the case, but when it finally came to court, the Chief Justice closed the hearing. The verdict would be released; so, too, would any sentence that was handed down. But the events leading up to the little boy's death would remain a mystery.

Few people were surprised to hear that the boy's mother and her boyfriend went to prison for the crime. Police declared themselves satisfied with the result, saying there was no doubt justice had been done. And yet for years rumours swept the Barrett Estate, passing from neighbour to neighbour and clinging like cobwebs to the long-vacant house: there had been a cover-up. The real perpetrator, at least according to local gossip, was the boy's six-year-old sister, Lauren.

PART ONE

PART ONE

Lauren Cameron

When a young woman lives by herself, it's assumed she must be lonely. I'd say the opposite is true. In fact, if anybody had asked me what it was like when I first started living on my own, I would have said, 'It was perfect.' I was completely alone – I had no close friends, and nobody I called family – and that was precisely what I wanted.

The place I moved into was basically a shed, and it was built on a battle-axe block behind somebody else's house. The property itself was on Sydney's northern beaches. There was a family living in the main house, the one that fronted the beach. They owned the block and, like many Sydneysiders who had beachside property in the 1980s, they decided to make the most of it by carving a driveway down the side, building a granny flat out the back and renting it to me.

After the first meeting, when they gave me the keys and we talked about the rent, I had nothing whatsoever to do with them. They were a family – a mum, a dad and two teenage kids – living in the main house, and I was the boarder. I could get to my place without bothering them. I just walked down the driveway, opened my door and I was home. I had my own toilet, shower and enough of a kitchen, so there was no reason to go knocking.

Before I moved in, I bought four things. The most expensive was a queen-size sheet set in a leopard-skin print, with two pillowcases. I bought a box of black crockery, with dinner plates shaped like hexagons. I had this idea, then, that I might one day have close friends who could come over for dinner. I also bought a new steam iron and ironing-board, these last things because it was a condition of my employment that my uniform be straight and clean.

I still remember the first morning I woke in my own place. I was seventeen years old. I padded into the kitchen in my moccasins, put the kettle on the stove top, and pressed the red button to make the flame ignite. I took the plastic cover off the new ironing-board and scrunched it into a ball. I was fiddling underneath the board, trying to find the lever that makes the legs stick out, when the kettle began to whistle itself into hysterics. I put the ironing-board down and took a cup from the crockery set, removing some of the cardboard that had been packed around it, and made a cup of tea – hot and sugary, with the bag taken out, not left in – and I thought to myself, 'This is just like playing house! I'm okay here. Things are going to be fine.'

When the family told the neighbours they'd rented out the granny flat, they probably wanted to know whether I was going to cause trouble – whether I was going to bring boys home and make a racket. But the answer was no, I was not. I amused myself in the granny flat by learning new and humble domestic tasks: sweeping the floor with a straw broom; bending to collect the mess in a dustpan and brush; buying garbage bags with two handles that tied at the top. My idea of a good

night was to eat Tim Tams in bed and to smoke cigarettes on the porch, although only after I saw the lights
in the main house go out.

The owners would have said, 'Oh, she's the perfect
tenant, like a mouse, so quiet, you never even know
she's there.'

From time to time, I'd bump into the mum – not
my mum, but the mum who lived in the main house.
I'd be heading out to work and she'd be on the nature
strip, getting shopping bags out of the boot of her car
or something, and she'd smile at me – probably because
everybody approves of hospital staff – and I'd smile
back at her.

I didn't see much of the dad. Perhaps he'd decided
that there was nothing to be gained from getting too
close to the girl who lived in his shed. I had nothing
much to do with the children, either. I was closer in age
to them than to their parents, but really, what did we
have in common? They came out from time to time, to
jump on the trampoline and to sit under the pirate flag
in the old tree house, but we rarely spoke.

I'd taken a job as a nurse's aide in a city hospital, and
I'm sure my co-workers at first understood why I lived
alone. I was new to Sydney so it made sense, at least in
the beginning, that I wouldn't have many friends. After
I'd settled, though, they must have wondered why I continued to live in a granny flat when I could easily have
shared a city apartment with one of the other aides.

The noticeboard at work often had handwritten signs tacked up, advertising rooms for rent. 'Outgoing girl wanted to share FUN FLAT!' one of the ads said. The truth is, the things the other girls wanted to do – going to nightclubs, drinking Fluffy Ducks and Orgasms and Harvey Wallbangers – didn't sound like fun to me.

Of course, I wasn't famous then, far from it. I was just the quiet girl, the churchy girl that lived alone, prayed in the hospital chapel, and never socialised. I'm sure they all got a shock when photographs of me started appearing in newspapers, just as I'm sure the family I boarded with got a shock when journalists swarmed the granny flat, waving microphones on sticks.

I got a bit of a shock myself. I took refuge in my bed, hiding under the leopard-skin sheets, trying to fight the urge to *run*. Because, really, run where? There was nowhere to go.

I don't know how long I would have stayed under the covers if Harley hadn't turned up. He walked down the side drive, past the windows of the main house. I heard the mum rap on the glass. 'Hey, you,' she said. 'Off our property!'

Harley said, 'I'm not with the media. I'm Harley Cashman. Lauren's my sister.'

She would have been startled. For one thing, the mum knew me not as Lauren Cashman but as Lauren *Cameron*, which was the name I'd given her when I moved in. She didn't know I had a brother, either. I'd told them what I used to tell everyone: 'I have no family.'

Harley knocked at my door and when I didn't answer, I heard him push it open. I didn't stir but I could feel warm sunshine pour across my bed.

Harley said, 'Mate, what *are* you doing? Everyone's looking for you.'

I didn't respond so he pulled back the doona and said, 'Lauren, seriously, this is ridiculous. Get up.'

I felt so frightened and overwhelmed that I wasn't sure that I could. I said to Harley, 'I can't.'

He said, 'Sure you can.'

We went on like that for a while, him saying, 'Come on, Lauren,' and me saying, 'Just go away, Harley,' until he said, 'Okay, look, I'm not going to hang around here forever. If you want me gone, I'm gone.'

It was then that I realised I didn't want him to go, not without me, not ever again. I rose from the bed, untangling myself from the sheets, and said, 'Okay, all right.'

'That's right,' he said. 'Get up, and let's get you out of here.'

I was wearing only a T-shirt and a pair of knickers.

'You're going to need to get dressed,' he said, and started picking up some clothes I'd flung onto the floor. Compared with him – with anyone – I was tiny. He held up a pair of my pants and said, 'How do you even get one leg in here?'

I snatched them away and went into the bathroom

to dress myself.

'Good on you,' he said when I emerged. 'Now, let's go.'

He ushered me to the door and we left the granny flat together, me with a jumper over my head in case there was a photographer still lurking, trying to get a picture. He'd parked his car on the nature strip. I couldn't see anything because the jumper was over my face so he guided me into the passenger seat. It was only once we'd started moving, once I was sure we were clear of the suburban streets and onto a freeway, that I took the jumper off, and said, 'Where are we going?'

Harley said, 'I've decided that you should meet the folks.'

I said, '*Whose* folks?'

He said, 'Mum is gonna love you.'

I thought, '*Your* mum. Not mine.'

I rolled the jumper into a ball and put it on the floor near my feet. I said, 'She doesn't even *know* me, Harley.'

He said, 'Mate, you're my *sister*. What more is there to know?'

I didn't answer. What more was there to know? What do any of us know? We think we know the basic facts about our lives: those are my parents and these are my siblings and this is my story, at least as I've come to tell it. But, really, how much of it is true?

Detective Senior Sergeant Brian Muggeridge

When I first met Lauren Cameron her name was not Lauren Cameron, it was Lauren Cashman. I don't know when she changed it, although I've got a pretty good idea why.

Lauren likes to tell people that she has no parents and no siblings. It isn't true. When I first met her she had a mother, a sister, and not one but two brothers, and all of them were called Cashman.

I met them on the evening of 11 November 1982. I remember the date because it was Remembrance Day and I'd been on parade since dawn with the old Diggers at the Cenotaph on the Barrett Estate. I was hoping to knock off early, but then I got a call to go out to the Cashman place on DeCastella Drive. A mum had called triple-O, screaming that her kid had been bashed, and although a young constable was on her way to the scene, a more senior police officer was going to be needed.

The Cashmans lived in a Commission house – quite a few of the neighbours later made a point of telling me that when I went around taking statements from them. They said, 'Those people, they don't own here. It's Housing Commission. They're just renting.'

What did they mean by that? Not that the family was poor. There were plenty of poor people on the Barrett Estate. I don't mean down-and-outs. We had quite a few old-age pensioners and a few single mums on the estate, but in those days, most people worked. We had labourers, hairdressers, panel beaters, and a good bunch of guys down at Barrett Glass. Nobody was flush. At a guess, the highest earner on the estate would have been the school principal, on something like $45,000 a year. It was a 'working-class' estate in the proper sense of the word: people worked, although not for much.

So no, the neighbours didn't mean 'poor'. They meant something else, something that in those days was harder to define. These days, we wouldn't hesitate. We'd say the mother was a bludger with four kids under six to three different blokes, none of whom were on the scene.

Anyway, I drove up to the house as fast as I could. I was in one of those white Commodores they gave coppers in those days. The idea was to give us the speed and the muscle we'd need to catch the crooks. Trouble was, every bloke under thirty on the Barrett Estate had a white Commodore, and they souped them up to make them go faster. There were a couple of Commodores already parked in the driveway of the Cashman house when I got there. At first I thought they were both police cars, but on second glance it was pretty obvious that one of them wasn't. The suspension had been lowered – in those days we used a beer can to check, and there was no way you'd get a VB under this car – plus the windows had been tinted. No, this one wasn't a police car. This car belonged either to a man who lived in the house, or to a man who at least visited often enough to feel comfortable parking in the drive.

The ambulance was already there and I saw the paramedics leap from it and move like lightning across the lawn, the white soles of their shoes flashing. I got out of the car and made my way up the path, expecting to find the house in a state of chaos. I mean, that's quite normal, isn't it? If a kid has come a cropper and the parents have had to call an ambulance, well, you can expect a lot of noise. The parents will be screaming and crying and it's my job to get them to settle down, so we can start figuring out what happened. But there was no panic in Lauren's house.

The mother, Lisa, was in the kitchen with the young female police constable. Lisa was pale and extremely thin, a chain-smoker, with hair that had been frizzed and dyed red so many times you couldn't tell what colour it originally was. She was twenty-six years old, but she had that worn-down look that women get when they've fallen pregnant for the first time at a young age. If I was to hold up a picture of her alongside pictures of today's twenty-six-year-old girls, fresh from university and still giggly, you'd have said she was forty.

Anyway, Lisa was standing in the kitchen when I arrived, holding herself up against the laminate bench and chewing the skin around her thumb. Like I say, I expected some kind of frenzy, but I got the feeling she was just plain irritated, like here was something she really didn't need; all these people in uniform in her house, it pissed her off.

In the lounge room a big bloke – a near-naked bloke – was holding this kid up under the arms like a puppet, trying to make his feet grip the carpet. It was hopeless. The kid's legs kept buckling, and his head was lolling about on his neck.

I could see what the big fella was trying to do. He was trying to make the boy stand up, but I could see that wasn't going to happen. The kid was all floppy and he had those 'sunset eyes' you get when the brain is gone, with the eyeballs not focused and the lids half-closed. The paramedics were trying to intervene. They weren't shouting at him, but they were talking loudly, saying, 'Please, put the boy down.'

There were other kids in the house: a boy of about three, and a girl who was still a toddler, both of them in the lounge room, all curious and afraid. And then there was Lauren. She's wasn't in the lounge room. She was in the hall. How did she look? Well, what can I say? In the looks department, she was blessed. She had buck teeth and freckles across her nose, and she was wearing a T-shirt that had some kind of cartoon animal on the front. She could have been anybody's little Aussie rug rat except that, like all the other kids in the house, she had this extraordinary white hair. I don't mean white-blonde, like some kids have, I mean white-white, like a Samoyed dog. It was curled all around her face and cascaded down her back, so long that she probably would have been able to sit on it. She had white eyelashes, and white eyebrows, too, but she wasn't albino – that would be going too far. No, she was more like a ghost. And it wasn't just the hair that made me think that. It was the way she was hovering in the hallway, like she was trying to decide whether it was all right to come and look at what was going on.

The first words I heard out of Lisa's mouth were: 'Get up.' I've got to say, it struck me as strange. The big bloke had let the boy fall to the floor and the paramedics were leaning over him, and I'd say it should have been obvious to anyone that the boy was in no position to stand up, but that's what the mother said. She came out from the kitchen, broke into the huddle around him, and said, 'Jacob, get up.'

'Is he dead?' Those were the first words I heard from

Lauren. She'd come creeping down the hall, wanting to get a good look.

'Don't be stupid, Lauren,' her mother said. 'Go get the heater.'

Again, it was such a strange thing to say. This was November, remember, so it was as good as summer in Melbourne. We'd been sweating out by the Cenotaph. Some of the school kids who'd been standing to attention while the band played, they'd actually fainted. Lauren didn't argue with her mother, though. She went off down the hall and came back with a portable heater. It was three orange bars in an aluminium shell, and it was covered in dust, but Lisa took it from her and plugged it in, and within seconds the whole house was filled with smoke from the dust on the elements. That didn't stop the mother, though. She put the thing close to Jacob's head, and his white hair began to steam. I realised his hair must have been damp.

The paramedics were working like crazy. One of the paramedics said, 'Please, get it out of the way,' and the other said, 'What's the boy's name? How old is he?'

'He's five,' said Lisa. 'He's Jake. Jacob.'

The paramedic said, 'We're going to have to get him to hospital.'

'Jesus,' said Lisa. 'I ain't got ambulance cover.'

I think that's when I stepped in. I'm pretty sure my first words would have been, 'Hello. I'm Detective Senior Sergeant Brian Muggeridge, Barrett CIB.'

Nobody paid any attention. One of the paramedics was trying to fit an oxygen mask over the boy's face, and the other was kicking the heater out of the way while trying to get the wheels out from under a stretcher, so they could get Jake off the floor and out the door.

'You won't need cover,' said the paramedic.

'You'll need to come with us,' said the other.

I said, 'Hang on, I'm just going to need a few seconds here.'

Lisa glared at me and then turned her back, so I went over to the copper in the kitchen and said, 'What you got?'

The young constable must have been a new recruit because her shirt was still sharp across the creases. By that time I'd been a copper for about eight years, I suppose, and maybe it was starting to show. My father had been in the force and he'd told me, 'The pay's lousy but at least you get to retire at fifty-five.' That appealed to me. All I could see myself doing as a young fella was working long enough to buy a boat and spend my retirement fishing. What I didn't know then was what I'd have to go through to get to retirement age. The human misery, it was already wearing me down.

The new recruit told me the mother had sent her boys to the shops for cigarettes. Jacob, who was five, and Harley, who was three, were on their way home when a man came up and told them to hand over the change. They refused, and so the man started roughing them up, knocking them to the ground and kicking them. The younger boy, Harley, managed to break away, run home and raise the alarm. Lisa had followed him back to the school grounds and found Jacob lying there, unconscious. She carried him home in her arms.

I thought, 'No.'

I can't tell you exactly how or why I knew the story wasn't true. Instinct, maybe. I'll admit that I was swayed by the condition of the house. It was slumped on its foundations as if the burden of housing so many fractured families had taken a toll on the frame.

I don't know whether Lisa had been listening to the constable who gave me these details, but when I moved again towards her, to try to ask a few questions, she got pretty agitated. She said, 'I gotta go with Jake,' and she came into the kitchen and started gathering cigarettes and other things off the kitchen bench. She had a Glomesh purse and a set of house keys with a plastic tag hanging off the ring that said 'Never Mind The Dog, Beware the Bitch Who Lives Here!' She stuffed those things into her handbag, and then she opened the fridge and took out a baby's bottle filled with orange cordial, which she gave to her boyfriend, saying, 'Make sure you give this to Hayley.'

The boyfriend said, 'Do you want me to come?'

She said, 'You stay here.'

I noticed straightaway that there was no tenderness

in the exchange. I mean, you might expect this guy to be comforting Lisa a bit at this stage, or at least to be saying, 'Don't worry, he'll be fine,' or something, given that they were obviously an item, but that wasn't what was happening. It made me wonder how long they'd actually been together, or even known each other. Later, we'd find out they'd been together six weeks.

I thought to myself, 'Did he do it?' Look, I know that sounds biased against blokes, but how many times had I been to a situation where a kid was out cold and the de facto was the one who'd done it?

The paramedics looked ready to leave and were starting to push Jake out toward the ambulance. Lisa was obviously going to have to go with them, but getting her out the door was going to be no simple matter because by now the media was all over the lawn. In those days, reporters had access to police scanners. They can't do it any more, not with mobile phones and scrambled messages and so forth, but in those days we basically had CB radios, and it wasn't illegal, not then, to intercept what you heard on the two-way system. So they would have heard the call – a child had been beaten on the Barrett Estate; paramedics required – and they'd have followed the ambulance to the house, and now they were outside, waiting to hear what had gone on so they could write it up for the next day's papers.

They wouldn't interfere with the paramedics. They'd be allowed to make their way to the ambulance, to get the boy inside, but Lisa . . . well, she wasn't injured, so they'd see her as fair game.

I said to Lisa, 'I'm going to have to help you get past the press. They'll be shouting questions at you but you just stick with me and I'll get you though.'

She was nodding her head and gripping her bag. We went out the front door and I tried to help her into the back of the ambulance, but she tripped and we had to make a second go of it, which gave the snappers plenty of time to get a picture. I thought she'd immediately fuss over the boy when she got inside, but she didn't. Instead, she looked out through the glass doors of the ambulance, towards the flashes from the cameras and the bobbing, fuzzy microphones, and she was wearing a very strange expression. If I had to put a name to it, I'd say she was thrilled.

I made a note of the time. The call to triple-O had been placed at around 5.40 p.m. and now it was getting toward 7 p.m. The deadline for the newspaper reporters was 10 p.m., at the absolute latest, and the photographers were at least an hour from their darkrooms in Melbourne's CBD, so it was clear that they'd soon have to get moving if they were going to get this story in the paper. I knew from experience, though, that they'd probably wait for a statement from the cops before they'd move. Lisa was shouting things at them through the glass doors of the ambulance, things like: 'They ought to lock 'em up and throw away the key!'

They knew they had a story – a good story – and now it was up to me to give the thing some context.

The other thing they'd want, of course, was a picture of Jake, not only of him going into the ambulance but a nice portrait, something good and clear, that they could whack on the front page. I scanned the pack, looking for somebody I recognised, and straightaway saw a guy from *The Sun* I remembered from some other job. I signalled to him to come forward, into the house, telling him I'd give him a photograph that he could share with the others. We stepped through the front door and walked straight into the boyfriend. He was standing in the lounge room, his massive legs and chest still bare, just looking like a stunned mullet, taking up all the space.

I said, 'I'm Detective Muggeridge. You're . . . ?

He said, 'Peter Tabone.'

I said, 'Right, Mr Tabone, can you help me here? I need a photograph of Jacob that I can give to the press, something we can copy for the newspapers.'

By way of an answer, he said, 'He's not my kid.'

I'd already figured that for myself, so I let it go and scanned the room, and immediately saw a portrait – a bright, white-and-blue portrait of four children – in a cardboard frame on the mantelpiece. I picked it up and said, 'Are these the children? Which one is Jake?'

Unaccountably, Peter brightened.

'I paid for that,' he said. 'Pretty all right, isn't it? Pretty good, actually.'

He seemed not to understand the seriousness of the situation. We weren't here to *admire* the photo; we were here to find Jake's attacker. Again, I said, 'Which one is Jake?'

Peter considered the photograph for a moment, then pointed and said, 'That one.'

Jake was seated in the middle of the group. Like all of them, he was wearing blue jeans and a white T-shirt, and he was flanked on both sides by siblings. Behind them was a cloudy background: not dull-cloudy, but a bright blue background with white clouds. I handed the photograph to the *Sun* photographer, who laid it down on the kitchen bench and said, 'Thanks, mate. We appreciate this.' He lifted up his camera and began photographing it. That was the easiest way to get a copy in those days, before digital prints and email, you'd just copy a photograph with your own camera, develop it in the darkroom, and send it by courier to colleagues from rival papers. The copies would be in colour, but in the newspaper they'd turn out black and white, which was a pity, because the thing that was most striking about the kids, the thing that any witness was likely to remember, was the hair.

Peter seemed very interested in the photographer and his gear, but he didn't seem too happy about his portrait being copied. He said, 'Why do they need a picture?'

I said, 'If anybody sees this picture, they might

remember seeing Jake on the way to the shops and they might remember something suspicious, and that's going to help us catch the culprit.'

Peter said, 'Yeah, okay, but remember, *I* paid for that picture.'

The photographer looked up, surprised. Was Peter suggesting that he should pay for the right to copy it? The photographer let it go. I remember thinking, 'These guys aren't bad. The press gets a bad rap but they've got a job to do and, on this occasion, that meant getting a picture, any picture of the kid, so people could look at it and say, "What a cute kid! How could anybody hurt a child like that? What's the world coming to?"'

When the *Sun* guy was done, I put the portrait back on the mantelpiece and went outside. The press was waiting for me, waiting for some kind of official comment to go with their stories. I stood in the forest of microphones and said, 'As you have no doubt gathered, we have a serious incident on our hands here.'

They nodded and waited.

'We've got a five-year-old boy who was sent to the shops with his brother, and it appears that they've been set upon by a man who has bashed him, possibly for the change they were carrying.'

I paused to give them time to write this down.

'I think you'll agree that's a cowardly crime, to beat an innocent boy, a five-year-old boy,' I continued.

'We are appealing for witnesses to come forward. We ask anyone who might have seen anything suspicious to please call Crime Stoppers. I think you've all got the number.'

One reporter said, 'Can we speak to the parents?' and I said no. Another reporter wanted to know what kind of injury the boy had suffered. I said, 'That's obviously a matter for the specialists. At this stage it's unclear, but I think I'm safe in saying that the young lad is in quite a bad way.'

They wanted to know the boy's name and I told them: Jacob Cashman. They wanted to know how to spell Jacob – was it Jakob or Jacob or, who knows these days, Jaycub? – and I confirmed it: It was J-A-C-O-B, Jacob. Jacob John Cashman. Referring to notes taken by the new recruit, I added: 'Born 1 August, 1977. He's five.'

'He's what?' The reporters hadn't heard me. Daylight was fading and the cockatoos that made their nests in Barrett's gum trees had taken flight. They were swooping and screaming, apparently furious.

I repeated myself, louder this time. I said, 'Five. The young boy, the victim, he's five.' And somehow, those words brought silence upon all of us.

I turned and went back through the front door. The boyfriend, Peter, had turned on the TV and the children were watching, of all things, *The Love Boat*. They didn't turn to look at me. There was a day coming when they'd have to face up to what happened in that house on DeCastella Drive, but it wouldn't be that day and, likely, not for years, so I let them go on watching.

Frank Postle,
Reporter

The minute I saw the photographs of Lauren Cameron in the newspaper, I thought to myself, 'I know that girl.' I couldn't remember the details at first so I got onto my daughter, who's a reporter herself these days, and asked her to have a bit of a search around the archives, and then I pulled out my own files to refresh my memory. I've still got a few of the old scrapbooks I used to keep, with my articles cut out and pasted in, from before the whole world went electronic.

It was a bloody horrible story, and I suppose it's reasonable to ask, 'A story like that, how do you forget it?' But, I mean, I've worked for newspapers for twenty-seven years and I can tell you now, I've seen plenty of bloody horrible stories. Kids getting beaten, kids getting dumped, kids getting *raped*, if you can believe that, and

I learnt pretty quick that if you spend too much time thinking about it, you'll go out of your mind.

The Cashman story, well, it wasn't in the worst category of crimes I've had to cover for the papers. I know that sounds rotten, but as far as I could tell, it wasn't a savage beating, and not systematic abuse, like you see these days, with kids starved to death and kids hogtied face down on the bed with rags. This wasn't one of those. There was barely a mark on the boy. I got a glimpse of him when they were putting him in the ambulance and he looked like he'd been knocked out. I remember thinking, 'What's happened here?' Maybe it was an accident, or maybe they'd just gone too far.

Look, don't get me wrong. I would have been affected by it. I'm not made of marble. I've got kids of my own. But the thing is, I was working for *The Sun*, and we had a couple of editions to fill every day, and news moves pretty quickly. We might have had a horse race one day – the Melbourne Cup, right? – and then a bashed kid the next day, and after that, an election, and then it's Christmas and it's time to do the cricket stories, and, well, life goes on, doesn't it?

By rights, I shouldn't have been out on the road the day that Jake Cashman got bashed. I was the news editor. That means I was supposed to sit at the desk at *The Sun*'s old headquarters in Flinders Street, ashtray to my left, keeping track of the stories coming in. On November 11, we wouldn't have had anything much, just the usual pictures from the Remembrance Day ceremony, standard fare that nobody much cares about any more. We covered it because we at the *Sun* had respect for the diggers. Then the call came through from the bloke on police rounds, saying, 'We've got something.'

Police rounds weren't based at the paper. They were down at Russell Street, where they had the scanners, so he would have called me up and said, 'Yeah, we've got a kid – a five-year-old – and the official story is he was grabbed by a man at the local school and left on the ground and his kid brother ran home to Mum and she had to carry him home.'

I would have thought, 'That's a good yarn.' I told the editor, 'We've got an ambulance on the way to a kid, and it looks like a bashing.' Probably he said, 'Beauty,' because that's what we would have felt. It's not callous, it's just, like I say, we've got a paper to put out and we need stories to fill it. The editor would have wanted to know where the kid lived and I would have said, 'Barrett Estate,' and he would have rolled his eyes because Barrett . . . look, I'm sure the people who live there will tell you it's a good neighbourhood, but it's got something of a reputation.

The editor would have wanted to know: 'You got anyone to send?' That was part of my job, to find a reporter to get to the scene, but I didn't have anyone, or maybe I did but I just felt like doing it myself. Sitting in the office all day, it used to get me down, so I would have rounded up a snapper – a photographer, an old hand – we'd have made sure we had a pack of smokes between us, and driven out to Barrett. We'd have had to step on it because if we left it too long, the ambos and the coppers would be gone and we'd have nothing.

I remember we had a bit of trouble finding the place because DeCastella Drive was not actually in the *Melways*. We had to ask a guy at the servo where it was, and he said, 'Oh, yeah, coupla weeks ago the council decided to create some chaos by renaming all the streets.' Apparently, they had a Main Road West, and a Main Road East and an Old Main Road or something and they reckoned that was confusing, so they were having a competition to rename the roads, and people could put forward suggestions. This was just, like, weeks after the Commonwealth Games in Brisbane, and everybody was all excited about all these gold medals that the Aussies had won in the pool, and the weightlifting, and the marathon with Deeks in it, so all the councillors went down there in their robes and put up new signs that said 'Lisa Curry Court' and 'Dean Lukin Close' and 'DeCastella Drive', which was where the Cashmans now lived, and the road we had to find.

Anyway, we needn't have freaked out because we were first on the scene. First reporters, I mean. When a kid gets in strife, it's not really a story for *The Age*. They'll cover it, but usually from some wanky social-justice angle, and two days after everyone else has picked it to pieces. Not like *The Sun*. We'd get it on the front page and make the most of it.

There were no TVs there – no TV reporters, I mean – because the call to the ambulance had come in late, so they wouldn't have bothered. No point going out there if you can't get it to air for the 6 p.m. bulletin, right? In those days, a story was only a story if Brian Naylor told you so. On the papers, we had a bit more time. It was actually better if something happened a bit late, because we knew we'd have it on our own, and if it turned out to be a good story the TVs would be onto it the next day.

The ambulance was still there when we arrived, thank God. The snapper jumped out of the car and got a shot of the kid getting loaded in. The coppers were there, too, so there was no point knocking on the door. There's no way they'd let us in, so we hung around the front of the house for a while, talking to the neighbours. I ascertained pretty quickly that a fair number of kids lived in the house, that the mother was on welfare, and that it was a Commission house. I would have been thinking, 'This isn't ideal' – not from a news point of view, because it's always a bit better when the family aren't bogans, but how often do kids in the good neighbourhoods get bashed? Not often, mate, let me tell you, not often. But then again, we always made a point at *The Sun* that half our readers were probably on minimum wage and just because people were poor didn't mean they were up to no good. We didn't look down on them like *The Age*.

I thought to myself, 'Hang around, Frank, and just see what happens,' but it was getting late and I didn't have much copy to fill out a story, so we spoke to the media guy – the police media guy – and he said, 'Yeah, you've got at least half an hour before there'll be any action here, so if you want to go for a quick lap around the block that'll probably be okay.' So we did that. We tracked down the kind of guys you can rely on to give you a couple of quick quotes – the priest we found at Barrett Anglican, for example, and the mayor – so that we'd have some kind of story whether the cops came out to talk to us or not. The cops were pretty helpful in those days, though, and we knew they'd give us a few quotes if we hung about long enough, so we went back and, yep, they were good to us.

First, they invited our guy in to copy the portrait of the kid, which saved us from tracking one down ourselves. It can be a real pain in the arse: you have to find classmates, you have to find grandparents, you have to try to talk them into giving you a snap, and it's not always easy. So it was good when the cops handed over a pic, and I remember when I finally saw it back at the darkroom, I thought, 'Yeah, that's all right,' because the kid, from a news point of view, was pretty much perfect: very Aussie-looking, pale and freckly, and not Aboriginal, which was good, because it's much harder to work up sympathy when the kid's Aboriginal.

After we got the pic copied, the cop came out and told us the story about the kid being bashed, which I took down verbatim despite thinking it was bullshit. What else can you do? You can't really write, 'Oh, the cops say this and this, but we reckon they're full of it.' That's not what a newspaper does.

I wouldn't have had a mobile phone with me. It was before mobiles, really. Some people had them but they were big, blocky things that you carried around in a suitcase, so I'd have had to find a phone box – preferably one that wasn't all smashed up, preferably one where the kids hadn't cut the cord, before they got the idea of making them out of that stretchy steel stuff – to let the editor know that we had the story and it was a goodie, and would run for a few days. Otherwise, he'd be sitting in the office, wondering what the hell was going on. Filing copy was a pain, too – no laptops in those days, only copy-takers back at the office, amazing old chicks who would sit on the phone with you, and take it down in shorthand, and then enter it into the system, which means you had to compose the yarn as you went, trying to remember what you'd already said, and trying to think where the comma ought to go. So, yeah, I would have got into a phone box, I would have balanced the handset on my shoulder – it would have been one of those black bastards that weighed a tonne – and

I'd have dialled with my pen and gone through my note-book, writing the piece on the hoof, and reading it out, and then reading the graffiti on the walls while I was waiting on the line for the editor to tell me it was all good, and all received.

The editor told me that if I got back by nine, he'd hold the press and get it on the front page, so that's what we did, me driving and the photographer stressing out, because it was his pictures of the kid that every-body was waiting on.

I have to say, I'm still pretty pleased with what we achieved that day. I've got the clipping in my scrapbook, so I must have been pretty proud of myself at the time, too.

'MAN BASHES BOY.' That was the headline. It ran across the top of the front page. I tried to get a touch of outrage into the copy. 'A five-year-old boy was savagely bashed by a man as he walked through his own school-yard near his home,' I wrote.

'Police say Jacob Cashman was sent by his mother to the shops to get cigarettes.'

Now, you see, most parents could relate to that. Send the kids to the shop, you assume it's all safe, you live in the neighbourhood, you know all the neighbours, and look what happens.

'The boy's brother, Harley, who witnessed the beat-ing, said Jacob was knocked to the ground, kicked in the head and the stomach,' I wrote.

'Little Jake is now fighting for his life in the Children's Hospital.'

The rest of it was pretty standard: police were appealing for witnesses. Neighbours were all upset and wondering whether to keep the doors locked. Inside the paper, we had the commentary from the mayor and the priest, both of them blaming television.

'There's too much violence on the box,' the mayor said. 'People see a murder every other day and they don't realise it's not real.'

We ran the picture of the kid right across the front, six columns (the seventh was always reserved for sport, like a footballer with a groin injury or something). Even though the picture was black and white, you could still see that the kids were pretty surreal-looking, and I wasn't the first to notice. One of the neighbours told me that the Cashman kids were known around the Barrett Estate as the 'Ghost Children'.

When I'd asked some of the other neighbours who were standing around whether they were good kids, they mostly said yes, but then one guy, he spun me out a bit. He said, 'Actually, mate, I've always found them a bit weird. You know, with that white hair scraped back. When you see them all together it's like the *Village of the Damned*.'

And that was actually dead on. That's exactly how they looked, and it must have stuck in my mind because I can't find it in the paper. Obviously I left it out of the story. Whether that was because of space, or because in the circumstances that would have been pretty inappropriate, I don't recall.

Mrs Margaret Cooper, Portrait Maker

The moment I saw the photograph of the young Cashman children on the front of *The Sun*, I recognised it as one of my own. I'd better explain: my name is Margaret Cooper – everybody calls me Marg – and from the years 1980 until 1987, I worked as a portrait photographer at the Barrett Regional Shopping Centre, on the Barrett Estate. It was a late-blooming career for me. I was already in my fifties when I took it up. You see, I was born in 1923 and educated at a Catholic girls' school in Kew in Melbourne's east at a time when photography wasn't really something that a young woman would consider a suitable profession. It wasn't quite right, somehow. Photographers were mostly men. Perhaps that was because the equipment was heavy, but more likely it was because portrait photography was something, like medicine, that a man would do.

Like most girls in my day, I intended to matriculate and then to teach, at least until I was married. So, after high school I went to the Melbourne Teacher's College, fully intending to graduate. It didn't quite work out that way because, of course, the Second World War came and it was all hands on deck, never mind about any dreams we might have had of teaching and what have you. I was assigned a position at the munitions factory in Melbourne's west and I won't say I didn't enjoy it. There was camaraderie – a sense that we were support-ing the men overseas – and I had a little money in my pocket, which is something my own mother hadn't had.

In any case, after the war the men took over the factory jobs and that's when I finally took a job as a primary teacher. In those days, all you needed was one year's study, which I had. The hoops they now make you jump through . . . well, I suppose it's a good thing, but it seemed so much easier for people then. Soon after that I was married, and Ken and I had children. I made it my business to raise our four girls. That wasn't a ques-tion then: you had children, you raised them. There was no childcare, except for the church hall, and that really wasn't considered ideal.

Ken was a good husband and, I must say, we had an exciting life together, we really did. Before the war, Ken had trained as an electrical engineer. Afterwards, he became involved in some of the big water projects: the Snowy Mountains scheme was one, and then we moved onto other things, eventually bringing water to people in other countries.

Anyway, by the late 1970s, Ken had retired and we'd moved to the Barrett Estate. It was Ken who suggested we move there, I suppose because we both wanted to be closer to the girls. They'd left the nest and were pursuing careers – two of them were in Melbourne – so it made sense to be nearby instead of out whoop-whoop where I couldn't help them with the grandchildren. Ken saw an ad for Barrett and said, 'Oh, they're building a new estate,' but it wasn't new to me: they built it on the land where we tested the munitions during the war. There wasn't a house to be seen in those days, only some concrete buildings we called the 'bomb shelters', although they had no actual purpose that we could see. Anyway, all that was taken down and it was remarkable how quickly the houses went up. I was quite impressed. We decided to build our new home on the part of the estate they called 'Barrett Riverview', which was a little quieter than the rest of the estate, but you still had the benefit of having the young families around. People were quite friendly – you could rely on the neighbours to keep an eye on things if you had to pop out for a while.

By the time we moved out there, of course, we were getting on. I had my interests – I had my roses, for example – but yes, I was looking for something else to occupy my time. I didn't want to go back to teaching. Although there were Catholic and Anglican schools on the estate I'm sure they would have regarded my skills as antiquated. In any case, Ken had had his first stroke, and I don't suppose I wanted to be away from the house all day. Before he had the stroke, Ken and I had taken a few courses together: dancing, theology and a short photography course. The photography instructor had told me I was quite talented and I'd enjoyed it, especially taking photos of the grandchildren. It was my daughters who said to me, 'You should go into business, start your own little empire.' They thought I might be the next Anne Geddes, taking photographs of children sitting on pumpkins and that kind of thing, and it did tickle my fancy.

My son-in-law – he's a solicitor, got quite a good little practice – he was the one who went with me to the Barrett Regional Shopping Centre. We talked about leasing some space in the forecourt. They wanted people to come on the weekends, and offer some different services. The banks and the Post Office and even the butchers were closed on the weekends in those days, but the department stores like Venture were open, and I suppose they thought some novelty stands would be interesting.

It was quite a thrill to be in business. I got a certificate of registration from the Department of Small

Business, which said, 'Proprietor: Marg Cooper.' That was something! Ken put it in a frame and it's still there, in the lounge room. My idea was to take portraits of local children and present them in a nice way, so that parents could display them in the home. I can imagine the rigmarole you'd need to go through to do something like that these days: a 'working with children' check, a police check, you'd need liability insurance. In those days, I had a sturdy table and a nice backdrop of blue sky and clouds. Ken helped me choose a camera, and off we went. I wasn't interested in becoming a millionaire. I've got my Lotto tickets for that! I charged what I thought was fair: $5 for one portrait and $10 for a package. If they wanted a plastic key ring with a small picture inside I would charge $7 extra for that.

Barrett wasn't a rough place. I will say that things have changed: I've moved out of our original house and I'm in a unit now, and you do get more Asians. I saw some young men the other day, as black as the ace of spades. I know what Ken would say, 'We're the white dots on the domino,' but they are perfectly nice people. A family of Somalis has actually moved into the unit next door and I have no problem with that. They're not Muslim. It might be different if they were, but these are Christians just like you and me, except they cook their food in the garage, and the smell is often quite strong.

Back then, when the thing with the Cashman boy happened, it was mostly young Australian families and people like Ken and me, retirees. You had your bad elements, but you get that everywhere. There was Housing Commission on the estate but not the old kind, not those ugly towers, just a house here, and a house there, designed to blend in. Unless you knew, you would never have realised it was Housing Commission, although I'd say everybody did know.

I read about the incident with the Cashman boy in the newspaper. I remember it, the same as I remember the day the mill burnt down and we all came into the street to watch. Perhaps it's because we weren't used to that kind of excitement.

Anyway, I was at home when I heard about it. I used to get *The Sun* home delivered. Kids would go out before dawn on a bike with a milk cart lashed to the handlebars, and deliver the paper. I suppose none would be bothered now. I'm told they have too much else to do already, what with the sports and the studies and the time they have to spend on Facebook. On that day, I remember, I picked up the paper from the lawn and turned to put the jug on, and when I turned back, *The Sun* had unfurled and there, on the front, was one of my photographs. I only had to look at it to know it was mine. I immediately remembered little Jacob. First, there was the hair. People today say, 'Oh, they were called the Ghost Kids,' but I never heard that, and anyway, against my blue-and-cloudy backdrop, they didn't look like ghosts. They looked like angels, really quite heavenly angels. Then, too, I remembered, the man who came with them, the one who went to prison. Maybe I'm embellishing it a bit now, but I seem to recall that he didn't have proper shoes, he had rubber thongs, and he had that way of walking where they'd slap across the floor. I just hate that noise. I feel like saying, 'Pick up your feet,' and maybe I did say that to him. I've said it to enough people, I know that.

I do remember that he was wearing football shorts – shorts, with bare legs, no socks, it's all okay now apparently. He said to me, 'How much for a pitcher?' No: 'How do you do?' and no: 'Excuse me.' Just: 'How much for a pitcher?' He wanted a photograph to give to the children's mother. He said, 'They're not mine,' and I thought, 'No need to brag about it.'

I told him the price and he agreed to buy a portrait, so I went about setting up the scene. The children weren't at all difficult to manage. I lifted them, one at a time, and put them onto the table, in front of the cloud backdrop, one behind the other, as though they were sitting astride a log. They were wiggling and jiggling but all children do that, and I had few tricks up my sleeve. If you're going to photograph children, you need a few tricks, let me tell you. I kept a rattling clown and often times, I only had to hold it up and shake it for most children to at least stop crying and stare at its face. I had some little jokes, too, designed to focus them. I would stand behind the camera – it was a monster of a thing, not the little digitals you have now – and I'd say, 'Now,

in your loudest voices, children, say, "Funky Monkey!"'
And that would normally get a giggle because they were
expecting me to say, 'Say Cheese!'

The boy who was bashed, Jacob, he was in a particularly excitable mood. He kept saying silly things like
'I don't like monkeys', and perhaps I did get a little
exasperated, but still, I was completely shocked when
the man walked over and belted him.

Don't get me wrong. I'm not the kind of person who
says, 'Oh, you mustn't smack the children.' I'm old-
fashioned. I believe that a swift kick up the backside,
as my husband used to say, can do a child the world
of good. I used to put my own children over my knee
from time to time. But this was something quite different. The blow made a sound like a cricket ball on a bat.
I was so startled I dropped the flash and ended up taking a picture of the light bouncing off the polished floor.

The little boy's hand flew to his head. I thought,
'Oh, poor mite, he's going to cry, and that will be it, no
portrait today,' but he didn't make a sound. There was
a look on the man's face that said something like, 'Don't
you dare!' And then he walked back to where I was
standing, and he said, 'They reckon you're not allowed
to give them a hiding. I reckon it's the only thing what
works.'

That's how he talked. I suspect he had no education
at all, not that I'd want to condone his behaviour.

I went on and took the photograph – the flash was

okay, thank goodness – but I was very distressed about the image. I liked the children to be happy, so the grandparents could be proud, but the Cashman children had these fake smiles plastered on their faces. Jacob said quietly, 'My head hurts.' He was clutching that part of his skull that had reddened under the blow. It was all I could do not to gather him into my arms, but the man, he said, 'Yeah, well, that'll learn ya. You're gonna learn to do what you're told, mate.'

So when I saw that photograph of the children in *The Sun*, I realised the police must have taken it off their mantelpiece or wherever it was kept and given it to the media, because at that stage they were still looking for the man that bashed the boy. That's when my daughter said the newspaper wasn't allowed to reproduce it like that, not without permission, and she said she would ring up and see if they would pay me, but I suppose it slipped her mind. Then, of course, the rumours about what really happened in that house started swirling, and I thought, 'No, better let it go.'

Detective Senior Sergeant
Brian Muggeridge

Sometimes I wonder how many times I've been called to a house on the Barrett Estate responding to a police matter, as opposed to being there as a guest at somebody's barbecue. I don't know exactly, but Barrett definitely gives me a steady list of things to do. Lately I've started to think I've seen inside every house on the estate. I've pulled up marijuana plants. I've broken up teenage parties. I've been present when the sheriff – the court sheriff, that is, not the American kind – wants to repossess the car. There's been the occasional house fire – there was a spate of them, actually, when those oil burners became popular and people went to bed with them burning under the curtains – and, yeah, I've had my share of domestic-violence matters.

The Cashman case was definitely a strange one, and

it kept getting stranger. I'd left the house on DeCastella Drive quite late in the evening and returned the following day. The little boy wasn't there, obviously. He was still in hospital. The story had been given good coverage in *The Sun* and, like normal, the shock jocks had picked it up and were reading it out on the radio, tut-tutting and referring to Jacob as 'Little Jake'. They were telling everybody he'd been bashed by a man and the listeners were upset. They were calling up the radio stations to express their rage and to offer assistance to the family. I thought, 'Great, once again the police station will be full of cans of Campbell's soup, stuffed toys and, for some reason, torches.' People always give soup, old toys and torches, don't ask me why.

Like every cop in Melbourne, I had my radio tuned to Triple M. Between 'Flame Trees' and the prize wheel, they were reading from *The Sun* and putting their own spin on the story. They described Lisa Cashman as a 'single mum' and said she was 'struggling by on the single mother's pension' and 'doing her best'. One of them said, 'You should see the photograph on the front of the paper! These kids are so clean you can tell they're properly cared for.' Another guy said, 'This family doesn't have much, but the mum – the single mum – always makes sure they have a proper lunch in a lunchbox for school every day.' And I thought, 'How on earth can you possibly know that?'

I found Lisa in the kitchen, pretty much where she'd been the day before. She was holding a mug of tea. The string from the bag was dangling down over the back of one hand. She had an Alpine Light in the other hand and she had that look about her, like she'd been up all night. Her hair was like a bird's nest. Although it was still early, there was a forest of cigarette butts sprouting from the saucer she was using as an ashtray. The TV was on loud and the kids were crouched around it. Harley's eyes were still crusty from sleep and he was still wearing last night's nappy. I hate that, when I see a kid wearing a nappy that's hours old, heavy with urine, hanging down between their legs. I've had kids of my own, so I can just sense the rash, and I know how it makes them scream. But he wasn't screaming. He was standing on plump feet, watching Humphrey Bear.

Hayley was there and she, too, had that goggle-eyed look kids get when the TV is on. I'd say she was no more than eighteen months old. I didn't see Lauren, but the boyfriend – the big bloke, Peter – was there, and still half-naked, wearing boxer shorts with cartoon reindeer. He was in good shape, I remember that: he had a line of dark hair running from his navel to the elastic band around his waist, and he was ripped, like he worked on his abs. He was sitting in a Jason recliner, one ankle across the other knee, and he was slapping the rubber of his thong against the sole of his foot. I had to avert my eyes because, from where I was standing, I could see up the legs of his shorts, where a testicle squeezed against its sac. The place smelled the same as the day before:

a bit like a nursing home, and a bit like an empty pub after a Friday night, when the beer hasn't been cleared from the troughs and the smoke still hangs in the air.

Now, I'd never pretend to be an expert on trauma, and certainly I'm not a psychologist, but as I've said, I've come to expect certain things from a house where there has been some kind of drama. It's like a particular atmosphere: people go into shock, and that pretty much puts a lid on their emotions, at least for a bit. Say a child has fallen into the pool, or gone and got electrocuted in the shed or, like in this case, supposedly been set upon by a man, in the first instance there's the wild panic as everybody tries to save the kid and blame each other – 'Why weren't you watching him? I thought he was with you!' Then, by the next day, the shock settles on them, and they go kind of numb. I've heard people say, 'Well, it takes a while for the bad news to sink in,' but it seems to me that bad news doesn't so much sink in as *press down*. You see it on their faces, even over the course of a morning. Their face will literally start to fall – the skin droops from the cheekbones, the mouth drops at the corners and the jaw slackens. Actually, now I think about it, the shock affects the whole body that way. The shoulders slump and the hands get heavy. You end up with grown adults standing there like dumb gorillas, their clothes hanging off their bodies, like they belong to somebody else.

That's what I was looking for in the house on

DeCastella Drive, that *pressing down,* that slumping look, and let me tell you, it wasn't there. The atmosphere in the house, it was just different. For one thing, Lisa was there, and I thought, 'My God, why isn't she still at the hospital? How did she get back?' But there she was, with Peter, and they were talking, and talking *quick,* and they weren't making eye contact with me, which also doesn't happen that much. The thing is, when there's been a genuine accident, people are relieved to see you. It's like they think you can help. They're excessively polite. They might not want to look at you, but they want to sit you down, make you a cup of tea, like they've got this idea in their head that if they're well-behaved, if they behave like everything's normal, the world will set itself right.

Like I say, Lisa wasn't in that kind of mood. She had a fierce temper on. The first thing she said to me was, 'Have you got 'im?' At first, I didn't understand what she meant. She had smoke coming out of her mouth and she was bending a cigarette into the ashtray and taking another from the pack at the same time. When I didn't immediately answer, she said, 'You find the little prick what did this to Jake?' And while the words might sound right, the tone was all wrong. It wasn't like, 'Have you really found him?' It was more like, 'Are you actually looking?'

She turned from me and hit the button on the base of the kettle. Her cup was empty and it seemed she was going to make more tea. That in itself was kind of weird. If you've ever been in any shock yourself, you'll know the last thing you feel like is putting anything into your body. Your hunger, your thirst, it just shuts down. I once heard it said, at one of the training courses we had in those days, that it's normal for the body to do that without you even knowing it. You're in shock, you see, and you're fearful, and if you think there's a chance you might have to run, you keep yourself light. I don't say people don't make tea. They certainly *make* it, but they don't drink it, is my point. They go through the motions and then they stand there looking into the distance while it goes cold.

Anyway, Lisa didn't rinse her cup. She messed about with some canisters, unfolding a tea bag and dropping it in, and leaving the old one in a puddle on the counter. She did say to me, 'Do you want a cuppa?' and I said, 'Thank you, that'd be great.'

She asked, 'How do you have it?' and I said, 'White, with two.'

She opened the fridge, looked inside for a moment and said, 'Yeah, well, you're gonna have to have black. We're out of milk.'

I said, 'Black is fine. Let's sit down, Lisa. Let's see if we can find out what's happened here.'

I was wondering how to approach the subject of the man in the schoolyard. There didn't seem much point saying, 'Look, I don't believe this, Lisa,' because then she'd just clam up, and anyway, that's not the way to approach an investigation. Our rule is: assume nothing.

She said, 'I wanna know what'chve got. I wanna know what you're doin' *here*, when that man is *out there*. I wanna know why you aren't out findin' 'im, and stickin' 'im in jail and throwin' away the bloody key.'

I pulled myself into my professional stance: clipboard in front of me, pen in my hand. I said, 'Lisa, you've said that Jacob and . . . is it Harley? . . . you've said that Jacob and Harley went out to the shops at around 5 p.m. to get cigarettes . . .'

'Yeah.'

'I have to ask you, is that unusual? Jacob's how old? Five? Does he go to the shops by himself quite often?'

She said, 'He's just started goin'.'

I said, 'Okay. Can I ask you: how much money did he have?'

She had a temper, that woman. Sharply, she said, 'I've told ya all this. I gave 'em some change, outta the jar. We needed fags. What I wanna know is what *you're* doin' about the man what done this.'

She'd moved out from behind the bench in the kitchen and was sitting with Peter, on the arm of his Jason recliner, flicking a Bic lighter with her thumb.

'You're obviously upset,' I said, twisting my body to face her again. 'I understand that. But what we need are a few more details so we can get this investigation properly underway.'

Peter took the Alpine Lights and began fiddling with the packet, trying to work a cigarette loose.

'Can you not pinch my packet?' said Lisa.

'You gone and smoked all mine,' he said.

I tried to focus their minds.

'Let's see if we can go over it again,' I said. 'Let's see if there's anything *I've* missed, anything I can do, to get this man under arrest.'

Lisa sighed, a great, melodramatic sigh, like this was the most boring thing she'd had to do in a while. She said, 'I told ya. Peter gave 'em some money. I said to 'em, "Get some Alpine Lights, and you can get some lollies with the change what's left." They left here at five o'clock. I know it because they were watching *Happy Days* and it was just finished.'

'Okay,' I said. 'And . . . Peter? Do we have a surname for you, Peter?'

'Tabone,' he said.

'Okay, right, Peter Tabone. You were here, too? Do you actually live here?'

'I been here a month.'

'Six weeks,' said Lisa.

'Jacob's not your son?'

Lisa snorted.

I said, 'Are you the father of *any* of these children?' I didn't mean to put the emphasis on 'any' but it came out that way.

'Nope,' said Peter.

'What's that got to do with it?' said Lisa.

I said, 'Whose children *are* they?'

It's a dangerous question, that one. You don't want the mum to think that you regard her as a town bike, or a welfare mum, or anything like that. I was still thinking that Peter likely had something to do with the bashing, and I was determined to keep Lisa on side, so I said, 'Where's the kids' dad? Did he do a runner? Shoot through?'

She dragged back on her cigarette and, breathless now, she said, 'Yeah, they shot through.'

She paused then, waiting for the smoke to clear her nose, and said, 'They all shoot through, don't they? They want the fun, but not the responsibility, right? They want to get in the sack, naturally, but not deal with the consequences.'

I said, 'What age is your oldest, Lisa?'

'Lauren's six,' she said. 'I had her at twenty and her father, arsehole that he is, wasn't even around on the day she was born.'

Peter put a hand on Lisa's naked ankle, a gesture I understood to mean: 'Yeah, but I'm here, aren't I? I'm actually a good guy, so don't shop me.'

I said, 'And Jacob came along next?'

'That's right,' she said. 'And his dad's a dead leg, too. Not welcome in this house. Then there's Harley, and you might as well know, Harley's actually got the same dad as Lauren. He turned up for five minutes when she was four, long enough to knock me up again, and me believin' all his bullshit, and then he's shot through again.'

I said, 'And there's another one? A fourth child?'

And she said, 'Yeah. Hayley's me youngest.'

'All right,' I said. 'And these blokes, they're off the scene but I've got to ask you. Is there any idea in your mind that one of them might have had something to do with this?'

Lisa said, 'Are you bullshittin' me? I ain't seen jack of 'em in years. If you find 'em, can you let Family Services in on the secret, because I'm owed child support.'

She lit another cigarette. Humphrey had disappeared from the screen and Hayley, the toddler, was getting restless and clingy. Lisa reached down and picked an old dummy up off the carpet. She sucked it for a minute, to clear it of lint, and put it in the child's mouth. I remember thinking, 'My wife would have a heart attack.'

I tried to get back to the events surrounding Jacob. I said, 'Okay. So you've given Jacob and Harley the money to go to the shop for cigarettes . . .'

'*I* gave 'em the dough,' said Peter. Why he wanted to make a point of that, I cannot tell you.

'Okay,' I said. 'Peter, you gave them the money. They left here around 5 p.m. Did you give them any instructions? Do you know which way they went? Do they always go the same way?'

'I told 'em, you go straight there and you come straight back,' said Lisa.

'Yeah, and they do whatever the hell they want,' said Peter.

Lisa turned sharply toward him. 'Nobody's askin' you, mate. If you gave 'em any discipline, if you'd get off your arse, instead of sitting there smokin' bongs . . .'

Peter shrugged and said, 'Not my kids.'

'Not my kids,' she mimicked him.

'Not my problem,' he replied, smiling in a slightly menacing way, his foot slapping against his thong.

'Not my problem.' Lisa mimicked him again. 'You bloody *live* here. You're the one hangin' around here, demanding to get your tea cooked . . . you're the one who decided to make 'em your problem.'

I thought, 'Now, that's a strange thing to say.' In what way had Peter made the children his problem? But Peter said, '*You're* the one that let 'em run wild.'

I let them go at it. Probably, I was thinking, 'How many times have I had to listen to a conversation like this? "They're not my kids, they're your kids." "You don't discipline 'em. You gotta smack 'em." "You smack *them* and I'll smack *you* and see how you like it . . ." How many times have I been to a house on the Barrett Estate to find, for example, a man with a bloody nose, head-butted by the woman in some dispute over her kids gone wild?' So I let them keep at it, and after a while, I said, 'Where's Jacob's bedroom?'

This seemed to startle them, at least into silence. I wondered why.

'What's *that* got to do with it?' Lisa said. 'Why do you gotta see Jake's bedroom? Why aren'tcha out lookin' for where Jake got *bashed*?'

'We're doing that,' I said. I would have kept my voice gentle. There was no need for Lisa to know, not yet, that uniformed police *had* walked the schoolyard where Lisa claimed to have found Jacob, and there was no flattened grass or scuffs in the dirt, no patch where a body might have fallen to earth. Also, why had the bloke in the shop said he'd have remembered two kids coming in to buy cigarettes, yet he couldn't remember Jake, and he couldn't remember Harley, not even when our uniformed guys had gone there and shown him a photograph of two of the most distinctive kids you're likely to see?

Besides, if Lisa's story was true, well, it would have been one out of the box. Kids just don't get bashed by strangers, or at least they didn't then, and certainly not at five years of age. You get your perverts flashing at kids in the park, you get your drug problems, but there isn't any research anywhere that suggests that five-year-old white kids in the Australian suburbs get beaten by strangers. No, the data tells us this: when a person who is what we call 'vulnerable' – a homeless man, for example – gets hurt, there's a real chance it'll be at the hands of a stranger. A group of drunks might lose their heads on the way home from the pub and give him a kick while he's lying in the doorway. But when you've got a person who is not classified as vulnerable – that is, when they are a five-year-old kid, enrolled in the local school, living at home with their mother and their siblings – and *they* get hurt, well, it's almost never a stranger. In almost every case, the perpetrator is somebody known to them.

I said, 'I'd like to see the bedroom.'

I'd moved by now to the sofa opposite Lisa and, although it was sagging and my knees were up under my chin, I could see most of the house. Directly in front of me, there was the hall where I'd first seen Lauren. I knew enough about houses on the Barrett Estate to know that if I walked down that hall, I'd find a bathroom, a toilet and three bedrooms. Nobody had anything else: there were no studies, no sewing rooms, no indoor gyms, not then.

When I was a kid, there were no houses like the Cashman place on the Barrett Estate. Come to that, there were no houses at all on the Barrett Estate. It was just land, acres of land. We used to get told that it would never be developed, that it would always be there for kids to roam across, and in any case, there were rumours that the land was contaminated because they used to test munitions there. Nobody could be sure how much lead was in the soil. Then demand for housing skyrocketed and some time in the 1970s, the

Commonwealth released the land to developers who carved it up and built upon it. These developers stuck billboards on the freeway, advertising the place as a new 'satellite city' that would be perfect for young families. In those days, a perfect estate was one with straight roads and proper kerbing, and nobody cared much about the natural environment. When they cleared the joint, they left exactly six gum trees standing.

I got up – it wasn't easy since I'm a big guy, and that sofa was collapsed – and walked down the hall. Lisa was right behind me. I did as I'd been taught to: I made mental notes of *everything*. On the left, behind the first door, there was the bathroom. It was nothing extraordinary, just pale pink tiles on the walls, shampoo bottles lined up on top of the shower cubicle. Behind the next door there was a toilet – a separate toilet, they call it now – with an empty Harpic Blu Loo hanging in the bowl. Next to that there was a pile of magazines in a basket: *TV Week, New Idea, Wheels,* that kind of thing, nothing that got me thinking anything was too weird. On the window ledge there was a can of air freshener. The smell was like lemons.

On the other side of the hall, to my right, there was the first of the three bedrooms. It was beige like all the rest, but still obviously a girl's room. The bed was pink and the curtain was a purple sheet, and in amongst the toys, well, there was Lauren. She startled me, maybe because she'd been so quiet. I'd totally forgotten about her, but there she was, sitting on her bed with a doll – a naked doll with close-cropped hair – both of them staring back at me. I didn't speak to her. It wasn't a good idea, not without a social worker, but I did catch her eye. Her expression was troubling. It was something like: *Am I in trouble now?* But you get that with kids who are always getting it in the neck from their parents, and I'd reckoned that these Cashman kids were always being told they were gonna get it. I didn't think to stay there and tease a story out of her. As far as I knew, she hadn't seen anything. I did think, 'You poor kid. You've got the bum rap with this room.' The door looked out across the hall to the toilet, and no doubt Lauren would have copped an eyeful of Peter whenever he sat there, flipping through *Wheels* and doing his business.

Two other bedrooms came off the end of the hall. One was obviously Lisa's. There was an ashtray on the side table and a shawl over the lamp. It was a bit scorched, like it had caught fire more than once. There was a dressing table with a tin of Impulse body spray. Shoved between the wall and the queen-size bed there was an old cot with rumpled sheets, which must have been where Hayley slept.

On the left-hand side of the hall there was the third bedroom, the one the boys shared, and I remember it well because it reminded me of my own boys' rooms. The Cashman kids had their precious things on display: there was a cardboard certificate from the Barrett Primary

School awarded to 'Jacob Cashman' (this, written in biro) for 'helping classmates' and 'good story writing', and there was a medal hanging from the chest of drawers on a stripy ribbon. Instead of beds, there were bunks. Jacob likely slept on the top, a privilege always granted to the older boy. It didn't look much like the sheets got changed. There was a dark patch on the bottom bed – a smudge of sweat and grime and urine, about the size of a child's body. There were figures from action cartoons and a model of a T-Rex. There was a book, *The Ancient World of the Dinosaurs*, borrowed, according to the sticker, from the Barrett Primary School.

From down the hall, Peter said, 'The bloody press are here again.'

I walked back to join him in the lounge room. There were glass panels on both sides of the front door, and through them I could see cameramen setting up tripods and adjusting their lights.

Lisa said, 'Can't you tell them to piss off?'

'I can,' I said. 'But they won't. I don't know if you've seen this morning's newspapers, Lisa, but what happened to Jacob is news – big news – and that's a *good* thing.'

She said, 'A good thing! You reckon, *Detective*?'

Was she mocking me? Yes, in the midst of this tragedy, she was mocking me.

I said, 'Well, Lisa, we're going to need the public's help . . .' and then I paused, before adding, 'You know, to find the man who did this to Jacob.'

I watched to see whether Lisa would exchange glances with Peter, and she did. A moment of silence settled upon all of us, and I suppose that was when it dawned on Lisa that I actually didn't believe her. I didn't want that idea taking hold too soon – I wanted her to be in cahoots with me, and not with Peter – so I continued, 'Look, let's make them welcome. Let's go outside and tell them again what happened to Jacob and we'll ask them once more to appeal for witnesses for us. I know most of these guys. I trust them. They'll put it on the six o'clock news, and in the newspapers again tomorrow, and maybe somebody who has seen something will come forward.'

I wondered whether she'd have the guts to do it – to lie to the press and to the city of Melbourne, I mean. She could tell me her tall tales, but it's not easy to stand in front of cameras and tell a lie like the one she was intent on telling. That said, I didn't doubt that Lisa knew how to tell a lie. She would have spent years lying to the welfare department about where the fathers of her children were; to teachers, trying to explain why the kids weren't at school; and to the boyfriends, because I've no doubt they overlapped. Lying like that, pretty much to everyone about everything, was probably second nature and came easier to her than the truth, which is harder. You can't really tell the Salvos, 'We're out of money because I spent it all on booze.' You've got to make something up. You've got to say, 'The welfare cheque didn't come.'

Or, 'I lost my purse.' You can't really tell welfare, 'No, there's no bloke living in my house. I'm a single mum.' You've got to say, 'That guy? He's my brother.'

But *this* lie – a man attacked my kid and left him close to death on the ground – well, that was a biggie, and it meant getting the kids to lie, too. I didn't imagine Lisa would have too many problems with that. How many times had I seen it? A mother will tell the kids, 'If you say Daddy hit me, the cops are going to put him in prison and you'll go to the orphanage.' It scares the life out of them. I mean, Lauren was only six and Harley was three, and you don't need a psychology degree to know that kids of that age will lie for their parents if they're told that's what they've got to do. Who does a kid love, more than anybody else? Their mum. What does a kid want, more than anything else? The approval of their mum. And in a house like this one on DeCastella Drive, what would the kids most fear? Two things. Mum, and not having a mum.

Still, I said to Lisa, 'I think we'll have to get the kids involved.'

She said, 'What kids? Not Lauren.'

Not Lauren.

I said, 'No, not Lauren. Lauren wasn't there, was she?'

Lisa said, 'No, she weren't.'

'Okay then, no, not Lauren, but Harley. He was there, right?'

'He was where?'

'At the school?'

'Yeah.'

'Okay, well then, if it's okay with you, I'd like to get Harley out in front of the press because somebody might remember seeing him with Jacob.'

Lisa said, 'All right,' and I thought, 'She's got more balls than I thought.'

She was a better actress than I'd figured on, too. I could actually see her, there in the house, working into the role she'd have to play. She'd started to tremble with indignation. I wondered about the psychology. Had she got to the stage where she was starting to believe her own story? Or was she still hoping that she could get others to believe it? Another part of me was thinking, 'I wonder how long she can keep this up?' I didn't want to have to go through the whole ordeal: crying Mum on TV one day, and then the boyfriend led up to the court in handcuffs the next, because when that happens it's the quickest possible way for a jury to lose any sympathy they might have for you when the trial gets underway.

I signalled to one of the blokes on the front porch. He wasn't a copper. Don't tell me how, but I can spot a copper. He might be wearing scuba gear, he might be in the middle of a fishing holiday, he might be up to his neck in waders, and I can tell he's a cop. This bloke wasn't a cop. He was the media-liaison guy, a graduate, probably from RMIT, trained to handle the press.

I was a bit suspicious of these guys when they first came into the force – you like your coppers to be coppers, if you know what I mean, you don't want too many outsiders around – but they'd proved themselves reliable and pretty handy at keeping the press behind the barriers.

The media guy opened the front door and I told him to tell the press to get ready because Lisa was about to come out and make a short statement. I said, 'Tell 'em, "Sorry, we can't have any questions. The mother is distressed, obviously. This will be an appeal for witnesses and you can take some photographs, and then we'll be getting Mrs Cashman out of here, to the hospital."'

The guy nodded and I closed the door to give him a minute to pass the message back to the press. Through the glass panels, I saw a young woman in a suit and a white shirt – no doubt she wanted to be the next Jana Wendt – get up out of the gutter and use a pocket mirror to check her make-up. When, I wondered, did reporters start to look less like cops than like bankers? When did so many of them become *women*?

To Lisa, I said, 'I've let them know that they'll have a few minutes and then you want to leave here and get to the hospital to see Jacob. I've told them that there won't be any questions, but believe me, they'll try to ask questions anyway.'

I warned her, 'It's important that you don't say anything we don't agree to say. Some of the information – what Jacob was wearing when he went out to

66

the shops, for example – we need to keep to ourselves because we might need it, to verify the accuracy of a witness report.'

'What?'

That came from Peter. I didn't feel much like talking to him, but I suppose I had to explain, so I said, 'Let's say somebody comes forward and says, yes, I saw those two boys walking back from the shops.

'We can say, okay, what was Jacob wearing? Now, if we know that Jacob was wearing a white T-shirt, and that hasn't already been all over the news, the witness might say, 'He was wearing a black T-shirt,' and then, well, we'll know that's not the witness we're looking for.'

Peter seemed impressed. He said, 'You think of that yourself?'

I told him, 'That's fairly standard.'

To Lisa, I said, 'Now, the important thing is to decide what we *will* say. The time, the details, who Jacob was with, that's all okay. And if you think Harley is up to it, if you think Harley can speak about what happened, we'll get him to speak, too. Harley can talk?'

'He talks good,' said Lisa.

'All right. And where's he gone?'

She turned and hollered, 'HARLEY! *HARLEY*!'

Harley came out from wherever he'd been. It seemed to me that he was more curious than afraid. I dropped to my knees in front of him, so we were eye-to-eye.

I said, 'Harley? My name is Brian. I'm a detective with the Barrett Police. I'm a police officer.'

Sometimes, with kids, it's good to say you're a police officer. They're fond of police. They hear about them on the TV and at school, and the message is mostly that we are the guys who can be trusted. Harley was being raised to be suspicious of police – no doubt, in this house, we were 'the pigs' – but he was still young so the process was only partly underway.

I said, 'Harley, I've got a very important job for you today. I know you are upset about what happened to your brother and, in a few minutes, I'm going to take you outside with your mummy. There are going to be people out there who work for the papers and the TV, people who make the news.

'Now, everybody is very worried about what happened to your brother. We want to *catch* this man, Harley. We want to make sure that he can't bash up any other little kids.

'What we need you to do, Harley, is to tell the people with the cameras and the microphones – to tell the media – exactly what happened.'

I knew that Harley would probably look at his mother at this point, and he did. I thought to myself, 'How much does he understand? If he understands anything at all, how will he process it? Tell the media *exactly what happened*? Or exactly what his mother told him to tell the *police*?'

Lisa stepped into the gap. 'You tell them about the man,' she said, nodding, and staring into Harley's eyes. 'You tell them what you told me and Pete.'

I straightened.

I said, 'All right. Lisa, are you ready? This – speaking to the media – it can be a very difficult thing.'

She said, 'I wanna do it . . . cause you gotta catch this man so he don't do it to no one else.'

I thought, 'She's well into character now.'

'All right,' I said. 'Let's go. I'll speak first. I'll explain the situation. Then, Lisa, you speak, and then Harley, all you need to do is say exactly what you remember.'

I wasn't sure how much he would be able to say. The boy's vocabulary stretched, probably, to ten simple words: Dog. Cat. Boat. So far, at least, he hadn't said anything to me.

I opened the front door. The beam from the TV lights came straight at us. Lisa winced and put up her hand to shield her face. Peter's eye was immediately caught by the reporter who was trying to look like Jana, and blow me down if he didn't look ready to flirt.

I opened the way I always do. I said, 'Ladies and gentleman, thank you for coming.'

I've always enjoyed that line. It's like, 'Thank you for coming!' As if they were invited! I went on. I said, 'I'm Detective Senior Sergeant Brian Muggeridge of the Barrett CIB and I'm here today to make a public appeal for witnesses to what I think we'd all describe as a particularly cruel attack on a young boy.

'I'd like to introduce you to Lisa Cashman. Lisa is the mother of young Jacob Cashman, Jake Cashman, who is the child that some of you might have seen yesterday, being taken to the Children's Hospital.'

'And the dad? What's his name?' said one of the reporters, signalling behind me to where Peter Tabone was standing.

I said, 'No, the dad's not here. This here, Peter Tabone, he's an acquaintance of Mrs Cashman, here to give Mrs Cashman some support. We've also got young Harley here, who witnessed the attack, and we're going to have both of them speak to you briefly this morning, and what we'd like you press people to do, if you don't mind, is get out an appeal for witnesses.'

I explained the details of the case again and then made an appeal to the public for information. I said, 'Jacob's got very serious injuries, and we obviously want whoever did this off the street. So we're asking people who might have seen these two boys on their way back from the shop at around 5 p.m. yesterday, or seen any strange men in the area, anything at all that triggers a memory, to come forward, to do as we said yesterday and call Crime Stoppers. It can be completely confidential, but any information could help us.

'And now I'm going to introduce you to young Harley, who was with his brother. You'll appreciate that it's been very traumatic, and you'll understand that we don't want Harley to answer any questions at this point, but he might be able to say something.'

'Harley.'

Harley had been standing behind my legs. I stepped to the side, so he could be seen. In the glare of the TV lights, his white hair gleamed. He put half a foot forward, but was mute.

I said, 'Harley, you can just tell these folk what it was that you saw yesterday.'

There was a moment of awkward silence, but finally, he said, 'We got bashed up, me and Jake.'

The press waited, but that seemed to be all Harley wanted to say. He dropped to his haunches to inspect something on the porch. Lisa lifted him by the top of his pants.

'He hit Jake, didn't he?' she said. 'Where did he hit him?'

Harley said, 'Tummy.'

I said, 'All right, Harley, that's fine, and now, Mrs Cashman, if you could just speak?'

Lisa looked at me and then stepped forward. Now, we are talking here about a time before obesity became the scourge of the working class. Lisa was scrawny and pale and wearing a dress that was basically a column of terry-towelling material, held up by a band of elastic. She was a mother of four, and four pregnancies had taken a bit of a toll. Whatever she'd had up top before the kids arrived was well and truly gone. There wasn't enough in her boobs to hold up the dress, so it was kind of hanging from her nipples. Later, when I saw the TV footage, which showed just Lisa's head and shoulders as she spoke, I thought, 'Oh no, she looks naked.'

What else can I tell you about her? Well, people don't like to admit there's a class system in Australia, but as a cop, I can tell you it's a fact. You've got crime at the top end, but it's white-collar crime and tax evasion and the occasional jealous rage. At the bottom, you've got Indigenous families living on welfare – frankly, nobody is all that surprised when their kids get it in the neck. Lately, you've got more refugees – Sudanese and Somalis, the tallest, blackest, lankiest men you've seen in your life, all spider limbs, and the women dressed up like pepper grinders. They get into their own version of strife, belting each other over some ancient tribal problem. And then you've got Australians themselves, the white ones, the bogans I suppose you'd call them, who it's apparently okay to have a bit of snicker at, who would snicker at themselves because they're quite proud of the fact that they've got no airs and graces. They're the people who wear ugg boots to the milk bar; they're the people who you see today draped in the Australian flag, naked but for their stubbies and the Southern Cross tattoo on Australia Day.

Lisa was firmly in the bogan camp, and I knew exactly what the good folk of Australia would see when she appeared later that night with Brian Naylor on the six o'clock news. She had that bad dress, that skinny body, and skinny fingers with cheap rings on all of them. Her nails were painted to look like the tail of a peacock, and her arms were bare from armpit to wrist. Her hair had been permed, dyed, bleached and then dyed red, and was now growing out like a mullet down the back of her neck. Her eyebrows were plucked into a single line of hair, and the smokes had forced her gums back so she had that witchy look that you get when your teeth are too long.

There would be a fair amount of sympathy for her plight – it was obvious she had no education and was struggling by with all those kids – but on some other level she would have been repellent. There would have been a feeling that she'd brought much of this on herself. The only thing that saved her, I think, was that her voice wasn't strangled. You know the way the mums in the suburbs whine? It wasn't like that. Lisa had a voice that was deep and smoky. It sounded kind of hot.

She looked out at the cameras and said, 'My boy Jake got bashed yesterday. I want to know who bloody did it, and why! Why bash an innocent five-year-old boy!'

I'd encouraged Lisa to appeal for information in a calm manner, to suppress whatever emotion she felt. I'd told her, 'Nobody likes a lynch mob.'

Lisa had nodded, but now, in front of the cameras, she was letting the tears come, and she was letting her anger show. Why wouldn't she? Lisa Cashman was generating more respect and attention in front of those cameras than she'd been paid in her whole life.

She said, 'I want this bloke caught! I want to find out what kind of mongrel would do this! He should rot in hell.'

She was crying now and her make-up had started to run. I put my hand on her shoulder and gently moved her back to stand with me.

'We've got time for a question or two,' I said.

To myself, I thought, 'Here come the cynics.'

A reporter from *The Sun* – from memory, it was old Frank Postle – was first to speak. He said, 'Where were you when this happened, Mrs Cashman?'

Lisa said, 'At home!' and Frank, quick as anything, said, 'Do you often send the boys to the shops *on their own*?'

Lisa was fired up. 'Whaddaya mean by that?' she said, but before she could say more, I stepped in to defuse the situation. I said, 'Look, I think you'll appreciate that Mrs Cashman is extremely upset, the whole family is very upset. You'll appreciate that we want to get Mrs Cashman back to the hospital to see young Jacob as soon as we can. Thank you very much.'

Frank tried to interject but the bloke from media liaison stepped in. I heard him say, 'That's it, folks. I know you've got more questions and as soon as we've got more information we'll let you know.'

I rounded Peter, Lisa and Harley into a group, and

pushed them back through the front door, into the lounge. I stayed on the porch for a moment longer. A cameraman, reaching down to release the hold on the telescopic legs of his tripod, said, 'Sounds like so much bullshit.'

Frank said, 'Stranger, my arse. It'll be the boyfriend. Always is.'

Did he mean me to hear these things? I suppose he did, but I wasn't concerned. His doubts were my own.

Robert John Bird,
Surgeon

I remember the day that Jacob Cashman, aged five, came to the Royal Children's Hospital, because it was Remembrance Day. I've observed Remembrance Day since I was a boy at school in the 1950s. At 11 a.m. precisely we were required to stand behind our wooden desks, a framed portrait of Queen Elizabeth before us. We were silent for exactly one minute, and then we would say, 'Lest we forget.'

As a boy, I wasn't quite sure what I was supposed to be remembering. Doubtless there were times when I spent the minute of silence thinking something inappropriate. Now I'm older I understand. My grandfather was an army cook and my father also served in the army, so I'm not exactly short of people to think about.

My own profession has been medicine. Like all the

boys at my school, I was given a choice of three professions: medicine, the military or the law. I chose medicine, and I am now a paediatric surgeon. My clients are children: I operate on them; I try to make them well.

In any case, on the day that Jacob came to the hospital the parade of retired servicemen from the Shrine of Remembrance on St Kilda Road to Young and Jackson Hotel on the corner of Flinders Street had taken place in the morning, and I had gone along to pay my respects.

I seem to remember that it was a hot day, seasonally hot, for this was November. There was a feeling that rain might come – storm clouds had gathered and darkened the sky – but that feeling had been with us for many weeks. Rain would not come to Victoria until December, ruining my wife's preparations for a seafood meal served outdoors on Christmas Day.

The clinical notes show that Jacob arrived at the Emergency Department shortly after 7 p.m. In those days, calls to triple-O were monitored by staff able to give basic First Aid instructions, but generally unable to make an assessment of the patient's condition.

Paramedics aboard the ambulance could tell us more: that a child had been found floating in a swimming pool, for example, or that a woman had gone into labour and was threatening to deliver. Paramedics aboard the ambulance with Jacob Cashman told me they had applied what we then knew as the PGCS scale or (Paediatric) Glasgow Coma Scale. Jacob had scored a five, and that was troubling. A score of three on the PGCS is a patient either dead or in a very deep coma, while a score of fifteen is a fully awake individual. A score of five meant Jacob was unconscious: his eyes may well have been open but he would not have been able to see; he would make no sound or movement; and he would respond to no stimuli. There were signs of hydrocephalus, or fluid on the brain, too. The boy's head and face were swelling, his fontanelle (almost fused, since he was five) was bulging; and the veins across his skull were engorged.

Then, too, there was the indentation to his skull, barely perceptible, except by touch.

My initial diagnosis, subsequently confirmed, was that Jacob had suffered more than a head injury. He had suffered a brain injury. Let me explain that distinction. The term 'head injury' is generic – it describes any type of trauma to the head or skull. It does not necessarily mean the *brain* has been injured. Indeed, there are two basic types of head injury, one of which is *closed head trauma*, which does not feature penetration of the skull. (This may occur, as an example, when a man in a fist fight is punched in the head. He is bruised and sore, certainly, but his brain is likely all right.) The second type of head injury is known as *penetrating trauma*, where the skull itself is broken open, such as with a gunshot wound or a knife.

As a general rule, Australian children do not get shot or stabbed in the head with knives – and for this may we remain grateful, and vigilant. The most common type of head injury in children is therefore a *linear* skull fracture: in other words, a simple break along the lines of the bones that form the skull. It occurs when a child is hit with a rock or a ball. Such injuries are not normally serious. Bed rest may be all that is required.

A *depressed* skull fracture is more serious. It occurs when the force is more significant, and it means what it says: the trauma results in a dent in the skull bone, often to the thickness of the bone itself. This type of fracture may be associated with a brain injury – in particular, an intracranial haemorrhage, or bleeding of the brain – and this is very serious indeed.

When a patient with a head injury arrives at the Children's Hospital, a simple X-ray will normally be ordered, to detect any fractures to the skull. To detect a brain injury, we need a *computed axial tomography*, more commonly known as the CAT scan, where a series of photographs of the brain are taken from many angles and then reassembled, by computer program, to make a three-dimensional image. An *intracranial* probe, or ICP, may also be used. This instrument measures the pressure caused by swelling of the brain tissue, a common side-effect of brain injury. On the other hand, we might try an electroencephalogram, or EEG, which will measure electrical impulses produced by the brain to ascertain how it is working.

For Jacob, I ordered all three tests: CAT scan, EEG,

and ICP, and the results were not encouraging. In short, there were few signs that his brain was actually working as it should. I operated within the hour, to drain some fluid from it, but I was not hopeful of a recovery. Indeed, I had no doubt that Jacob was lost to us.

Jacob's mother had travelled to the hospital in the ambulance and rested in the waiting room while her boy was in the operating room on a ventilator. She was given permission to see Jacob briefly in intensive care. By then Jacob had the appearance of a child who was deeply asleep: his chest rose and fell, and his skin was pink. I suggested to Lisa that she go home, get some rest and return early the next morning for what I imagined would be a difficult discussion.

I left the hospital at midnight. The following morning, while still in my kitchen, I skimmed through coverage of Jacob's injuries in *The Sun*. I noted that Jacob's mother was claiming that her son had been set upon by a person unknown. I made no comment about that to my wife – she had peppered me with questions while I prepared her orange juice and porridge – but I had my own point of view. Upon arrival at the hospital, nursing staff had stripped Jacob's clothing from his body. I'd run my hand lightly over his limbs and his collarbone, and formed the conclusion that somebody had tortured this boy before. There were signs of damage – bumps and breaks – that had been left to heal, probably without medical attention.

I returned to the hospital at the normal time, around 8 a.m., and checked on Jacob. I recall now how moved I'd been by the quiet dignity of his small body. Jacob was the marvel that is a child of five. He was slimmer than boys today; his chest was a perfect cradle of bone, his jaw was delicate, his hands as smooth as soap. I remember the great regret I'd felt at shaving his hair, which was white and fine, almost like that of a distinguished gentleman of eighty, and at having to leave a jagged line of stitches, black and fierce as bull ants, marching around his ear.

His condition was unchanged except that now he had a white turban of bandages. I left him in peace.

I did rounds. Perhaps I saw to a broken bone or to a child who needed a transfusion. Perhaps I conversed with a set of worn-out parents slumped in cushioned chairs. Lisa arrived for her meeting with me mid-morning. I understood that she was delayed because she had already conducted a press conference from home. Part of it had played on the TV at the nurses' station. Lisa had reiterated her claim that Jacob had been assaulted by a person unknown. From her voice, I deduced that she was in an agitated state and I told nursing staff that I would be available to her upon her arrival.

When Lisa and her partner arrived they were directed to the office put aside for me. I gave them time to compose themselves before entering the room. I took my chair out from behind the desk so there would be no barrier between us. We sat in a semi-circle, facing each other. It's difficult to recall every detail but I would have been wearing a surgical apron and had mesh socks over my shoes, and this would have been a matter not of haste but of choice. I believe that a parent whose child is going to die not only deserves but *wants* to see a proper surgeon, somebody with some seniority, and the message that I'm that person can most quickly be conveyed by my wearing the surgeon's costume. For much the same reason I take care with my appearance. I have barely any hair at all any more, only a ring of white that my wife, perhaps cynically, describes as my halo, but I keep it short and neat, just like my fingernails.

Lisa had changed her clothes since the press conference. On the television she had appeared to be nearly naked, and I'd wondered what she was wearing, since so much skin was exposed, but she was dressed now in a vinyl suit with shiny iron marks on the fabric. I could tell that sexual allure was important to Lisa: the stocking-socks underneath her suit were fishnets, and she was overly made up.

Lisa's partner, Peter, was a young man – essentially, he was a very large boy – and he had a disconcerting way of abruptly raising one shoulder when he talked. He tapped his feet constantly. The back of his neck was pock-marked; here was a man who once suffered terribly from acne. His hair already receded at the forehead; to compensate, he wore it long and curled at the back.

I began by saying, 'Let's start with the nature of the injury to Jacob's brain.'

They did not speak so I continued.

'Often, in very young children, when the skull is still soft and the bones have not fused, there can be a blow to the head from one direction – say, if a child falls from a tree – and although the brain can be pushed from one side of the skull to the opposite side of the skull, the softness of the skull provides some cushioning.'

As I said the words, I knew they were misleading. That circumstance was irrelevant to Jacob. His skull was not soft. The bones had basically fused. In attempting to explain, I had put myself at risk of blurring the message. Lisa's face was full of confusion.

I moved to correct myself.

'Jacob is an older child,' I said. 'His skull is well-formed. His skull is not soft enough to allow the brain to swell or to move without injury.'

Lisa said, 'Will he be okay?'

I wanted to be as clear as I could.

'There is a great deal of swelling in his brain,' I said. 'Jacob's brain tissue has been pushed up against his skull, and in the process Jacob has suffered a brain injury. I believe he is brain *damaged*.'

Lisa said, 'What can you do?'

Now came the important part – and the hardest part. I said, 'I'm sorry, Lisa. Jacob will not recover.'

I expected at that moment that Peter would reach

for Lisa's hand. Such a movement between couples in trauma is so common that I've come to regard it as a reflex. Where there is a diagnosis of cancer, for example, the partner who is least invested – and that may be the cancer sufferer – will reach for the other partner's hand, and press down upon it. The idea, I suppose, is to anchor both people to the room, to prevent either of them from fleeing. It did not happen between Lisa and Peter, and I was so used to seeing it that I was momentarily caught short. I rose from my chair and took the leather-bound box of tissues, a gift from my colleagues, off the desk. This, I handed to Lisa. She set it upon her lap, like a child might hold a pet.

I continued, 'In a situation like this, I would like to be able to give you a best-case scenario. Unfortunately, today I have only a worst-case scenario. Jacob is currently breathing with the aid of a respirator. When the respirator is removed, he will be unable to breathe on his own.'

Peter said, 'He's not breathing?'

I said, 'That's correct. He is not breathing unassisted, and he cannot breathe unassisted.'

Lisa said, 'Can you keep him on the respirator –' It came out something like *respa-rader* – 'until . . .'

I waited.

'Like, until he comes around or whatever?' she said.

The tissue box was still on her lap, and Lisa had begun to wrap herself around it. It was to me a familiar pose: a human being under attack will cover their central region as best they can, to shield the tender organs, not least the heart.

As gently yet firmly as I could, I said, 'Jacob's brain injury is irreversible. He will not recover.'

In forty years in the medical profession, I've never overcome the guilt I feel at having to break news of this type. Obviously, children die every day, and it is surely *conceivable* to every one of us that one of our children will pre-decease us. Nevertheless, it is the thing we most fear. It is the thing we in modern medicine devote our greatest energy toward preventing. In modern times, it still seems to most of us that the death of a child is a gross violation of the pact we have with our God. He gives us children. We should, therefore, be allowed to raise them. That is the natural order of the world.

Lisa said, 'I've heard of people waking up from a coma.'

I knew what she was doing. She was holding out hope, even where there was none. My role, then, was to help her move quickly through the stages of loss – the disbelief, the denial, the bargaining, and the acceptance – so that Jacob would be allowed to die.

I said, 'He won't wake up, Lisa.'

Peter said, 'How do you know that?'

I met his gaze. Perhaps some more information *was* necessary. I had a common metaphor up my sleeve, one I often used to explain a brain injury to people, and although by using it I would run the risk of trivialising Jacob's injury, I decided to employ it now.

I said to Lisa, 'Have you ever had a swollen ankle?'

Lisa nodded, as I knew she would. Most Australian girls have twisted an ankle on the netball court. It is normally no great trauma and once the pain subsides it can be amusing to be bandaged and on crutches, essentially unharmed and yet the centre of attention.

I continued, 'Good. Then you know that when you have an injury to any part of your body, it swells?'

She nodded, yes.

'Your ankle is able to swell with fluid because its capacity to swell is essentially limitless,' I said.

Now she was confused again.

'Your ankle is not encased in your skull,' I said. 'The brain *is* encased in your skull. Your skull is like a hard shell. When the brain swells, it comes up against that shell, and there is a limit to how far it can swell.

'Pressure builds up, Lisa, and blood vessels that supply the brain with oxygen become constricted, which means they get squashed.

'The swelling pushes down on the brain stem, which controls the breathing and the heart. The damage is permanent. Part of the brain dies, Lisa. The skull protects the brain but in a case like this, it can also damage the brain, and that is what we have found with Jacob.'

Peter said, 'Can't you do something?'

I said, 'We have taken some of the fluid and drained it to the abdomen, to reduce the swelling. That will make Jacob more comfortable. The damage to Jacob's brain cannot be reversed, however. It is permanent.'

We sat for a moment in silence. Lisa said, 'There must be something you can do.'

I said, 'No.'

The weight of this news appeared to be settling on Lisa's spine. She had become a curled ball of agonised flesh upon her chair. She had pulled her knees up to her chest, and her feet were now resting on her seat.

Peter remained combative. He said, 'How much do you really know? We'll get a second opinion, thank you very much.'

This, too, was common: a second opinion was another straw at which to clutch.

I had my answer ready. I said, 'I want you to know this is not a personal opinion. This is the opinion of this hospital's experts, all of them. If there were a shred of doubt, if there were anything known to medical science that would be useful to Jacob, I assure you, we would grab it. I do not want to lose him. I know you cannot bear to lose him, but lose him we will.

'That said, you are of course able to seek a further opinion. I am certain you will find it is the same.'

I was aware, obviously, that the death of Jacob would have consequences for this couple. While he lived, police were dealing with a case of abuse, or neglect, or even assault. If he died – when he died – it would become a case of manslaughter, or even murder.

I had not, until that point, talked to Lisa about what, precisely, had happened to Jacob to so disable him. It was not my business to investigate. But I wanted to know. Of course I wanted to know. Jacob was, by appearances at least, a lovely boy. He was also my patient. I did not believe that Jacob had been beaten. His parents claimed he had been kicked and punched, but if so, where were the scrapes and the bruises? No, he'd taken one blow to the head – but who did it, and why?

Lisa said, 'I want to see him.'

This was an important development. Lisa's desire to see her son was very closely related to her need to accept the circumstance before her.

'Yes,' I said. 'We can arrange that.'

We walked the hall to intensive care together. The police were close behind us. I opened the door to Jacob's room. Even in the few moments I'd been away, his small body had shrunk a little. He was deeply asleep and comfortably hydrated, lying on a pale blue sheet, his naked chest rising and falling, his eyes closed. Lisa stepped forward. The Royal Hospital employed counsellors specifically to assist parents in a moment like this: parents who needed to say goodbye to their children. This person had been summonsed and I was grateful to see her put a plump hand over Lisa's long fingers.

Lisa said, 'I want a priest.' That, too, was a request easily accommodated. The hospital had its own chapel.

I allowed Lisa to stay in the room, briefly, without me. I am neither a guardian of the courts nor the coroner. I understood that an investigation was underway, but in my view a mother should not be prevented from saying goodbye to her child.

A police officer – a detective, I assume – approached me in the corridor. He was perhaps thirty-five, and in the process of surrendering to middle age.

He said, 'What's the prognosis?'

I gave him my diagnosis. 'Blunt-force trauma.'

He said, 'Will he make it?'

I said, 'No.'

'Priors?'

He meant: has Jacob been injured before? As I've said, in my examination of Jacob's body I had noticed that his collarbone was marked by a small nodule, suggestive of a fracture left to heal without medical attention, and there was evidence of other breaks. All of this I would put in my final report. At that moment it seemed useful to say only, 'Yes.'

The detective said, 'We don't want her in there too long.'

'I'll see how it's going,' I replied.

I returned to Jacob's room. Lisa was weeping. She turned to me and said, 'He can't die.'

He could and he would . . . and so do we all. Some

of us at the age of 100, bored to tears by the length of our lives; some of us at the age of eighteen, after living in a blaze of glory and then burning out in a car crash; some of us in middle age, wishing we had just a few more years to enjoy the grandkids; and some of us, like Jacob Cashman, gone to God at the age of five.

I said, 'I'm sorry.'

I can't remember how long Lisa continued to sit with Jacob, although I suspect we didn't sit for long. There is only so much to say to a person lying unconscious on a hospital bed. People say 'Goodbye', and some, maybe most, also say 'I'm sorry' – for what, I'm never sure, but it seems we're always sorry for the things we didn't do for the dying.

Lisa said, 'What now?'

I said, 'With your permission, I will give a directive to end the artificial life support. The respirator will be taken away.'

'And then what?'

'He'll slip away.'

He'll slip away. Oh, how I wish that were true. If only death were like that! Instead, Lisa would leave the room. I would sign the necessary paperwork. The nurses would turn the lights down and remove the machinery. Then, in the darkness, Jacob would begin to fight for his life. His small body would jolt. His chest would heave off the bed. His jaw would clench and his small hands would grope the air, trying to hold onto something, anything, in this world.

He wouldn't feel pain. Morphine would be administered immediately, and continuously, through a drip in the back of his hand. Still, his death would be agony. I don't mean that in the traditional sense of the world. No, when I say that death is agony, I mean it in the true sense of the word. Agony comes from the Greek, from 'agon', which means 'struggle'. That is what we do at the end of our lives. We struggle. We rage, as Dylan Thomas put it, against the dying of the light . . . and we lose.

We all lose.

Detective Senior Sergeant Brian Muggeridge

I didn't think Jacob was going to die. He was in a bad way, that was obvious, flopping around the way he was that day in the house on DeCastella Drive, but it didn't look like a fatality. There was no blood. No bruising. It was the paediatrician at the Children's that set me straight. He was an older guy, balding on top and blue scrubs, like every doctor you've ever seen. He told me, 'Blunt-force trauma.'

I said, 'Will he make it?'

He said 'No', or something like it, or maybe it was the way he'd said 'Blunt-force trauma', I just figured he was telling me there was no hope.

I wondered what was going through the bloke's mind. I mean, he'd had to operate on the boy, cut the kid's head open, work half the night trying to save him, and then he'd got to spend another hour in the waiting room with the people who likely put the kid in the hospital in the first place. It boggles the mind. The nurses, too: they'd had to tend to the kid, and they'd had to look at Lisa falling about in the corridor, and at Peter trying to hold her up. Surely they knew. But they never said anything.

As for the parents, well, how must they have felt, seeing all these good folk, these professionals, the counsellors and whatnot, fawning over them? Did they feel any guilt? I wouldn't rule it out, but the victim mentality is pretty well entrenched in some people. If they felt sorry for anyone it was mostly themselves, and I'm sure if Lisa was thinking anything that day at the hospital, it was basically that this wasn't her fault. Sure, her fella might have hit the kid, but how was she to blame? That's how she would think.

Anyway, it wasn't up to me to right the wrongs in the world. I had to get to the bottom of the matter and I wanted to do it quickly. All the papers, all the radio, they were still running with the story that Jacob had been set upon, and it's not right to have a community believing that kind of thing can happen. It wasn't fair on the people of Barrett, for one thing, and it has a knock-on effect. Parents start driving their kids to school and picking them up instead of letting them walk, and nobody is allowed to go out and play because they think the neighbourhood's not safe.

Jacob's life support was removed at noon on November 12, and he would have passed away shortly after that. The death certificate records the time of death as 12.30.

We got the bloke from media liaison to type out a quick statement for the reporters in the foyer. It was brief enough. It said, 'Jacob Cashman's life support has been withdrawn.'

They would get that, straightaway. It meant: the kid's dying.

The statement went on, 'Jacob's mother, Lisa Cashman, and her defacto husband, Peter Tabone, are assisting police with their inquiries.'

They'd get that, too. Take it from me, whenever you see the words 'assisting police', it means they're being questioned and the cops think they did it.

I watched the media guy hand the statement around, and I heard a couple of reporters chatting. One of them said, 'Him or her, do you reckon?' and his mate replied, 'Him. Definitely him. Whadda you reckon?'

'I reckon her.'

'Come on, mate. It's always the bloke.'

They were packing up their gear. There was no point hanging around the hospital, not if the parents were going to be at the police station. One of them turned to me and said, 'Are we going to get an arrest today?' and I said, 'I don't know, mate.'

'Where are the other kids?'

'Welfare.'

Welfare. That's what we used to call the state government department that is now referred to as the Department of Community Services, although officially it's called the Department of Child Protection and Family Services, I think. To me, it's basically the welfare department, and it's never been any good, although apparently there's also a new slogan: 'Every Child, Every Chance.' You can read into that whatever you like.

'God help them,' the reporter said.

I agreed with him, but I said, 'That'll do.'

The media followed us back to the police station at Barrett; we were all there by 2 p.m. They weren't going to get inside. That would be ridiculous. The story was getting bigger; there were heaps of them. They'd have to set up on the footpath. The media guy was trying to herd them.

'Leave a spot clear for pedestrian traffic,' he said, opening his arms to show how much space he wanted around the front door. 'I'll come out when we've got a development. I think we all know it's gonna be a while.'

That was fine by most of the hacks on the footpath. It's hard to believe now, but news was once something that was revealed twice a day: first in the morning newspaper, and again on the six o'clock news. It wasn't something that was posted on the Internet as it happened, all hours of the day and night. These guys were seriously permitted to sit in the November sunshine all afternoon, twiddling their thumbs and waiting for developments. Naturally enough, their big concern was food. They'd been at the hospital all morning, drinking instant coffee and looking for a place to take a leak. Now they'd have to wait some more, and they were hungry.

'I'll do the run,' said one. 'Who wants what?'

'Is there a place with hamburgers?'

'I really need some water.' That came from the TV girl, the one who looked like Jana.

'Where's the nearest milk bar?'

The media guy proved his usefulness, again. He stepped up and said, 'The best place for you guys is the joint on the corner of High Street. I know the bloke there. He'll take care of you. Listen, can you get me something, too?'

They probably settled down to greasy burgers, cigarettes and Coke – a Coke and a smoke and a choke, they called it – and we brought Lisa and the boyfriend through a back door. The idea was to shield them from the cameras, although you never get away with it, not entirely. There's always one bloke, usually from *The Sun*, snooping around the back, trying to get the picture, and yeah, he got one.

The Barrett Police Station was not a sophisticated operation, not then, and not now. We had three people to interview – that would be Lisa, and the boyfriend, and Harley. I didn't even think about Lauren. Why would we want to talk to Lauren? No, that wouldn't come until later. But every one of the people we did want to interview would have to be taped, and Harley would need to have a social worker on hand, or else the evidence we collected would be inadmissible. Everybody's got their right to a lawyer, and all that. Barrett didn't have an endless supply of rooms. There was no two-way mirrored glass. You see that on TV but you didn't get it at Barrett. One of our interview rooms was actually converted from the storage cupboard. We had to sit with plastic drums storing liquid for the photocopiers, and does anybody remember how that smells?

Anyway, we stuck Lisa in the main room, and Peter in the room with the photocopier. The two kids we didn't want to talk to – Hayley, who was just a toddler, and Lauren – got their social workers and were told to have a bit of a play, Mum would be out soon.

I wanted to start with Lisa. It would have to be formal. My feeling was still: it's got to be Peter. So I went into the room where Lisa was and sat opposite her at the table. I stared into her face. She looked ragged. Bone dry, if that makes sense. She was stained with cigarettes, and she was still smoking. We at Barrett were trying to get our heads around the idea that cigarettes weren't the best idea. There was a new ban on smoking in city offices, up in Melbourne, but at the Barrett cop shop, you could still smoke – everybody smoked – so we let her smoke, too.

I'd been watching her over the course of the day,

and I'd decided that Lisa wasn't stupid. She was defensive; she was uneducated, but not stupid. She knew her rights, too. Straight up, she said she wanted a lawyer. She wanted to say 'nothing to nobody' that might be used against her. I'm no genius at the interview thing. I'm not going to pretend we had a *Silence of the Lambs*-type operation going on at Barrett, where we'd get inside people's heads and make them crack. We didn't. In fact, all we knew about the criminal mind was that if we ever came across a proper psychopath, somebody with a real bit of evil or a touch of nous, we'd be stumped. Happily, we didn't come across that kind of crook. The sad and the violent, we had a lot of that. The plain stupid, you bet. That was our lot at Barrett. Psychopaths, not so much.

I had a pretty good idea what Lisa's take on the situation was going to be. First up, she was a grieving mum who'd just lost her son, so she was going to play that card. Next up, she'd deny everything, and that's where I figured I'd get her. That's where she'd trip up. Let me see if I can explain. Let's say you've got a bank robbery in Bourke Street at 9 p.m. on Saturday. A police officer will take his suspect and say to him, 'Were you in Bourke Street at 9 p.m. on Saturday?' If he's a smart guy, a good crook, he'll say, 'Certainly, sir. I was indeed in Bourke Street at 9 p.m. on Saturday.'

Now, that might sound counterintuitive. Why does the guy want to put himself at the scene of a crime? But that's the thing. Chances are, we've already placed him at the scene. These days, we've either got him on the CCTV, or we've got a witness, and he knows he's easy to place there, so he says, 'Yeah, that was me.'

A dumb guy, an inexperienced crook, he'll deny everything. He'll say, no sir, not me, and then we pull out the CCTV, and we've already caught him lying.

Now Lisa, I was guessing she fell into the second category. She was smart, but not an experienced crook. She was the type to say, 'Nope, wasn't me. I weren't there,' and land herself right in it.

What I needed to do then was find some facts that were incontrovertible, and see if she'd deny them. I had a little something up my sleeve, something that didn't quite make sense, and I was mulling it over when Lisa said, 'Where are my kids?'

I said, 'They're all here. We're going to have to talk to them.'

She sat up straight and downright snarled at me. She said, 'Who do you got to talk to? You talked to Harley already. Hayley's a baby. And where's Lauren? You don't got to talk to Lauren. She weren't even there.'

I said, 'Lauren was at home, wasn't she?'

She didn't trip up. She said, 'Jake wasn't bashed *at home*.'

I said, 'Lisa, can I get you a coffee?'

She said, 'No, but I need the loo.'

I thought, 'I bet you do.' Like I've said, a person

under pressure will find themselves lightening their load, whether they realise it or not. I signalled to the guy working the tapes to shut them down. I said, 'It's at the end of the hall. I'll come with you.'

Lisa said, 'I don't need a *chaperone*. Why you gotta watch me take a piss?' I followed her out anyway, and stood at the cubicle door. I listened for tinkling, but there was none.

After a bit, I said, 'Everything all right in there?'

'Bloody hell,' said Lisa. I heard the sounds of a woman pulling up her knickers and fastening her belt.

'I've got to organise the funeral,' she said upon exit. 'We haven't got no money. I want something special. He deserves it. Jacob's a good kid.'

I noticed that she was speaking in the present tense. Jacob's death was barely a reality to her.

'I want to talk to the priest,' she said. 'I want to get one of those headstones shaped like a teddy bear, one of those big ones, all marble.'

We walked back to the interview room together. It was time to get serious. The reporters would have to file something soon and I didn't want another round of newspapers going out with the same story on the front. I waited for the tape deck to start rolling. I made sure I could see the cogs turning, and then I got straight to it. I said, 'Sit down, Lisa. For the record, I am Detective Senior Sergeant Brian Muggeridge, Barrett CIB. You do not have to answer any questions. Anything you do say may be used in court against you. Do you understand, Lisa?'

She looked startled, and then it kind of dawned on her. All these formalities – I could see her thinking, '*Shit, I'm a suspect.*'

'I got nothing else to tell you,' she said.

I said, 'Do you understand, Lisa?'

She nodded yes, but I had to make her say it out loud for the tape.

'Okay,' she said. 'Yeah, I get it.'

I said, 'There are a couple of things we need to go over. I'm going to tell you straight up, Lisa, we don't believe that Jacob was set upon by a stranger. It's not credible.'

She said, 'You've got no right holding me like this when I've got the funeral to do.'

She opened her handbag, took out a cigarette. She said, 'I can't believe this.' She was rolling her thumb over the ball of the lighter.

I said, 'Lisa, we're talking here about a homicide.'

It was the first time I had used the word. There are a couple of things that have to be in place before you can prove 'murder'. There has to be intent, pre-meditation. I had no idea what happened to Jacob, beyond the fact that he was now dead and going cold in the hospital, and my patience with his mum was wearing thin. Maybe the boyfriend did it. Maybe it was an accident. Manslaughter was a possibility, but surely it was time to quit the bullshit about the stranger.

I said again, 'Homicide, Lisa. Serious business.'

Her foot began to tap, rapidly, against the floor. Now was the time to make my move.

I said, 'Lisa, why was Jacob's hair wet?'

She looked up.

'Wet?'

'When Jacob went into the ambulance, his hair was wet. Why was that?'

She said, 'I don't know.' Then she said, 'I think there was a puddle in the yard.'

A puddle in the yard? Ladies and gentleman of the jury, the alarm bells should have rung right there. It was *November*. A total fire ban had been in place since September. The entire state of Victoria was tinder dry. A year from then, I'd be fighting the Ash Wednesday bushfires with the Barrett volunteer brigade. Seventy lives would be lost. That's how hot, how dry, it was in Victoria in November 1982. And to explain why Jacob was wet, Lisa says, 'There was a puddle in the yard.'

I said, 'No, there wasn't.'

'There might have been,' she said.

'No, Lisa, there wasn't. Jacob's *clothes* were dry. His clothes were dry, but his hair was wet. How do you explain that? How did Jacob's hair get wet?'

I waited. It was time for Lisa to admit one of the *incontrovertible* facts of the case: Jacob's hair was wet because they'd put him in the bathtub, or doused him with water to try to bring him around. There was no other explanation. Jacob wasn't marked. It wasn't as if they were trying to wash away any blood, but for some reason, Jacob *had* been doused in water at some point before the ambulance arrived. Presumably he'd also been dressed in clean, dry clothes.

Now, if Lisa had been a smart crook, an experienced crook, she could have handled that fact. She would have said, 'Yeah, all right, we put him in the bath. He was so weak, or so hot, when we carried him home that we needed to cool him down.' That would be plausible. That's something you or I might do. But Lisa's instinct, her habit of a lifetime, was to *lie,* to lie about *everything*, and so she did.

I said, 'Did you put Jacob in the bath?'

She was on automatic pilot now. The automatic, knee-jerk, lie-to-the-cops pilot. She said, 'No.'

I said, 'Lisa, when I'm done here, I'm going to speak to Harley. We are also talking to Peter. Do you think either of them will tell us that actually, yes, you did put Jacob in the bath?'

She was worried. They probably hadn't gone over that detail. They probably had no story to cover that. Peter might say anything. The kid would certainly own up to it, and why not? It seemed an easy enough question for a child: did Mummy put Jacob in the bath? Sure she did.

So, Lisa now had a choice: she could either speak up and save herself, and give up Peter, or she could carry on with the charade. I was thinking, 'Give him up, you stupid woman. He's an arsehole.' From the moment I'd seen him in Lisa's house, not with his arms around her but reclined on the Jason, tapping away at a cigarette, I'd thought, 'You've got nothing to lose by losing him.' I was hoping she'd see things the way I saw them. She had a shallow, sexual bond with this guy. They were living together because it suited his animal instincts: he was getting a root. She was probably thinking, 'Yeah, but I want to have a guy around, someone to party with; to drink UDL and smoke bongs and help keep the kids under control.' But that wasn't love. That wasn't even the basis for any loyalty. *Give him up*.

I said, 'Lisa, did Peter do something to Jacob?'

I said it in the voice I use when I'm trying to get a woman to crack. I like to think of it as my compassionate voice. It goes: confess to me! Own up now, say, 'Okay, Jacob *wasn't* bashed by a stranger. Peter kicked the shit out of my kid and the reason I'm covering up for him is because I'm bloody terrified!'

I said, 'Lisa, we know that Jacob has been injured before.'

She didn't say anything. Instead, she went through what I call the motions. She pushed back her chair. She dragged her decorated fingernails through the front of her hair and then threw her head back. She got to her feet and found she wanted to be sitting again, so sat down. I let her go; it was just stress playing out.

'I want to see a lawyer,' she said. 'I'm gonna get him to ask you why you aren't out *there* trying to find out who did this, why you're in *here*, hasslin' *me*.'

So, she wasn't ready. Not yet.

'Okay,' I said. 'Let's call a halt to proceedings for a moment. For the benefit of the tape, we are suspending the interview.'

I prepared to leave the room. Lisa was wide-eyed. She said, 'Where you goin'?'

I said, 'I want to give you a bit of time to think.'

'In case you forgot, I got a funeral to plan.'

'I understand that. There will be time. There will be an autopsy. I'm really urging you to use this time to think hard about how you want us to proceed.'

I left her alone – not strictly true, since a uniformed officer would have remained in the room – but essentially alone, to plan her next move. I walked down the corridor toward the staff canteen. I had the feeling, or maybe I'd been told, that Harley would be there. Now, as a rule, the courts don't let cops like me interview little kids. You've got to have a specialist and the whole thing has to be strictly regulated. Kids have a tendency to tell adults what they think they want to hear and, besides that, who knows what goes on in the brain of a three-year-old? They can sense trouble as well as the older kids, and they're keen to dodge it, like anyone is. Their Achilles heel – if you want to call it that – is that they don't self-censor. They aren't cautious. The other thing is, if they're conditioned to lie – and a lot of kids we deal with are conditioned to lie – you can catch them out pretty quick. Their made-up stories have a fantastic quality. They keep adding details, stuff that doesn't fit, and the whole thing soon unravels, and you think, 'Bingo!' And then the counsellors come in and say it's all inadmissible because you tried to trick the kid or something.

I figured it would be all right to have an informal chat, though. Harley had a social worker with him. I'd make like I was gathering information about the attacker, and nothing to use in court.

The moment I entered the canteen, the counsellor said, 'This isn't official, right?'

'Right,' I said. 'I'm just up for a chat.'

Harley was like every three-year-old you've ever seen. He was moving around the unfamiliar room, examining coffee cups and reaching for the sugar spoon so he could stick it in his mouth.

I said, 'Harley, can you sit here?' I held a chair out for him. He wandered over, climbed up on it and sat down, his feet swinging.

I said, 'Harley, we need to ask you about what happened yesterday.'

He didn't say anything. I continued, 'Harley, your mum has told us that a man bashed you and your brother.'

'Jacob was bashed by a man,' he said, happily enough. He wasn't being flippant – what does a three-year-old know of flippant? – he was merely uninterested. He'd answered these questions before. He couldn't see why it was important. He was looking at the ceiling, looking at the walls, wondering when he might be able to get up and resume exploring the room.

I said, 'Harley, did somebody hurt Jacob?'

He said, 'No.'

'No?'

'Jacob got bashed by a man.'

He inched forward in the plastic chair, moving on his buttocks, the way kids do, shuffling until his feet touched the floor. Then, before I could stop him, he was out of the chair and making his way toward some new object of interest. Technically, I wasn't allowed to touch him, but I couldn't help myself. I rose and ruffled his hair – I swear, it was irresistible, that hair – and left the room.

I saw no value in tracking down Hayley. How old was she? Eighteen months? She couldn't even talk. But I did want to give Lisa more time to come to her senses. So, rather than go back to the interview room, I tracked down Lauren. After all, she was six years old. If something *had* happened in the house on DeCastella Drive, as opposed to in the school, she would have to know about it.

Almost by accident, I found her in the corridor. She was in the company of another counsellor. What can I say about how she appeared? I've thought about that so many times. Was she distraught? I don't think she was, not then, anyway. She was quite interested in what was going on around her. The events of the previous day – the police and the ambulance – would have been pretty exciting, and now she was being treated the way kids are treated when there's a tragedy of some kind: she was being spoiled. She'd been offered a Happy Meal from McDonald's and now she and the social worker were off to the Coke machine. She was being allowed to handle the change. Probably, she'd be allowed to feed the coin slot, choose her drink, press the buttons, and make the can fall. If she was anything like any other kid in the world, she would have been thinking, 'Wait until I tell Jake. Oh wait, Jake's gone. Do I want Coke, or something else?'

In saying that, I don't mean to imply that she was a callous child. Let me stress that, actually: I don't believe for a minute that Lauren Cashman, or Cameron, or whatever she now calls herself, was a callous or uncaring child. In my experience, you can tell a six-year-old that their *parent* has died and they'll go straight back to the TV, and look at it blankly. Ten minutes later, they'll be giggling or fighting with a sibling over what to watch.

It will come for them – the grief, I mean – but it takes *years*, not hours.

Anyway, what happened in the corridor shocked us all. I was standing there, and Lauren was maybe two metres away, coming toward me. She was shaking the change in her hand, in step with the social worker, and then, suddenly, out of the blue, her mother was there. Now, let me assure you, that wasn't supposed to happen. We were trying hard to keep them apart. They may well have been mother and daughter, and they may well have needed to be together right then, but the mum was linked to a serious crime, and there was no way we were going to let them collude, not once it became clear that the story was bogus.

Anyway, for some reason they let Lisa out of the interview room at the same minute that Lauren was being escorted down the hall, and they ran right into each other.

Now, in the twenty years since then, I've thought a lot about what should have happened in that moment. Had Lisa's account been true – if Jacob truly had been set upon by a stranger – then mother and daughter would have run toward each other, surely? Lisa would have bolted down the hall and taken her surviving child in her arms, and they would have sobbed together, grieved together, held each other up. Lauren would have run to her mother, confused and afraid, and seeking comfort.

What actually happened was the opposite. They stepped *back*. They looked startled to see each other. Lisa, in particular, got a fright. And then, get this, Lisa *hissed*. She raised her voice and said, 'I hope you're not telling any lies in there, Lauren.'

Lauren didn't bat an eyelid. In a voice just like her mother's, a lazy, husky, adult drawl, she said, 'I ain't said *nothin'*.'

She was speaking the truth. Lauren *hadn't* told us what happened on DeCastella Drive, not yet, anyway. Her mother hadn't told us anything, either. And yet, the look they gave each other, it was like: *Can I trust you?*

We didn't know it, not then, but they had an agreement. How it was reached, I can't tell you. Maybe, in the moments before the ambulance arrived, Lisa sat her little girl down and spoke to her calmly, saying, 'This is what we are going to do . . .'

Maybe the opposite is true. Maybe she took her by the shoulders and shook her until her eyes rattled and said, 'If you so much as whisper a word about this . . .'

I don't know how it happened or even, really, whose idea it was. What I do know is that they entered into a pact, and sealed it, before any of us arrived. They concocted the story about the attack. They went over the details, as best they could, and as far as I can tell, they all agreed, 'If we stick to this, nothing can happen to any of us.'

It didn't last, though. One of them reneged.

The Reverend John Ball, Anglican Priest

I must admit I was surprised when the police told me that Jacob Cashman's mother wanted to have the funeral for her young son at my church, St John's Anglican Church, on the Barrett Estate. It wasn't so much that she wanted a *church* service that surprised me. It's quite normal for people to seek out the priest when it comes time to bury someone, even on an estate where nobody under the age of seventy goes to church. No, what surprised me was that Mrs Cashman wanted an Anglican service for her son. I'd been following the case in the newspapers, and I knew for certain that the Cashman family had never set foot in my church. I'd also assumed that they were Catholic. The boy's name – Jacob – seemed to suggest it. In my experience, when you're dealing with a family that has named their child Jacob – or, for that matter, Joseph or Sarah or Rebecca – you're normally dealing with Catholics, but no, the police told me that the mother said they were Church of England, and so the Anglican Church was where the funeral would be.

I don't kid myself that Lisa Cashman was making any kind of political or theological statement in saying that she was Church of England. I don't imagine that she had any idea about the Reformation or the history of schism in the Christian churches. No, Church of England is simply what so many Anglo-Saxon Australian families that aren't Catholic claim to be, when pushed on the question of religion. Come to that, I don't believe that Lisa Cashman knew, not in any spiritual sense, that she had endowed Jacob with a truly Christian name. It's entirely possible – quite common, actually – to find people who have no idea that Jake is a short form of Jacob, and that Jacob comes from the Bible. Parents these days present their children to be christened because they want to have a nice party with some formalities, they want to celebrate the baby and have photographs taken. It's become something of a sad joke in the Church, though, that they don't actually know why they are doing it. They don't understand that a child when baptised is entering into a life of Christ. They don't understand the significance of the names they give their children. At a conference on faith, I heard about a baby girl who the parents wanted to call Jezebel. Thank heavens, their priest managed to talk them out of it. 'But it's so pretty!' they said.

There is no point complaining, I suppose. Just as there's no point complaining about the church building we had on Barrett. There might well have been a time – indeed, there was a time – when the tallest building in any Australian town would have been the church. A time when the steeple would have risen higher than any other structure on the landscape, when the church would have provided a focal point for the community. Those days are gone. Churches now are dwarfed by office blocks. On new estates – places like Barrett – well, they're often out on the industrial estate. If we hadn't taken the lease, the building might have ended up a branch headquarters for Medicare. St John's was visible to no one but the staff at Barrett Glass who had to walk past to get a sandwich from the milk bar next door. It was neither the biggest nor the most impressive structure on the estate – that would be the shopping centre – and from one Sunday to the next, the pews – the plastic chairs – were mostly empty. There was no shame in Barrett in skipping church. In fact, young people felt quite embarrassed if they did want to go to church. It was daggy. That's what the kids told me, 'Church is daggy.' Their parents thought the same. They filled their lives with work and sport and barbecues, and if they ever did feel empty, they'd buy some new possessions. If they yearned for a spiritual experience, they'd get out the Tarot cards or scented candles, or have a séance. They would not turn to Christ.

When I started at St John's I did make an effort to get people through the doors. I was of the view then – less so now, I don't mind saying – that if church was daggy, if it was gloomy, then we should make it less intimidating. I put a signboard out the front, next to the wooden cross, and I changed the letters every week, to make the place seem alive and welcoming. Like everybody, I was inspired by the sign that once went up outside a church in Hawthorn: 'What would you do if Jesus came to Hawthorn?' Some wag had written, 'Move Peter Hudson to centre half forward.' It created much mirth and people flocked to see it. I wanted to show people that church isn't all about guilt, and that a priest can be a modern person with an interest in football and a sense of humour.

On a very hot day, I'd write, 'If you think it's hot here, imagine Hell!'

My favourite, though, was, 'Looking for a sign from God? Here it is!'

It didn't work. Attendance at St John's stayed low, except at Christmas and Easter, or when somebody wanted to get married.

We charged $100 for a wedding, and for a funeral it was $50. For Jacob Cashman's family, I waived the fees. I could see from the newspaper coverage that this was a family with limited funds, and I knew it would be a big funeral, with media coverage. I might as well be honest: a big funeral, with journalists and cameras, is as good an opportunity as any to get out the church's message, so I was on some level pleased when the Cashman funeral came my way.

Police told me that Jacob's mother wouldn't be present. I thought that was cruel. I don't believe any charges had been laid. I thought it was important that she be there, regardless. But the authorities declined on security grounds.

'She'll be lynched.' That's what the detective told me. 'They'll string her up outside the church and tear her to pieces.'

I won't deny that emotions on the estate were aflame. The story about the man attacking Jacob had shocked people, and their hearts went out to the Cashmans, but then it quickly began to fall apart and people started to gossip and come to their own conclusions, and of course the mother and her boyfriend were 'assisting police', as they say, and people were enraged. They were angry that the parents might have done something to the child. Then, too, there were early rumours that there was more to this story than people even realised.

I was conscious of my responsibility to both the community and the Church. I would remind the congregation that God alone judges us. In days to come, when Lisa and her boyfriend were formally charged, newspapers would be filled with comments from people thirsting for revenge. One mother would say, 'You don't bash your kids. They drive you up the wall but you don't bash 'em,' and another would say, 'I just don't get how you can do that to a little kid. Have you seen the pictures of him? The boy's an angel.'

Police had given me the portrait of Jacob that had already appeared in the newspaper. A lady in the parish office, one of our volunteers, had it framed, and we stood it upon the coffin. Jacob had very white hair, and he also had a white coffin. A state government department – I don't recall which one – provided a quick injection of cash to Jacob's family. They do this for all welfare recipients who need to bury a family member, and since Jacob's mother had been on the single mother's pension, she qualified. She had been allowed to choose the colour of the coffin. I was pleased she chose white. Once, in a country town, the parents had requested fire-engine red for a small boy knocked over by farm machinery, but generally I suggest white for children. It lends the ceremony a degree of solemnity, reminds us that we are burying a child.

The police said the boy's siblings – Hayley, Harley and Lauren – were to be present, and I was conscious of including them in the service. I asked the volunteer we had in the office to seat them on the plastic chairs nearest the altar so I might address them directly.

In retrospect, I didn't do enough for the children. I was prideful. I was too conscious of the media attention, and too interested in the impression I might make. The mayor was there, as was the principal from Barrett Primary. I was also too young. This was nearly thirty years ago; I had virtually no experience with small children. It did not even occur to me that the service for Jacob would be well underway before the children realised that Jacob was actually with us, that he was *in that white coffin* at the front of the church, under the photograph of him.

We make that mistake, don't we, of assuming that children will understand things that adults automatically comprehend? It's not that I should have said, 'Here we are, and there are Jacob's earthly remains, in that box,' but I wonder if I could have done something to help Lauren, at least, understand what was going on. Because with children it dawns on them slowly: He's in there, and he's *dead*. If we opened the lid he would not sit up as we remember him. He's dead, and dead's *forever*.

There was no sign of Jacob's father. His identity had been determined from documents held by the Department of Social Security. He was named in paperwork demanding that he pay child support, but an attempt to find him before the funeral had failed. Who did turn up, in large numbers, were children from the Barrett Primary School. They wore blue polo shirts, with a crest on the right breast, and white socks and school shoes. Their teachers had supplied them with white balloons and, at first, we let them carry the balloons and even hold them in the church, but then they started to do what kids will do when armed with balloons – belt each other – so the teachers had to take the balloons away again. We stored them out the back to release later, when Jacob's coffin was loaded into the hearse.

The media was there, too. I made an effort to make them feel welcome. There were some people who looked at them gruffly and I thought, 'You're probably the same people who will later go and pick up a copy of the newspaper and see who you can recognise!'

The sermon was one of the more difficult I've had to deliver. I tried to focus the mourners on the good that had come from the death of Jacob Cashman. That might sound strange, but I do believe that we must try to find the good in all circumstances, and perhaps also try to understand what God is trying to tell us, or to show us, or expects from us, when a small child dies.

The community had come together to comfort each other. That was something positive. It may not have been immediately apparent – especially not with so many people bristling with indignation – but I do believe that a sudden death provides us with an opportunity to comfort each other.

I reminded the congregation that we were in no position to judge.

I talked about suffering, too. I said that we, as human beings, don't always understand why God makes us suffer and, in particular, why he makes small children suffer. If you believe as I do that all things that happen on earth are the result of God's will, and if you believe that God loves us, then it is difficult to understand why He would allow a small child to suffer, and so we must simply accept that God has a plan, and that we must trust in God.

I heard one or two people snort with derision during that section of the sermon. I imagined them thinking, 'Is that the best you can do?' In truth, though, suffering is something to which I've turned my mind. People forget: a fair swag of the Bible – Old and New, and all of Job – is concerned with suffering. It's a common complaint from the lapsed and the agnostic: 'If God exists, why would He allow this to happen? What could possibly justify the agonising death of a small child?' The way the media sometimes thrusts this question at me, it's as if they think such a question has never dawned on the Church.

Let me assure you, it's something to which I've turned my mind, and I do have some thoughts on the matter. Firstly, we in the Christian religion believe that suffering is real. Buddhists might say that suffering is an illusion, but that is not our opinion. Anguish, distress, pain – none of it is imaginary. The Lord Jesus Christ suffered, and his suffering was real. Jacob Cashman suffered, and his suffering was real.

Why, then, do we suffer? The oldest explanation comes from the Gospels: we suffer because of the Fall of Man. We are sinners; therefore, it is not helpful to blame God for our suffering.

Then, too, there is the idea that suffering plays a corrective role, enabling us to more quickly recognise bad behaviour. God allows His children to experience the consequences of their actions. If we ignore God's teachings, the results are painful. If we sin, we are punished.

I can see how those explanations are not particularly helpful when considering why a child like Jacob must die. It seems absurd that a child of five must pay for a sin committed by Eve in the Garden of Eden. Likewise, it's impossible to imagine what Jacob might have done – not eaten his lunch? Skipped school one afternoon? – to deserve his fate.

What, then, was the purpose of Jacob's death? I only know this, and it's a variation of what I've said before: God's purpose is often not immediately available to us, and when we are perplexed, ultimately we must trust in the God who loves us.

The Bible says, 'Suffering produces endurance, and endurance produces character, and character produces hope' (Romans 5:3–4). Peter says our suffering is not endless: 'He will wipe every tear from their eyes. There will be no more mourning and crying or pain.'

If, as a priest, you didn't believe that, you'd go mad.

Jacob's siblings did not speak at the funeral. I'm not sure they listened, either. I kept one eye on them while I was speaking. Hayley was squirming around the way a toddler will do. The social worker beside her tried to hold her down, but after a while we all gave up and let her scoot about the floor on all fours, gathering up lint.

Harley was restless. Lauren was mute, except when some friends from the Barrett Primary School came up with some balloons. They were crying, and she began crying too, and they formed a circle and hugged each other.

Quite a few of the children had made cards and signs saying 'Farewell Jacob' and 'We'll Miss You Jacob', and there were piles of flowers in aluminium foil crowded around the door.

After the funeral, the volunteer from the parish office took the Cashman children to the unit where I lived. They took off their shoes and we got them some cream biscuits and sat them down on the carpet in front of the TV. The three of them sat quietly until the commercials came on and they started squabbling among themselves. We gave them some crayons and they drew pictures, nothing nightmarish, just normal things: Harley scribbled; Lauren drew stick figures under a rainbow; and Hayley, well, she chewed the crayon and let coloured spittle run down her chin.

We waited long into the afternoon for a social worker to decide what should happen next, and at some point Lauren got up and went into the garden. We had a plastic swing set, the type with a hard swing and a see-saw under an awning for the Sunday-school children. Lauren didn't sit down on the seat of the swing. She bent herself over the plastic seat and, while she was upside down like that with her face toward the earth, she moved herself back and forward, leaving scuff marks in the dirt with her shoes.

I should have gone out to speak to her, but to put a question about Jacob . . . it seemed not to be my place, and in her confusion would she have heard me, anyway?

Besides, there was a reporter from *The Sun* on the telephone, wanting to get a few more quotes about the impact on the community, and by the time I finished the call Lauren was gone.

Detective Senior Sergeant Brian Muggeridge

I didn't go to Jacob's funeral. I'd spent a lot of time on the case already – I was at the place on DeCastella Drive until late the first day and then early again the next day, and then I was at the station all afternoon – and as important as these things are, my wife was getting annoyed. There was no reason to go to the funeral. What was to be gained by going to the church? It's a whole lot of grief, is all.

I caught a bit of it on the news, of course. I saw the priest, a bloke not dressed like a priest at all, just in ordinary pants and a shirt, which doesn't really do it for me. I wouldn't mind some more solemnity, if that's the word. He was giving some kind of sermon and, in my opinion, he was not that convincing. He waffled on with the usual stuff: 'It's God's will.' I mean, surely it's up to a priest to say something uplifting. But then, the death of a child, what can you say other than, 'Well, there must be a reason and I'm buggered if I know what it is.'

They played a bit of what they said was Jake's favourite song – an ACDC song, 'Back in Black', and I remember thinking, 'Lucky it's not "Highway to Hell"!' I mean, what's wrong with the hymns? The TV made a big deal about Lisa not being there, but she'd sent word that she wanted them to play 'I've Never Been to Me' and she wanted Jacob buried in a Batman suit.

It wasn't long after the funeral that the Cashman case was off my hands. Pretty much the day after Jacob was buried, I took his mum up to D-24 – that's to Homicide, in the Melbourne City Watch House on Russell Street – to be charged. There wasn't the heavy security at D-24 in those days. Remember, this was before the Russell Street bomb exploded outside the headquarters, blowing out the ground-floor windows and taking the life of Constable Angela Taylor. You could park out the front and walk right in, and take your prisoner up to the counter. It was at least two metres wide and might even have been marble, although probably not.

People who were going into the cells used to have to wait while the cop behind the counter got out the old ledger with the leather cover. Computers were in operation but nobody was connected, not the way we are now. So I walked in with Lisa, holding her by the elbow, and the cop behind the counter got her name, address, date of birth, and wrote it all down in pencil. Lisa had to give up her cigarettes and lighters and lighter fluid, and she got photographed and fingerprinted, and led into a back corridor where she would have been stripped and searched.

All the time it was happening, I could sort of see her shrinking. I can't explain it better than that. She was just getting smaller and smaller as the hours went on. She was pale and shaking and . . . yeah, shrinking.

I didn't watch the strip. There was a time when the male cops could have watched a woman strip at D-24, but then it all changed and if you had a woman prisoner, you had to get a woman guard.

This is probably the wrong thing to say, but I wanted to see Lisa strip. Not because I had the hots or anything like that, I just wanted to see her squirm a bit. Blokes don't care about getting their gear off. Most of them have been naked with other blokes before, at the urinal, in the change room, whatever. The women take it harder. By this time, I knew her story was bogus, and I knew – or thought I knew – what had happened on DeCastella Drive. Part of me wanted to see Lisa shaking and suffering, like Jacob must have been shaking and suffering. She would have had to take off that vinyl suit, stand in her undies and her bra, and a female police officer would have felt around her breasts, briefly between her legs, run her hands around her skull, asked her to lift her feet. About then it would have dawned on her: 'I'm in deep.' I wanted to see that.

She asked for a lawyer and I knew she'd get one, not immediately, but certainly before she got to court. If history was any guide, Legal Aid would see to it that she'd have a QC, a silk, because that's what always happens: down-and-out people get lawyers the rest of us working people could never afford.

The female officer would have gone through the normal drill: 'Could you please point out any identifying marks?'

According to the file she had a rose tattoo on her left ankle, a dolphin on the right shoulder blade and a band of roses around her left wrist.

Lisa was then taken into the women's block. It's like you see on TV: heavy doors at either end of a hallway, the whole thing made from bluestone, covered in twelve layers of creamy paint. The cells come off the hallway. There's a peephole in every door and a heavy bolt at eye level. Reformers would look at those cells now – brick with no windows, a stainless-steel toilet and no lid – and they'd say 'It's macabre' or 'It's cruel', but they're reacting to the stone and the iron bars. In actual fact, I know quite a few crims who preferred the old watch house. The new lock-up, out on Spencer Street, there's no stone, it's all air-conditioned and low ceilings, and you can hear the bloke in the cell next door farting.

The officer who was leading Lisa down the corridor said, 'Wet cell?' I was a bit surprised. The wet cell was for drunks. It had a drain in the floor so they could hose it out. Lisa wasn't drunk. She wasn't vomiting. But then I understood: the wet cell was slightly larger than the other cells – none was bigger than a wardrobe – and the guards were being kind. Lisa was a mother who had lost a child, after all.

She didn't go into the wet cell, though. Another officer said, 'It's full. Why, you got a D and D?' He was referring to a drunk and disorderly.

'Child deceased,' the first officer said. 'What about Number 12?'

Number 12 was the padded cell. People think they don't exist but they do, and they're like on the TV, too, with white foam and rough material on the walls and on the floor. Again, it was bigger and more comfortable than a normal cell, but it was full as well.

'Jesus,' said the first officer. 'Number 15?'

Number 15 was the smallest cell, one of the few that had only one bunk. They were trying to find a cell where Lisa could be alone, trying to find a room where she wouldn't have to share with two prostitutes and a junkie going cold turkey. They were treating her like a human being.

The guard on duty said, 'Yeah, okay, Number 15.' They walked Lisa down the hall. I fell into step behind them. I suppose I wanted to see her go into the cell. I wanted to see the door close. I wanted to look through the peephole, to see if she'd slump down or just stand there, bewildered.

She said, 'How long are you gonna put me here?'

I said, 'You'll have a bail hearing in the morning.'

She was lucky. It was a Friday. In normal circumstances, there would be no bail hearing until Monday, but the Cashman case was special. It had been on the news.

'I don't wanna stay here,' she said. I noticed her fingers were stained with ink from the fingerprinting and she couldn't stop rubbing them.

'I've got something I want to say,' she said.

I wanted to hear it but the female officer said, 'You can tell the court tomorrow.'

I walked back to reception in time to see Peter coming through. We'd been holding him in the back of a divvy van so he didn't run into Lisa during the admissions process. The cop behind the counter went through the same drill: name, age, fingerprints and photographs. Strip. Bend over. Open your mouth. Okay, down to the cells. All the way down the hall I could hear him saying, 'This is nothing to do with me. This is an effin' injustice,' and that kind of thing.

The story was in the newspapers the next day. *The Sun* had gone ballistic. The headline was: 'Little Jake's Mum ARREST!'

The copy said:

Little Jacob Cashman's mother has been ARRESTED in connection with his MURDER! Earlier this week,

Lisa Cashman made a TEARFUL PLEA to the public to find the MAN who bashed her boy, but police now believe THAT STORY WAS FALSE.

Cashman's boyfriend, Peter Tabone, who had been living in the HOUSING COMMISSION house for JUST SIX WEEKS has also been arrested in connection with THE MURDER.

Lisa Cashman will appear in court TODAY!

I suppose it was that story that brought the crowds to the court. Lisa arrived in the back of a police car. She had a windcheater over her head and she was flanked on both sides by uniformed officers. This was just a bail hearing, remember, the 'Have-you-got-a-case-to-answer?' hearing, yet they needed a flying wedge to get her through the doors. The mob that turned up couldn't have been from Barrett, because Barrett is a fair way from Russell Street, so I think it's fair to say that this case had the whole city enraged. There were mums with prams there. One guy had a sign that said, 'An eye for an eye!' and another guy was holding a noose. That's the kind of fever we're talking about.

That first hearing was open to the public. It must have been, because the press reported what police told the court. They said Lisa Cashman and her boyfriend had 'concocted a story' about a strange man when, in fact, Jacob had succumbed to injuries 'sustained in the home'.

The Director of Public Prosecutions applied to have

the rest of the hearing held *in camera*, which basically means 'in private'. He said the strong public feeling had already created a ruckus outside the court and he wanted to prevent a trial by media. He also wanted to protect the boy's siblings from any further trauma. That's something people would take for granted now – that the identity of kids before the court would be suppressed – but back then it wasn't a given.

The magistrate got the message. Of course, we'd already told him what we knew, and that probably swayed him, too. He agreed to hold the hearing in secret. He told the court: 'Any reporting of this matter would, in my view, be entirely inappropriate.'

He scheduled a committal hearing for March 1983. By then, all the other Cashman kids would be in foster care. I kept an eye on proceedings, as much as I could. I was pleased with the verdict and the sentence was about right. Lisa got fifteen years. There was some kerfuffle about the fifteen years that the boyfriend also got, with his family saying he had been in Lisa's house only six weeks when the incident occurred, but frankly, you can do a lot of damage in six weeks. It was best for everybody that he was taken out of circulation.

Elizabeth Costa,
Social Worker

I realise that some people have some valid questions about the way the Department of Human and Family Services in Victoria handles its most difficult cases. The Cashman children were certainly a difficult case, and I am pleased to take this opportunity on behalf of the Department to explain the manner in which it was handled.

Allow me first to introduce myself. My name is Elizabeth Costa – my colleagues and friends call me Liz – and I am Divisional Head at the Department's Metropolitan and Western Region Office. I guess you could say I'm a career public servant. I joined the Department at twenty-two, after graduating with honours from LaTrobe University. My degree is in Literature. I have served nine ministers and six state governments and, in my current role, I have overall responsibility for some 3000 children in state care and 600 staff. Plus I oversee a program involving some 250 foster parents.

Much of what I can tell you comes from the Department's files. The Cashman children came into the care of the Department in November 1982. I was not then in a position to oversee their case, but I have reviewed the file and I believe the matter was handled in an appropriate way.

Police on the Barrett Estate contacted the Department shortly after 1 p.m. on November 12. They had a situation on their hands: a five-year-old boy had died in the Children's Hospital, and his mother was assisting police with their inquiries.

There were three other children, and no known relatives.

The Department applied to the Supreme Court in Melbourne for a temporary care order, which would allow us to take the three children into foster care while the case against the mother was heard. Two social workers went to the Barrett Police Station to collect Lauren, Harley and Hayley.

There may be some criticism of our decision to place the children in different foster homes, but remember, if these children had come into care in the 1950s or 1960s, as opposed to the 1980s, they wouldn't have been placed in private homes at all. They would have been put in an institution, where they would have stayed until adulthood. The main homes in those days were 'Turana' – officially, it was the Victorian Children's Welfare Department Receiving Depot for Boys, but everybody called it Turana – and Winlaton, which was a similar institution for girls. It did not matter if a child was abused or neglected, or if they were a delinquent serving a custodial sentence after committing juvenile crime. All children went to the same institutions.

By the late 1970s, the Department adopted a new model of care, known as 'out-of-home' care, for children who weren't delinquents and therefore shouldn't be sent to institutions with young criminals. As I've said, the Cashman children came into the Department's care in 1982, and that is why they went into foster care, and not into an institution.

Foster care is a temporary arrangement. It is *not* adoption. Most of the children who go into foster care in Victoria do so for a short time. The Department aims to reunite them with their parents. They might be removed from their homes because they are at risk of abuse or neglect, or perhaps because the mother is suffering mental problems, or because there is drug abuse in the home, but very, very few children are in foster care for longer than a year. Foster care is a stop-gap measure. The ultimate aim is to get children home with their parents.

So, what kind of people might take children into their homes on a temporary basis? Well, some of the foster parents we had in the early 1980s – and still today, to some extent – are people who have a bit of extra room, a desire to do good works, and perhaps they are also in need of a bit of extra money. They might be on some kind of disability pension or unemployment benefit, and if they take in a foster child they can get a stipend from the Department, which is tax-free.

We do have *some* affluent families on the books, but not many. No, wealthy couples don't often inquire about becoming foster parents. They'd rather go on IVF, or adopt from overseas. They want a child of their own; one they can keep, if you like. Those who do apply to take a foster child seem to have this idea that they can *make a difference*. In many cases, they believe they can improve a disadvantaged child's life. As a social worker, whose job it once was to vet these couples, I'm cautious of this group. Children who come into the Department's care aren't exactly cute. They often display a range of challenging behaviours. Not to put too fine a point on it, they might bite or kick or swear. They may come with lice. They may be unable to use a knife and fork. They might steal money. These behaviours are confronting. I find that when these children are placed with affluent foster parents, the relationship frequently breaks down.

So, no, the homes are not affluent, but the foster parents must be in good health and, where possible, they must also agree to maintain the children's routine. In other words, when we place a child, we try to find a good, solid couple, in a home near the child's school and near the child's friends.

The Cashman children lived on the Barrett Estate. When they came into the Department's care in 1982, the first port of call on the Barrett Estate for needy children was the home of Mrs Edna Islington.

Mrs Islington is now deceased. Shortly before she died in 1995, she received an AO – an Order of Australia – in recognition of her efforts, having taken more than 100 of Barrett's needy children into her home over a period of thirty years.

I did not meet Mrs Islington but, based on information in the files, she was clearly a model foster parent. She understood the role. She provided shelter for children on a temporary basis, always hopeful that things would 'come good', as she used to say in her reports to us, so that the children would be able to return to their parents. She was not the type to seek attention. Like everybody in Barrett, she would have known exactly who the Cashman children were – their photograph had been on the front of the newspaper, after all, and the case involving their mother was the subject of ongoing attention – but I feel certain that she would have put all of that to one side, and cared for the Cashman children as she cared for all the children who came into her home.

I believe that Mrs Islington provided a haven for the Cashman children, at least when they first came into care, and, in particular, for Lauren. Indeed, there is no question that Lauren settled happily at Mrs Islington's. She did not seem unduly troubled by the separation from her mother, and Mrs Islington's reports to the Department, compiled on a monthly basis, suggest that Lauren was able to stay at the Barrett Primary School, where she continued to do well. Lauren had a good relationship with many of her peers. She had an astute and inquiring mind. Lauren did not complain about Mrs Islington. She did not wet the bed, or destroy her books and toys. She did not have tantrums. On the contrary, she became devoted to one of Mrs Islington's special dolls, a doll that was popular then, with hair you could retract and pull out of the head again. There is actually a photograph on file that Mrs Islington took with her Polaroid. It shows Lauren at seven, some several months after she came into the Department's care, hosting a tea party for Mrs Islington's dolls.

Mrs Islington introduced Lauren to books, and Lauren soon became an avid reader. At seven, she was working her way through *What Katy Did* and *The Secret Garden* and *Little Women* – opportunities, I suggest to you, that she would not have received in institutional care, and perhaps not even in her own home.

The Department monitored the psychological development – in those days, it was called 'the mental health' – of all the Cashman children while they were in Mrs Islington's care and, indeed, until they were discharged from the Department's care. They attended group therapy, where they were encouraged to use textas and poster paper to express themselves, and those drawings were later analysed for such things as colour, spacing, positioning and themes. Lauren was also chosen to be part of an exciting new program known as 'Think Good, Feel Good', in which she was observed during a period of guided play. She was encouraged to express positive emotions such as through smiling, laughing and clapping, and taught to recognise signs of stress. There was no indication from Lauren's drawings, or from Lauren's program reports, that she was a troubled child.

Now, when the Cashman children came into the Department's care, they were assessed as having 'short-term' needs. In other words, we did not know how long they would need to be in foster care. Then, in March 1985, the Cashman children were moved from the Department's 'short-term' list to the 'long-term' list. It seems that this occurred because their mother, Lisa Cashman, had finally exhausted her appeals and would be incarcerated for an extended period of time.

When a child moves to the long-term-care list, they do not necessarily become available for adoption. A child who is orphaned, whose parents are deceased, might be adopted, but the Cashman children were in a different category. Their mother had pleaded not guilty to charges laid against her; she had been found guilty and then appealed, and appealed again. At any time in that process, she might have been released and would have wanted – and had the right – to be reunited with her children.

The Cashman children, therefore, became available for long-term care but not for adoption. From the photographs and the notes I have on file, I believe it would have been a fairly simple matter to adopt the Cashman children out, had that been permitted. None of the children exhibited behavioural problems. The children did not have Down syndrome, they were not autistic and they were not Indigenous. On the contrary, they were bright, happy children, none of them older than six, but their mother was alive, and as long as that was the case, they couldn't be given up for adoption.

Obviously, it is much more difficult to place a long-term child than it is to place a pre-adoption child. Most foster parents will take a group of siblings for one or two weeks, but who wants a group for years on end? Only people who want to adopt, and they tend not to be the kind of people who will accept and understand that the children we've placed in their care are technically theirs for the long-term, but may in fact be removed at any time.

The Department did search for a 'long-term' placement where all the Cashman children could be kept together, but ultimately they were placed with three different families. I can explain how that happened: first, Hayley's father was located through dental records. His body had been found in a forest outside Melbourne. Apparently, he'd hanged himself shortly after Hayley was born. We don't know why. He had an aunt who had raised him, and she was both able and willing to care for Hayley.

Given that the aunt was a family member, the Department agreed.

It is reasonable, I suppose, to ask why Hayley's great-aunt did not also take Harley and Lauren. The answer is: she was under no obligation to do so. She was Hayley's father's aunt, and therefore no more than a half-great-aunt, if there is such a thing, to the other children. The Department did *ask* whether she wanted to take all three children, but she was a single parent herself, with children ranging in age from six months to sixteen years, and she did not want the other children.

So we had on our hands something of a conundrum. On one hand, the Department strives to keep children together. On the other, it seeks to place children with family members, where possible. A decision was taken to send Hayley to the great-aunt, since that would mean that one of the Cashman children, at least, was with kin. Once that happened, of course, the other Cashman children fell into an interesting place, policy-wise. They were now children who had already been separated from two siblings: their brother, Jacob, was deceased, and Hayley was with her great-aunt. The requirement to keep the siblings together was therefore breached, and so began the search for long-term carers for Harley and Lauren.

The Department found a foster carer for Harley first, probably because he was younger and easier to place. The record shows that he went into the care of a first-time foster carer, Mrs Ruby Porter, in December 1985. Mrs Porter lived on a property some hundred kilometres from the Barrett Estate. She was initially approved to care on a permanent basis for just one child because she had what the Department defined as a significant disability.

Lauren stayed with Mrs Islington, at least for a time. Then, when Lauren was about ten years old, an attempt *was* made to reunite her with her brother on Mrs Porter's property. Ruby Porter was conscious of the fact that Harley had an older sister and the moment she was approved to care for more than one child, she applied to take Lauren. The file shows that Departmental officers did visit the Porter property on the outskirts of Melbourne in 1986, with a view to moving Lauren into Ruby Porter's care. It was Lauren *herself* who declared that she was unwilling to go to the Porters. She was adamant. Why that was so, I can't tell you, but Lauren said she would rather run away than go to the Porter property.

It was suggested to her – I have the notes here – that it really would be in her best interests to be raised with a sibling. Harley was settled and happy at the Porters, and Ruby Porter was very anxious to have both children under her wing. But Lauren said – and again, I have the notes here – 'No, I want to stay on the Barrett Estate.'

I can see that some people might think that was strange. Why would Lauren not want to be raised with her brother? At the Department, we try to consider things from the child's point of view. Lauren was at school on the Barrett Estate. It's reasonable to assume that she had friends there. Had she been forced to move to the Porter property, Lauren would have had to start at a new school, make new friends, and adjust to a new home setting with a new foster parent. The Department is mindful of the fact that children don't always adapt well to change, and given that Lauren was adamant that she did not want to move, the plan to relocate her to the Porter property was dropped, and so began the process of trying to place her elsewhere, a process I think we'd all agree didn't work out so well.

However, I wouldn't say, and it would not be correct to say, that Lauren, Hayley and Harley were *forcibly* separated from each other. The fact that they were raised apart was simply a product of the way the Department's policies worked, and of the homes that were available at that time. It would not be correct to say that the Department discouraged contact between the siblings. There were occasions – at least one, possibly two occasions – when they met. The children could themselves have requested further contact, but apparently did not.

It is a matter of record that Harley's placement with

Mrs Porter endured to adulthood. That is something of which we can be proud.

As for Lauren and Hayley . . . well, I believe it would be wrong to say that the Department failed the Cashman children. As I said, Hayley was placed with a great-aunt because she was kin. It was a matter of deep regret to everybody, I'm sure, when that placement failed.

Hayley is now an adult. Her current circumstances are beyond the Department's purview.

As for Lauren, well, it is true that the Department was never able to find a long-term solution to her housing problems. It is also true that a secure home should have been found. Whether a secure home *would* ever have been found, given the circumstances, I just don't know. I remain of the view, therefore, that the Department acted at all times with Lauren's best interests in mind.

Mrs Karen MacInerney,
Foster Carer

We were driving in heavy traffic. Hayley was in the backseat. From memory, she was about seven years old. She said, 'Mrs Mac?' I had one eye on the traffic, but I looked at her in the rear-vision mirror and said, 'Yes, Hayley?'

She said, 'Mrs Mac, are uncles allowed to get into your bed and do things to you?'

I nearly ran into the car in front. Honestly, it was all I could do to swerve.

I parked the car and said, 'What things, Hayley? What uncle? Has somebody done something to you?' But she wouldn't say anything further.

I was concerned. Of course I was concerned, and of course that's what Hayley wanted: for me to be worried. As far as I knew, she didn't *have* an uncle. She has one female relative, a great-aunt, with whom she lived for a few years when she was a very young child. I can't be sure that the great-aunt didn't have a man around, a man that Hayley called 'uncle', but look, I doubt it. I doubt it because Hayley was forever making up stories. I'm not exaggerating when I say that most of what came out of that girl's mouth was a lie.

Beyond that, Hayley Cashman was the most sexually aggressive child I've ever encountered. If I had to take her word against that of a man or a boy she claimed to have been molesting her, well, I would say it was probably the other way around! She simply had no idea how to behave, no idea what was appropriate. She pushed everybody's buttons, including mine.

Hayley came into our care a few days before Christmas, 1986. The Department told us that she was five years old and she had been living with a family member – her great-aunt, the woman I've just mentioned – in a quite chaotic home for two years, waiting, apparently, to see what would happen to her mother in the courts. When her mother went to prison and the placement with her great-aunt fell apart, she came to us. A social worker from the Department drove up with her sitting in the back seat of the car. It was like looking at an orphan from *Oliver Twist*. She had silver curls, long curls that had been left to grow wild. It took me a week to get a comb through it. We took her inside, and so began the journey.

I can't tell you the resources we poured into that child. Endless resources; and all for naught.

For background, I'm not the sort of foster parent who says, 'Oh, I will love this child like my own.' I have my own children, and I love them unconditionally, with a mother's love. The foster children I've had over the years . . . it's different, and I'm not ashamed to say so. I don't know why it's so hard for some foster parents to admit that they love the foster children differently. It's like the big taboo. If you've had a child for six or seven or ten years, you have to say, 'I love them like my own.' It's not been the case with me, and I don't believe it's the case with many foster parents. I know a bit about foster care. I've been a foster parent for more than twenty years. I have taken more than fifty foster children into my home, and I understand the role I'm supposed to play. You take care of them, you give them back. That is the way the system is supposed to work. They do not belong to you. They are not your children. They are somebody else's children, and the goal is to get them back with their parents. But you can't get people to admit it. I've heard people tell me, 'I love all my children – my foster children, and my biological children – exactly the same way.' I think to myself, 'Oh yes? And if two of them – your child and the foster child – were hanging off the edge of a cliff, and you had one in each hand, and you could only save one of them, which would you save?'

You don't have to tell me the answer. I know the answer.

No, you don't love them all the same, and that's why I don't encourage the foster children in my care to call me Mum. I'm not Mum. I'm Mrs Mac. They have mums, most of them. That's not to say that I didn't develop a very strong bond with some of them, over the years. They might think I'm strict at the start, but I believe that children actually need boundaries, and many of them still come to visit me, still come through the door like it's their own home, singing out, 'Hey, Mrs Mac, it's me!' They give me a kiss, and that's okay. I don't mind that. But they are not my children. I understand that, and they understand that.

This is how I see my role: I provide foster children with nourishing food, and I put clean sheets on their bed at night. I enrol them in school, and I make sure they know the rules of the house. They must use their manners. They must eat with a knife and fork. They are not allowed to break things.

I get a small amount of money from the Department for each child, something like $300 a fortnight. It does not cover the cost of having the foster children in the house. I find myself buying things with my own money. In most cases, they need a school uniform. I send them all to the school nearest me. It makes no sense to be driving around to different schools. The Department might say, 'Well, don't get them a new uniform, they might only be with you for a few weeks,' but I say, 'No, they will wear the uniform.' They come with so few clothes of their own, what else are they going to wear? Some of them come with just the clothes on their backs. If you think they come with a small suitcase of summer and winter clothes and several pairs of shoes, you'd be very wrong indeed.

I have an arrangement with the local school. I can get second-hand uniforms at five dollars a piece. But it adds up. Five-dollar pants, five-dollar shirt, socks, shoes, hat, bag. It adds up. The school has excursions. I pay for that. I won't have the children sitting at school while the other students go off on excursions. That's not the way I operate. Most of the children I've had over the years have come only for respite care. They might have a disability, or their mother might have some kind of problem, and they come for a weekend or a week, a fortnight, or perhaps a few months, but still, I try to make sure they fit in, here at my home and at the school.

When Hayley came to me it was supposed to be temporary. She needed somewhere to go. I don't generally take children long-term. One child – Ben – I've had for eight years. He has a learning disability. It would be difficult to find another place for him. He has the mind of a two-year-old. He cannot tie his shoes. He has stayed and stayed, and that's fine. I didn't want another child permanently. It's not that I get attached – I don't – but I believe the foster parent plays only a temporary role.

It's a safe place to land. That's how I see it. A safe place to land, and then back to Mum or, if that's not possible, to a permanent family.

When the Department delivered Hayley, they told me, 'The great-aunt can't have her any more.' They didn't say why. They said, 'It will be for a few months. We're trying to find another relative.'

They did not find a relative. They had to move Hayley to the 'permanent care' list. It took a while. She was getting older. Her time with me was extended, and extended again, and before long a year had gone by, and then another. If I could have looked into the future and seen that I'd have Hayley until she was sixteen, I might have approached things differently. I might not have taken her at all. But I took her, thinking, 'Let's get through the holidays. Things always look better in the New Year.' It was three days before Christmas. She was a child. She deserved a present and a nice meal, like everybody else on Christmas Day. Then she was still here when the next Christmas came around. I bought another present. Then came autumn, and another spring. She outgrew the old uniform. I got her a new one. That's the way we went on: one season to the next, playing it by ear.

From the start, Hayley was difficult. 'Challenging' is how they put it. But that was okay. I'd had that before. It wasn't her behaviour. Not at first. That came later. At first, it was physical. Hayley had poor fine-motor skills. She could not hold a pencil. She could not catch a ball. The Department sent her to an occupational therapist. She said Hayley had poor muscle development. She needed to play on the monkey bars. They had monkey bars at the local school. I told the staff to make sure she played on them.

She started to bite. I've had biters before. Mostly, it's something they grow out of. They don't know it's wrong until you tell them. But Hayley was still biting when she was nine.

The Department wanted Hayley to stay in touch with her mother, in the prison. They want all children in state care to have a relationship with their parents. Mostly, I support that ethos. If a mum is having a bad time, if she's been on the drugs and she goes into rehab, and she really proves she can do it, then of course, send the children back. That's what everybody wants.

Now, Hayley was eighteen months old when her mother went to prison. There was a trial, an appeal, and then another appeal. During that time, Hayley lived first with a foster parent and then with her great-aunt. Then, when the placement with the great-aunt fell through, she came to me. In my view she should have been adopted. The Department disagreed. They wanted her to stay on the short-term list and to stay in touch with her mother, and for a while she did. At first, she would get letters. Her mother would write to her from prison, and the Department would pass on the letters. Initially, I agreed to read those letters to Hayley, but they said the strangest things, these letters. They said, 'I'll be out soon and we'll live together again.' That wasn't going to happen, not without a miracle. I said to the Department once, 'Why do you bring these letters? They just upset Hayley. Her mother isn't coming out to live with her.'

They said, 'We believe that Hayley and her mother have a relationship that should be encouraged. It is Hayley's *right* to have a relationship with her mother, whether or not she's incarcerated.'

I said, 'She doesn't have *any* rights. She's five years old.'

But they had their mantra. They said, 'A child has a right to know her mother.'

I said, 'But what if those letters are upsetting this little girl?'

They waved me away. 'We're the professionals,' they said. 'We're skilled in social work. We make our decisions in the best interests of the child.'

I didn't agree with them. I may not be a social worker but I'm not an imbecile. I didn't need a degree to know that it wasn't doing Hayley any good to get those letters. The Department wasn't interested in that, however. They continued to deliver the letters. Then, a few years later, they also arranged for Hayley to speak to her mother on the telephone from the prison. It was my responsibility as the foster carer to take Hayley to the Department's offices on the Barrett Estate to receive a fifteen-minute telephone call from her mother once a month. On almost every occasion, the mother would either not be on the end of the telephone at all, or she would be late to the line, and the allotted time would be eaten away.

On one occasion, when the mother did come to the line, late, she said, 'Sorry, I was having a durry.'

A durry! Her daughter was waiting on the line to speak to her, the only conversation they'd have that month, and she stepped out for a cigarette. Ten minutes of the fifteen minutes, gone.

After the phone calls came the visits. Once Hayley got to age six, we were told that she should visit her mother in prison, twice a year. It happened in February, and again in September. The first time, I was driving her to the Department's offices – they were going to take her out to the prison; not just Hayley but other children whose parents were locked up – but she was so anxious, she got a stomach cramp in the car and threw up.

They travelled to the prison in a white minibus, these kids. Hayley never liked the bus. She called it 'the spastic bus'.

'You're driving along, and kids in cars make faces at you.' That's what she told me. I thought it was wrong: a bus full of kids swinging into the prison, with the towers and the lights. They had to pass through security checks. Even the babies. The Department told me that some mothers got their children to smuggle in their drugs. They got their friends, or their boyfriend, to tuck the drugs into pooey nappies, and they would change the nappy in prison and take out the drugs.

Hayley was too big for nappies, thank God.

Her mother shared a room with other women, other mothers. They had hair dryers and a TV and a kettle and a microwave. She had a microwave before we did!

After the visits, Hayley would get sick. She couldn't go to school. I could never work out exactly what happened to her during those visits to prison, but I gather that the mother was not always there to see her, or else would be late . . . or else she would be 'shitty'. That's Hayley's word.

'She was shitty with me.' That's what she said.

The mother wouldn't want to hear what Hayley had been doing. We took Hayley to Guides. She got to a certain level and she received a badge and she was proud of that badge. She wore it to show her mother on a prison visit, but when she came back it was no longer pinned to her blouse. She had put it in her pocket. She wouldn't wear it again and she wouldn't go to Guides again, either. I asked her why not. 'Guides is for posh people,' she told me, and I know where she would have got that from.

Her mother taught Hayley bad habits, and bad manners, and Hayley was impressionable. She took the lead from her mother. She copied her. It was a bad model to copy.

Hayley's sexuality started to be a problem when she was about seven. We let her have a sleepover and she invented this game that involved getting the other girls to take their clothes off. We'd put mattresses down on the floor in the lounge room, so they could watch a video on the Betacord. I walked in from the kitchen. I'd been making the popcorn in a pot and I wasn't paying attention to what was going on in the lounge room. I came in holding a bowl of popcorn and dropped it on the floor. They were all stark naked and one of them was crying.

'What's going on!' I said. They were grabbing their sleeping bags and trying to get inside them. They said, 'It was Hayley's idea.'

I took her aside, into my room, and I said, 'Hayley, what are you *doing*?' And she said, 'Strip Jack Naked.'

I said, 'How do you know about Strip Jack Naked?' She just shrugged at me. I told all the girls to get dressed and hurry and not to play that game any more, and got them on to Pass the Parcel – thank heavens I had one already made up. Then we played Pin the Tail on the Donkey and the little girls loved it – they just do! – but all the time I could see Hayley sort of looking at me, like I'd ruined her fun.

Another time, I got called to the school because she was tormenting a girl from her class. Basically, she was taking her away from the other children at recess and tying her, with shoelaces, to a tree at the back of the oval. She told her that she was the prison guard, and the little girl – a kindergarten kid! – was the prisoner. She'd decide when the girl could eat and what she could do.

I explained to the principal about her mother, and I think we got away with that one.

And then one day, I was looking out the kitchen window when a car pulled into the drive, and there was a woman behind the wheel. She was furious. She got out of the car as I was coming into the driveway, and she said to me, 'Tell your freaky kid to keep away from my daughter.'

There was a little girl in school uniform in the back seat, looking absolutely terrified.

I said to Hayley, 'Who is that girl?' She had nothing to say about it.

After a while, the children stopped coming. Nobody wanted to play with Hayley and I could understand that, she was completely unpredictable . . . and the lies! The lies she told; she could not stop lying. The simplest thing: 'Hayley, did you put that thing there?' 'No.' Just flat out, 'No.' And I'd say, 'Hayley, I saw you do it.' And then she'd burst into tears and run into her room and slam the door.

When she was about eight, she started rifling through my drawers. I thought that was extremely strange. I mean, I'd had kids, I knew they loved to go looking for some old pair of heels and a shawl I hadn't worn since my twenties, maybe an Avon lipstick in a vivid colour, and they would come tottering down the stairs and we'd all be laughing. With Hayley, it was different. This was clandestine. I'd come upstairs and find her with her hands in my underwear drawer; she'd have taken out some bras and be trying them on. I am not a racy woman. I did not keep a stash of G-strings and push-up bras. I could not see the appeal of taking my beige tummy pants and putting them on. I'd say, 'Hayley, what *are* you doing?' She always fled. I'd go to her bedroom door, but she'd sit with her back to it, her feet against the wardrobe, and there was no way to get it open.

Hayley would also play with herself, if I can put it that way. Not just in the bath – look, again, I've got kids, and I've had dozens of foster kids staying here – I *know* what's normal. A bit of exploration, I expect that. But this was incredible. Hayley would sit on the floor in the lounge room with no underpants on, and study herself. I'd say, 'Hayley, that's not appropriate. That's a personal thing, and you do that in private.' And once she said to me, 'Like you pick your nose?'

She would take my pads out of the bathroom cupboard. I scolded her. Another time, she went through a box of tampons. I guess we had them from a girl who was menstruating – and she popped them all out of the applicators, and was standing there, swinging one around when I walked into the bathroom and caught her.

I spoke to the Department about it. As I say, I'm a regular foster mother; I've had plenty of kids and there have never been those kinds of problems. The social worker said to me, 'Well, do you have sex in the house when Hayley is home?'

I had no idea how to respond. I'm a married woman! My husband and I, we're all fine in that department. It's healthy and it's completely private. Did they imagine that I assembled the whole family to sit and watch?

We persevered with Hayley. Honestly, we did. Whatever her problems were, she was still a little girl, a lost little girl, and I'd have to be made of steel not to feel some compassion for her. But it soon got to the point where we couldn't take her anywhere. One example: we went to a lunch once, a lovely buffet. There were platters of meat and chicken and bowls of salads. She started helping herself with her hands. That is not the way we eat. We taught her to use a knife and fork. Hayley knows perfectly well how to conduct herself in public. But she loved to shock. She needed extra attention. She was scooping up handfuls of potato salad and dumping it on her plate. She knew I would be humiliated, and that seemed to be the point.

She wasn't always like that. At other times – the times that really broke my heart – it was like having a baby in the house, a sobbing baby. I could be sitting, knitting, watching some TV, and Hayley would come and crawl into my lap, even when she was quite big, and she'd sob, and sob, and sob. She would be completely inconsolable, and at those times, I admit, my heart just went out to her. But then, just when I was feeling some sympathy, she'd climb onto my husband's lap and try to kiss him on the neck, open-mouthed. I mean, really. She was absolutely uncontrollable regarding her sexuality. It got to the point where people just would not visit us, not even family. My brother – he is a very sensible, very decent man – told me he would not come into the house if Hayley was there. He told me she rubbed herself against his leg. 'I'm sorry, she just terrifies me,' he said.

It wasn't that she could actually *do* anything. She obviously couldn't overpower a grown man and force him to have sex with her, but they – my husband, my brother, my son – were absolutely terrified of being accused of abusing her. It happens. A foster child will point the finger at a foster parent. And one of my nephews, a boy who would I suppose be a cousin to her if she were my own child, came running out of her bedroom breathless one afternoon and said, 'Hayley tried to rape me in there!'

I went in and she was leaning back on the bed head, her legs wide apart, clothed, but with a leer on her face – a leer that I don't ever want to see again.

There were times when I wished the Department would take Hayley away, but they didn't and so I suppose we played the hand we were dealt. I wasn't going to say, 'It's too hard, take her back.' I have done that, with one or two kids who stole from me. With Hayley, it never got to the point where it was criminal, so what could I do? I could hardly have said, 'I don't like her. She frightens me.'

Hayley got her period at eleven. Not that she told me. I only found out because I was cleaning her room one day, and I found a drawer full of bloody pads, and bloody underpants, reeking. They were stuffed in there behind her clothes.

I said, 'Hayley, there's a way to dispose of these things. You wrap them up and you put them in the rubbish bin.' But she was always a bit strange when it came to bodily functions. As a smaller child, she would wipe herself with her hand, and smear her poo on the wall.

A short time after I found those soiled pads, Hayley told me, 'I've had it off, you know, Mrs Mac.'

I said, 'Had it off?' And she said, 'Yeah, I've had it off with a guy.'

I did not believe her. I thought she was too young.

But still, I agonised over what to do: tell the Department or not? And in the end, I really had no choice because you can't take the foster kids – not even the long-term placements – to see a medical practitioner without permission from the Department, and I thought, 'What if she's pregnant?' I wanted somebody to talk to her about sex, before she had it.

They said, 'We will have a counsellor talk to her,' but

it seems the counsellor only talked to her about 'safe' sex, not about *not having* sex. That didn't seem to be part of it.

'It's all right to give a blowjob without a condom,' Hayley told me after one of these sessions. 'It's anal sex that gives you AIDS.'

I couldn't believe the Department would discuss these things with such a young girl, but they said, 'It's her sexuality, Mrs MacInerney, not yours.'

They said, 'We're going to put her on the contraceptive pill.'

I said, 'What, at this age? She can't even remember to brush her teeth every day.'

The other problem was that from a very young age, Hayley was aware that she was about to come into some money. She used to say to me, 'I've got a victim's payment coming, when I'm older.'

I said, 'Who told you that?'

She said, 'My mum.'

It was true. Hayley would, when she turned sixteen, come into money. Not a huge amount, just a few thousand dollars, but it would certainly seem like a lot to Hayley. It was money to compensate her for the crime committed by her mother: the loss of her brother, Jacob. In the eyes of the law, Hayley was a victim of crime, and entitled to compensation.

To my mind, these victim's payments cause more trouble than they are worth. What was the point of giving a large amount of money to somebody like Hayley, who was essentially a troubled child? It would be a sum far too large for her to manage; she would blow it all in a very short period of time. I knew it would provide her with the illusion of security where there was none.

Look, I know, I know, *I know*. What happened to Hayley when she was a child – the loss of her brother, the break-up of her family – was extremely unfortunate. It must have been terribly upsetting. It shouldn't happen to any child. But honestly, to instil in these children a sense of themselves as victims and to give them a 'victim's payment' is in my opinion very wrong. In my opinion, they should be encouraged to *get over it*, to *move on*. They should be told, 'You cannot let this control your life. *You've* got to control your life. You have to say: "I *will* pull myself up. I won't let this beat me."'

Hayley was never encouraged to do that, not by her social worker, anyway. Oh, *we* tried. My husband and I, we tried. But I could not find a way for her to focus on something other than herself. The number of times I said to her, 'Hayley, it's not all about you. Other people have trauma. Bad things happen to people all the time. It's how you respond that matters.' She would say, 'And what would you know?'

I told her, 'Hayley, we've had children come through this house who have been involved in the most horrific child abuse. We've all seen it on the news; we've all heard it on the radio.' But Hayley wouldn't listen. She needed to be the one with the *worst* problems. She would go off, wailing, 'You don't understand. You don't know what it's like . . .'

Was she *actually* affected by what happened to her brother? You assume so, and that's the thing you reach for, when things go wrong. It's the first, and the obvious excuse for why a child might be behaving badly: they are troubled. But sometimes – and it's not easy to say this – foster kids don't actually remember anything about the abuse they've suffered. They hear it from the Department and they use it as an excuse to behave badly. I can't tell you the number of children I've had come through here who say, 'I'm not going to be like my mum' or 'I'm going to finish school. I want to make something of myself, not like my deadbeat dad.' It's their quiet determination that gets them through. They've seen what happens if you don't apply yourself and they refuse to play the victim.

I wasn't sure how much Hayley genuinely remembered about the house on DeCastella Drive or how much she'd been told. My best guess is that she didn't remember anything at all. I do know she *adored* telling people the story about her brother. She loved it when they were completely shocked that he had come to an untimely end and that was how she ended up in foster care.

Her delight in this was troubling. Honestly, she never

said, 'Oh, I miss Jacob,' or 'It hurts me, what happened to Jacob.' None of those things you might expect. No, Hayley seemed to use the story of what happened to Jacob to make *her* own circumstances, and her own life, more special and interesting. It also gave her an excuse for otherwise unacceptable behaviour. 'Oh, you can't discipline me. I've had a hard life!' Well, that didn't work with me, but it has worked with others.

We raised our concerns with the Department. I told them, 'There is no way she will be ready to live independently, not at the age of sixteen, and certainly not if she is about to come into a large sum of money.'

I found that my advice was unwelcome. They told me, 'We appreciate all you've done, but once Hayley is sixteen and can live independently, that is her right.'

Again, with her *rights*.

More troubling, to my mind, was this: *their* contact with Hayley would also cease on the day she turned sixteen. By that time, of course, her mother had died in prison. Hayley will tell you that she did not get to see her mother before she died, and I'm sure she blames me for this, but it was not up to me to make sure she went. The Department told Hayley that her mother was ill. Hayley said she could not care less. Afterwards, Hayley was offered the opportunity to go to the funeral. Hayley did not want to go. Hayley was offered the opportunity to meet with her siblings, to discuss the funeral arrangements. As far as I could tell, she shrugged off that meeting. She went along, and never mentioned it again. She was not upset by it; she didn't afterwards express any desire to see Lauren or Harley again, and if that seems strange, well, it shouldn't, because Hayley Cashman has very little interest in anything other than her own tragedy.

In any case, I said, 'Here is a child with very limited life skills, a very troubled, very unhappy girl, and you are saying she can just take control of her life at the age of sixteen? It will be a catastrophe.'

The Department said, 'We will provide Hayley with information that will enable her to transition to independent living.'

It was all jargon, useless jargon, and tell me, who was right? Me, or them?

I know what people think: how could we have let her get pregnant? It's not a matter of *allowing* it. You tell me how to stop it. I didn't want her to go on the pill; I certainly wasn't going to be asking her whether she was actually taking it. My own children wanted nothing to do with her, so they weren't in the loop. I couldn't blame them. She'd go into their rooms, take their diaries and try on their clothes. They screamed at me, 'Why does she have to live here?'

Half the time I didn't know, but I had to say, 'She's got nowhere to go.'

At about the age of thirteen, Hayley had started writing boys' names on her arm with a thick black marker, a wash-proof texta. I told her, 'That looks absolutely appalling, Hayley, you should scrub that off. And who is that boy, anyway?'

She'd say, 'We're in *love*, Mrs Mac.'

In love! One day she was *in love* with one of the Veal boys, then it was one of the Crumps – first Shane, then his brother – and then somebody else, all of their names scrawled onto her forearm, and all over her school books, and even on her school uniform!

The first time she came home with love bites on her neck, I nearly had a fit. I said, 'Hayley, what's that on your neck? I wasn't born yesterday. I know what that is. That's love bites.'

She said some nonsense about being bitten by a spider and then getting a rash, and I said, 'I didn't come down in the last shower, Hayley.'

I peppered her with questions, 'Are you having sex?' 'Who is he?' 'Are you being careful?' But she was always on about her rights. 'You've got no right to ask me those questions,' she'd say, and of course the Department was totally in cahoots, telling me to mind my business. She hacked off the hem of her school uniform, made it so short that her knickers touched the table when she sat down. I told her, 'That's not acceptable, Hayley,' and she said, 'I'm entitled to *express myself*.' Tell me where she got *that* from?

I saw she was pregnant before she told me. She was the tiniest thing. She never ate anything as far as I could tell; she was always bringing her lunch home, exactly as I'd packed it. I don't know what she lived on. Suddenly, there she was, in the kitchen, and I could see, under the uniform, clear as day, a baby bump.

I said, 'Hayley, are you pregnant?' And she just burst into tears and ran into her room.

I didn't know what to do. I stood at the door for ten minutes or something, saying, 'Let me in, let me in,' and asking my daughter whether she knew what was going on. And she said, 'Mum, I just pretend I don't know her. I don't hang around with her.'

When she finally came out, I don't know if it was the same day or the next day, I said to her, 'Hayley, sit down, we have to talk about this,' and she said, 'I'm having the baby.'

I implored her, 'Hayley, how can you have the baby? You haven't even finished school. You don't think I'm going to stay home with the baby, do you? That's not going to happen.' I didn't even know whose baby this was, for goodness sake, and although I pestered her about it, she wouldn't tell me, and to be honest there were times when I thought, '*She* probably doesn't know who the father is.'

And even though she was pregnant, everything just stayed the same. She would vomit in the morning, go outside, have a cigarette, come in again, wrap a scarf around her waist to try to hold her stomach in, put her uniform over the top, and go off to school with her cigarettes in her bag. I was in a state about what to do, and then it was taken out of my hands. The principal called me up to the school and said, 'Well, it's obvious that she can't stay on. She's starting to show and it's not exactly the right message for the other girls in the school, is it?'

And I said, 'And what am I supposed to do?'

He said, 'Well, we don't want that sort of thing at the school.'

And I said, 'You can't expel her. She hasn't broken any school rules.'

He didn't care. He said, 'She can't be walking around in a St Michael's school uniform, eight months pregnant.'

I contacted the Department, obviously, and their first question was, 'Who is the father? Is it anybody in the house?'

I said, 'Excuse me. We didn't do this to her! She did this to herself!'

I never said – never, not once – that I would turf her out, although I did say, I admit, that I wouldn't be taking care of the baby. I wanted her to have an abortion. I won't pretend that I didn't. She told the Department, and they said, 'Hayley does not want to have an abortion. We will set her up for independent living.'

I said, 'You cannot be serious.' This was a girl who could not cook a piece of toast or boil an egg. But they said, 'Yes, we have a place.' They took her to a high-rise building, a housing-commission building, filled with drug addicts and the homeless, and put her up in a one-bedroom flat.

I went to visit her. I looked around and said, 'Hayley, you cannot bring a baby in here,' but she thought it was marvellous.

'My rules now, Mrs Mac,' she said. The apartment was terrible, and she'd made it worse. In fact, I could hardly believe what she'd done to the place. She and some new friend of hers from down the hall – another single mum – had taken a black texta and basically drawn a whole household-full of furniture on the walls. In the lounge room, she'd drawn a sofa; she'd drawn a mantelpiece with a clock on it; she'd drawn a cat; she'd drawn a table with a vase with flowers, all over the walls.

She had blown the victim's compensation on a ridiculous bed – the salesman must have seen her coming – with a stereo and rolling lights in the bed head. She also had a kettle and a toaster, and a few other things. I gave her some warm clothes and some things for the baby. I said, 'Hayley, what are you doing? You can't bring up a baby in here, how on earth are you going to manage?'

Look, I admit, part of me was thinking, 'If I have to take the baby, I will take the baby.' I'm not made of stone, after all. But she was cocky. She said, 'We'll be getting the single mother's pension. We'll be fine here, thank you, Mrs Mac.'

I stayed for less than half an hour. While I was there, the girl from the other flat came by with a baby – it was a well-dressed baby, I admit that – and they sat on the floor with texta furniture on the walls, smoking, with Hayley swollen like a basketball.

I thought, 'Good God, is this really the best we can do for these kids?' Because here's the truth: I care about Hayley Cashman, I really do. For all I've said, I do have fond memories of her as a small child. There are memories I still treasure, memories of her curled up, allowing me to stroke her hair, or tuck her into bed with a hot-water bottle.

Once, when she was about fourteen, she even said, 'I love you, Mrs Mac. I know I don't always show it, but I do.'

And I said, 'Oh, Hayley, you could make life so much easier for yourself, if you just put away your claws.'

She didn't want to have an easy life, though. That was the problem. Hayley Cashman enjoyed the fact that she brought a world of chaos with her wherever she went. She was like a jack-in-the-box: we tried to keep the lid on, but she was wound tightly, under constant pressure, and always ready to pop.

Ruby Porter,
Foster Mum

When people ask me how Harley Cashman came into our lives, I say, 'He was delivered.' I like the double meaning. Someone else delivered him into the world, but then he was delivered, as if by a stork, to me. Harley was four years old and he had been in Department care for about a year. He had two siblings, both sisters, one of whom was younger, and one older. The Department told me there had been an 'incident' in the family and Harley and his sisters had to move out. They told me his mother was in prison and was not likely to be released before Harley finished school. They warned me that Harley might have some problems 'settling' with me, as they called it. He might have night terrors or wet the bed. They gave me the number of a twenty-four-hour service and said I should call if he was too much to handle.

They gave us a suitcase with some of his T-shirts in it, and said, 'Okay. Good luck.'

We put Harley in the back of the car. We intended to drive him back to our farm at Exford, out the back of Bacchus Marsh. We're not a wealthy family and our car was ten years old. It was a hot day; the air-conditioning was really struggling. I said to my husband, 'Open your window.' I opened my window, and I opened the back windows, too, and that's how we drove home, all the windows open, like we were in a wind tunnel.

Halfway home, we stopped to get a closer look at him. My husband found a clearing, near the Melton weir, where we could park the car. I took Harley out of the back seat, stripped him down to his nappy, and let him toddle in the eddies, his feet as round as the stones in the river. Everything about him was perfect: he had a round head – the biggest smiling head I'd ever seen – and bow legs, with rolls of soft flesh padding his inner thighs, down to his knees. His hands were still fat across the back, like a baby's hands. His palms had no creases.

The first night I put him into bed, I stayed with him, reading by a Smiley night-light. I stroked his hair until I thought he was asleep, but when I tried to leave he reached up, as if in panic. I'm a big woman. I don't move easily. He put his arms around my neck, pressed his face against my cheek and clung to me. I tried to draw myself away. I unhooked his hands from behind my neck, put his arms by his sides and tucked his blanket tightly around him. I backed out of the room, saying, 'It's okay, Harley. I'm just down the hall.'

He didn't say anything, but I could tell he was afraid. I closed the door gently behind me and tiptoed down the hall. I stood in the kitchen, my heart pounding. I was listening for his cry, but there was no sound at all. I went back into the hall. Harley had got out of bed and put his hands under the door. His fingers were coming out from underneath. They were blue and luminous, like starfish. When I opened the door – I was careful not to scrape the skin off the back of his hands – he looked up from where he lay on the floor with saucer-eyes and implored me, 'I want to sleep with you.' I put out my arms and he climbed into them. I carried him down the hall, in his singlet and his Kermit underpants. I put Harley down onto the middle of our mattress. He curled like a kitten into the hollow. Tony said to me, 'It's not allowed, Ruby.'

I said, 'We can't let him sleep on the *floor*.'

Tony replied, 'You know what they said, *Don't get attached*,' and I said, 'It's too late.'

The Department had told us that Harley would not be allowed to stay forever. He wasn't available for adoption and, in any case, we weren't eligible to adopt. The girl – that's all she was, a young girl, barely a woman – who handled adoptions at the Department told me in a tone that all of them seem to use that 'the

Department has guidelines and unfortunately your application to adopt places you beyond those guidelines and therefore your application can't be considered'.

I said, 'What does that mean?'

She said, 'It's to do with the *disability*.'

I *do* have a disability. I don't shy from that. I have a congenital deformity, a condition known as *spina bifida cystica* (in Latin, that's 'split spine'). I was born with part of the spinal cord exposed. I had several operations when I was a child, to cover the bone and to straighten my back, but I still don't stand completely upright. Nevertheless, that makes me comparatively lucky. Some people with *spina bifida* can't walk at all; some use a wheelchair. I have some numbness in my lower body. I don't walk in a particularly elegant way. My condition makes it difficult to exercise and the Department had told me that *technically* – that is their word, *technically* – I'm morbidly obese. In fact, although I'm a large woman, I'm fit. I work on the farm. I walk for an hour a day. I didn't understand why any of this – my gait, my weight – precluded me from adopting a child.

I said to the social worker, 'Would you stop me from having a child of my own?'

Of course, they wouldn't have been able to do that. I could well have had a child of my own, and there would be nothing they could have done about that. Anybody can have their own child. Doesn't matter if they are drug abusers or prostitutes or paedophiles, but when you want to adopt they put you through hoops, like infertility makes you less capable of being a parent.

My other problem was my age. I didn't meet Tony until I was thirty-eight years old. I had already been married. I wasn't keen to marry again. My first marriage was abusive. I allowed my first husband to make negative statements about my appearance. I allowed him to control me. He did not want to have a child, and especially not with me. He said it would be a cripple. My self-esteem suffered. It took a long time to break free. I didn't think I would get married again, but when I met Tony I knew it would be different. I told my mother that I would get married again and this time we would have a child. My mother's Catholic. She said, 'Ruby, what will be, will be.'

I'm not Catholic, not any more. Obviously, I was raised Catholic, but these days, I'm more of a spiritual person. I've investigated many different religions and I've taken parts of all of them, for my own spiritual identity. I studied Buddhism. I suppose I'm more interested in ethical living than in structured religion. I'm a vegetarian, a feminist and a socialist. I believe in reincarnation, in positive thinking, and that human beings belong in tribes. I've long worked with women, in particular, for the rights of minority women: migrant women, lesbians and Indigenous women. I must have used a lofty tone when I told my mother about the career I intended to have after university, fighting for the rights of women, because she said, 'Don't you tell *me* about rights. I've been fighting for your rights all your life.'

She has, too. She refused to put me in a special school. She told the Department of Education: 'There's nothing wrong with my daughter's *brain*.' She enrolled me in the local Catholic school. When she told them that I occasionally had to use a wheelchair, depending on whether or not I was recovering from an operation, they said, 'But we don't have a ramp.' My mother said, 'You'll have to get one, won't you?'

When I told my mother that Tony and I planned to adopt a child, she said, 'God will decide,' but actually, it seems like the Department decides. I'd moved onto Tony's property at Exford. I was completing a degree in women's studies, and I was advocating for the rights of women and disabled people, using Equal Opportunity legislation and the Disability Act.

Tony had a full-time job. He worked as a clerk. I thought we had much to offer a child who needed a home. But the Department told me it was impossible. I told them, 'You're not allowed to discriminate against me on the basis of my disability,' and that's quite right, but the girl told me, 'Put aside the disability for a moment. The fact is there are very few babies available for adoption.'

She was right about that. In the 1970s, the Department had plenty of babies. There was no single mother's pension and there was no childcare. It wasn't easy to get an abortion, and certainly not a safe, cheap one. But by the time we started thinking about adoption in the 1980s, things had changed. Gough Whitlam – who is my hero, by the way – had brought in a single mother's pension, and abortion had become less of a taboo. With the arrival of Bertram Wainer, the doctor who opened the first legal abortion clinic, you didn't have to get a backyard abortion any more; you could just go to his place at East Melbourne and have it done with dignity, so there weren't that many babies around.

The Department told us, 'Look at foster care. Plenty of kids need a temporary place to stay.'

I wasn't sure about it. I couldn't accept that I would be given a child for a period of time and then have to give it back to the Department, who might place it with parents who were not in the best circumstances. Nevertheless, we filled out the forms, attended the meetings – we were very self-conscious because Tony, who is much smaller, could fit in the plastic school chair but I could not – and we stayed and watched the social workers giving the whiteboard a work-out in front of us. Eventually, we got ourselves approved for 'respite care', which meant the Department could send us a child with a disability, a child with Down syndrome or cerebral palsy, whose parents might need a break, and we could care for the child for a weekend and then send it back.

I'll be honest: it was harder than I thought it would be. We had to patch holes in the fence because the little kids, especially the Down kids, got through them like lightning. We had to move things onto the top shelves. One child got her fingers caught in a mousetrap in the kitchen. And then, out of the blue, we got Harley. He had no disabilities. He was entirely perfect. I couldn't believe that I'd be allowed to take him home, but then I realised that some greater power had put him on earth for a reason, and until that reason revealed itself, I would be entrusted with him.

We knew from the outset that Harley had sisters, and we were willing to care for them, but the Department said no, the younger sister had been placed with a family member, and the older one, Lauren, had 'issues that need to be sorted out'. I was very curious to get the facts, but they would not say more.

So, from the first day, it was Harley alone, and I suppose I did come to think of him as an only child . . . and as my child. I probably should have been afraid of creating too strong a bond. The Department reminded us every day, or so it seemed, that Harley had been placed with us temporarily, and that we would have to give him up once the case against his mother had been decided by the courts. I ignored their advice. I loved Harley passionately, on sight, and he loved me. Neither of us, I'm sure, could abide by the Department's order not to love each other. How could I stop myself from loving the child that bolted across our fields in pursuit of rabbits; who leapt, startled, into my arms the first time he spotted a tawny frogmouth; who fell asleep on my lap, with his hands in his ice-cream bowl, three nights out of five?

There were things about parenting that I had to learn on the go. Harley would turn on the taps in the bath if I did not keep an eye on him. I was worried that he'd scald himself and I would get into a panic, wondering what the Department would say, so I would sit on the toilet, with the lid closed, and watch him in the bath. He would fill up an ice-cream tub with water and pour it over his head. Sometimes he'd sit for an hour, playing with his little pecker, studying it like it was the most fascinating thing he'd ever seen.

'That's the start of a lifetime love affair,' said Tony, when he observed him one day, and I shooed him out of there.

I had a strong faith that the universe would sort things out . . . and I was right. After two years, when Harley was five, turning six, the Department told us he had moved onto the long-term list. Adoption was still out of the question, but I felt that we had a wink and a nod from the Department that Harley's mother wasn't coming for him any time soon. I don't mean to sound awful when I say that, but I couldn't bear the idea that I'd had him for a few years and might still lose him to who knows what kind of future.

I'm biased, of course, but I believe Harley's childhood, with Tony and me, was idyllic. I didn't rely on toys or TV to keep Harley entertained. We had a mulberry bush that took over one whole corner near our house, and we were always saying we were going to cut it back, until it became clear how much Harley loved to pick the mulberries and squash them between his fat fingers. We had a dog – a succession of dogs, actually – and we had chooks. We tended the veggie patch. Sustainability is all the rage now. I'm reading in the newspapers all the time about a sustainable earth, but we had that idea twenty years ago. We were first on the bandwagon. Tony and I were trying to make ourselves self-sufficient, with our own water, a compost heap, horse manure on the garden, in the 1980s. We dug up potatoes and pulled up carrots, and Harley helped us with all of that. We had pea-shelling competitions. I'd take down two bowls and we'd sit on the verandah, each trying to fill the bowl before the other.

Every six months, we had to take Harley to the Department for some kind of inspection. They called it a 'progress report', but I was never of the opinion that we were all on the same side. I can say this now because Harley is grown up: I never quite lost the fear that they would spirit him away at any moment, for no reason at all. It seemed to be so arbitrary. We heard horror stories from other foster parents of children being taken away and placed back with their parents. Some of them were then mistreated, and were placed with a new set of foster parents. I knew I couldn't live if that happened to Harley.

I warned Harley not to call me Mum when we were at the Department. I told him not to say he called me Mum at home, because that kind of thing could trigger them.

When Harley was six, we enrolled him in the local public school, Exford Primary. It was a small school. It was one white wooden schoolroom with children from Year 1 to Year 6. Harley had blossomed, and with the older children around he soon turned into a confident child. He seemed so certain that everybody would love everything about him – and if they didn't, I certainly did. Here's one lovely memory: when Harley was in Year 2, he made a sculpture from Icy Pole sticks. He had to put it up for sale at the school art show; all the other kids' sculptures were put up for sale, too. Harley implored me to get to the show early. He was fearful that someone else would buy his sculpture before me! It didn't occur to him that they would want the sculpture made by their own child. And when I got to the show, Harley was standing very protectively in front of his Icy Pole sculpture, ensuring that no other parent bought it. When he saw me walking in, his face showed such relief and he said, 'Mum, quick, it's still for sale.' I paid my five dollars and Harley said, 'I really wanted you to have this because I know it's the best one here.' And it was. Truly, it was.

By the age of seven, Harley was probably the most popular child in the school. He made friends incredibly easily . . . and often with the strangest characters. I remember once, when he was about ten, I went out to the letterbox and saw Harley standing with a small boy who seemed to be hiding behind a tree.

I said, 'What's that boy doing, Harley?'

He said, 'That's Dominic. I met him in Speight Street the other day.'

They were using a slingshot to shoot cans off the letterbox. I watched for a while and then said, 'Hello, Dominic. It's very nice to have you come over.' And he said, 'I was run over by a car.'

I was a bit startled. I asked him if he was okay, and he shrugged his shoulders, and off they went again, with the slingshot.

So it was like that. Harley would bring home these strays, not just dogs, but *kids*, and he kept himself thoroughly occupied. Even as he got older, he was never one of those boys that wanted to stay inside. He wanted to be out and about, and he'd find other kids to go off with for hours, and I'd have to get used to the idea that it would be dusk, or dark, before I'd hear his bike come down the gravel drive. Then he'd eat pretty much everything in the fridge – four or five pieces of bread, one on top of the other, vacuuming it down, no time to even put on butter. I'd say, 'Harley, do you want me to butter that, make a cheese Toastie?' And he'd say, 'Nah, Mum, she'll be right.'

She'll be right.

Harley's mother died in prison when he was an adolescent. There was a flurry of Departmental activity at that time – he had to go to counselling and he met with his siblings, who he hadn't seen for years – and then life resumed, as normal. I searched for signs that he was unsettled, but there seemed to be none. Harley did what every other kid in the town did: got caught wagging school and didn't do it again; got caught smoking and then took it up; he dropped out of the local high school at sixteen and got an apprenticeship as a roof tiler. At the age of eighteen, he started his own business and he was doing well . . . until the accident. Even then, when I had to stumble into casualty in the middle of the night, thinking to myself, 'So, *this is how it ends. This is how we lose him* . . .' I found him sat up in the hospital bed, covered in bandages and in blood, flirting with the nurses.

And what did he say? He said, 'Come on now, Mum. Enough with the waterworks. It's no big deal. *She'll be right.*'

PART TWO

PART TWO

Lauren Cameron

I wonder if I might begin by asking an impertinent question: how many times have you had sex? I mean, with how many different men? You may not know the answer. Many women these days have no idea. They have to stop and think about it. I can tell you exactly. If you don't count the last time, then I've had sex with nineteen different men. Does that sound like a lot? It depends, I think, on when you were born. If you were born in the 1930s, or even the 1940s, then nineteen lovers probably sounds like more than is decent. Working, as I've done, on an Old Timers' Ward (it's the Alzheimer's ward but I can't help thinking of them as the Old Timers), I've met plenty of women who assured me they met the love of their life at a dance hall when they were seventeen, and never again looked at another man.

Who can say if they're telling the truth? Maybe they had a fling when US troops came during the Second World War or something. I don't know, but I do know this: the rules about women and sex changed around 1970. It was to do with Germaine Greer, apparently, and with the arrival of the Pill.

These days, it's easy to find women who would happily admit to having nineteen lovers over their lifetime, and maybe they're not yet done.

I didn't have sex with nineteen men over a lifetime. I had sex with nineteen men in a very short period of time: in the four years between the ages of thirteen and seventeen. Then, for ten years, I didn't have any sex at all. It's not that there was anything special about Number 19. Truth be told, I can't remember Number 19's name. I didn't give up sex because I found the right man. I gave it up because I recognised – finally, and too late – that it wasn't helping me get where I wanted to go, which was up and out of the Barrett Estate.

Some people are puzzled as to why – not to mention *how* – a girl of thirteen might embark on a series of sexual relationships. Well, I had no parents: my mother was in prison for the murder of my younger brother; and my father – well, I'll get to him, but let's say he was mostly off the scene. When I was a little kid I lived with foster parents and they didn't really instruct me about men and boys. What I learnt, I learnt from books. My first foster mum, Mrs Islington, used to tell me, 'Nobody can be lonely if they've got a book in their life,' which is true, but when you get life's lessons from books – especially the books on Mrs Islington's shelves – well, real life can be astonishing.

Mrs Islington started me off with *Cinderella*, and then *Snow White,* and from there we got through *The Secret Garden, What Katy Did* and anything by Enid Blyton. As I got older, I moved on to *Jane Eyre*, to *Madame Bovary* and *Anna Karenina* and *Lolita.* You can imagine how my mind developed, with nothing but these books to guide me. I thought men and women had sex with each other only when they were in love. Therefore, every time I met a man who wanted to have sex with me – they were really boys, of course, none older than twenty, desperate for a bit of experience – I figured they were in love with me.

Were they? What do you think?

I'd meet a guy, agree to sex, and afterwards, the bloke would be up and out of there, before I had time to put on my pants.

The first time, I was living in a unit in the caravan park outside Barrett. I was thirteen and I was living there alone. Now, that might sound strange, but let me tell you, lots of state wards live in caravan parks. I landed at the park when I was twelve, after yet another 'long-term' placement at somebody's home had broken down and I'd been temporarily put in a motel. That had been the story of my life: one placement after another.

My first foster placement had been with Mrs Islington. It ended when I was around ten. We'd all gone there – my siblings and I – while the courts sorted out the charges against my mother. After she went to prison, Hayley went to stay with a great-aunt, and about a year after that, when all the appeals had been exhausted, my brother, Harley, went to a new carer called Mrs Porter, in Exford.

I went to a couple who had no children.

I used to think of them as 'the Childless'. I suppose they took me because they wanted a child and hadn't had one of their own. Maybe they didn't like to do what you have to do to have a child. Maybe they thought sex was rank. They were pretty clean people. Prim people. Anyway, it was probably for the best that they didn't have a baby. I'm not sure a baby would have been welcome in their house. The Childless were house proud. They had doilies on the armrests of their chairs, and plastic running up the stairs so the carpet wouldn't become worn down.

I wasn't a messy baby. I was almost ten years old. I suppose the placement made sense to the Department: 'Neat, house-trained Lauren, meet the Childless. We're sure you'll be perfect together!'

'How do you do, Lauren?' That's what Mrs Childless said to me, the first time we met. She spoke like nobody else I'd ever heard. Who says, 'How do you do?' Nobody, not any more, but she did. She also liked to use big words, *obscure* words – that's one of them! – and then ask me if I knew what it meant, and if I didn't, we'd have to look it up in the dictionary together.

To really drive her mad, all you had to do was drop your Gs.

I didn't drop my Gs. Or maybe I did at first, but I certainly didn't for long. I learnt a lot from the Childless. Not simply not to drop my Gs, but other things, too, like how to keep a house clean. It still didn't work out, though. I only found this out later, but apparently I offended their *cat*. They had a Burmese with eyes like sapphires and a coat like mink. Mrs Childless told me it was a *show* cat. It wasn't to play with; it was to be shown, or should have been, except there was some problem with its overbite, something that caused an enormous amount of grief to Mrs Childless.

I do remember stalking the cat. I remember that it would try to hide under the patio. I would get down in the dirt. It would bare its teeth and hiss in protest. It had claws like needles; when I grabbed for it, it would scratch my chest and my forearms, leaving droplets of blood in long red lines.

Mrs Childless would say, 'Now, Lauren, Augustine doesn't like to be handled.' *Augustine*. They named the cat after a saint. Mrs Childless told me that Augustine had another name, too, a show name, but Augustine was what they called it – and picking up Augustine soon became the ambition of my life.

'It isn't working out,' Mrs Childless told the Department after the last time she had to pull me, by the ankles, out from under the house, where I'd gone in search of the cat. 'I'm sorry but there is something very strange about that child.'

And then, I suppose, she went back to polishing the buffet.

From Mr and Mrs Childless, I went to a couple who already had a child, a girl who was already a teenager. They were churchgoers so I called them The Christians. It occurred to me, after a time, that I was some kind of Christian project, too. Whenever they had guests – people from the church, or the pastor himself – I would be called from my room and be asked to stand under their plasterboard arch while they explained the latest developments in the life of The Girl They Had Fostered.

'She came with nothing,' the mother would whisper. 'Her mother is in *prison*.'

Mrs Christian was a hairdresser but she didn't work in a salon. Clients would come to the house. The thing then was perms. She had a trolley with blue plastic rods that she strapped hair around; and a bottle of what she called 'the perm solution'. The women came in with flattened hair; they left with springs upon their heads, like Steelo. Once, when Mrs Christian called me down to help with the solution – I was allowed to paint it on, while she held part of the hair around a curling rod – the client said, 'Isn't she one of the children from DeCastella Drive?'

Nobody was supposed to know that; Mrs Christian wasn't supposed to say, but I saw her open her eyes wide, and a faint smile of satisfaction came across her face and, when I turned my back toward the sink, she whispered, 'Yes, she *is*.'

After a while, I refused to come out of my room and participate in the salons. I sat on the floor and read. It must have troubled The Christians, because I was sent for what they called an 'assessment'. I had to sit in a group of six other foster kids, with a large piece of poster board and crayons between us. We were told to go ahead and draw. I remember being terrified. Was something specific expected of me, and, if so, what was it? Did they expect me to sketch the house at DeCastella Drive, to draw stick figures representing my mother and my siblings? I wasn't going to fall for that.

I stayed with the Christians for about two years. I guess I knew it wasn't really working out, but still, I was surprised when they came and sat on the edge of my bed one day to give me some 'exciting news'. Mr Christian had been offered an 'amazing opportunity'. They were going to live abroad. Mrs Christian said, 'Lauren, we really have to take it.'

I got the message. *We* did not include *me*.

'They wouldn't let us take you, anyway,' Mrs Christian said. I heard the word 'anyway' much louder than the others.

'You understand, don't you, Lauren, that we're your

foster carers and that gives us *some* rights, but we can't take you overseas. We wouldn't get permission to do that . . .'

I could have finished the sentence for her: 'even if we'd asked.'

The Department told me the Christians would be leaving in ten weeks. I was eleven years old by then, going on twelve, and getting harder to place. A child is one thing; a girl on the cusp of adolescence, that's another. A caseworker came to the house. She was the fifth or sixth I'd seen. She had to read through all her notes to figure out my history.

'You're getting older and it gets harder,' she said.

'Will I stay on Barrett?' I asked.

'That's the goal,' she said.

I wish I could explain why I wanted to stay on Barrett. Maybe I couldn't bear to leave the place where I'd lived with Jake, but that doesn't sound completely right. More likely, I felt I didn't deserve to be with Harley.

When no home turned up in the next ten weeks, I went into 'emergency care', meaning I moved from one house to the next, with foster parents who took children on a Friday night, in an emergency, and kept them for a week or so, and then moved them on. It was like a merry-go-round, but as a foster child you soon get used to it. You start to see the same faces around, and you say to each other, 'Where have they had you?' I'd say,

'I was last week at the Shellays, or the Coopers, or the Lindrums,' and they would have been there, too, although not always at the same time. Some of these temporary places were awful: there was stuff stacked all over the house; no food in the refrigerator; no toilet paper in the loo; debris strewn across the yards. If they were clever, these respite carers didn't let the Department near the front door. They'd stand out by the gate when the social workers would come, and they'd say, 'Here she is.' The social workers, being harried, would tick us off, and go on to check on the next house.

After a few months of this, I ended up at the Barrett Motel. There were supervisors licensed to the Department who were supposed to keep an eye on me and the other kids who lived there. They worked in eight-hour rolling shifts. The woman who ran the motel told me that when she took over the business she could barely believe that her best customer was the Department of Family Services.

'I cannot conceive,' she said, 'that this is the best we as a society can do.' I heard her asking the Department one day, 'Are you sure this is normal? One of these girls is only twelve.' The caseworker sighed and said, 'All the homes have closed down. What else can we do?' It was supposed to be a state secret. The Department didn't want people to know that adolescents were living in motels because there was nowhere else for them to go. I wasn't supposed to talk about it. Secrecy compounds shame, of course, but nobody thought of that.

Actually, it wasn't that bad. I had my own room, with a TV and an ensuite. One afternoon, the woman who owned the motel came past my room and saw me sitting outside, my back to the wall. She was collecting sheets and towels. She said, 'Do you want to come and help?' My caseworker had disappeared, as usual, and who could blame her? Nothing was more boring than sitting in a motel out on Barrett all day. The lady said, 'I'll just be folding the towels.' I could tell she felt sorry for me. I wanted to show her that I had manners, and I was capable of things. I said, 'I can help.' I followed her back to reception and marvelled at the set-up: there was a set of swinging doors behind the reception desk that led to the family's lounge room. If a guest came in to register they could ring the brass bell on the desk, and the lady would come out from her lounge and assist them.

I sat on the floor with the towels. The lady watched TV while folding the towels into a perfect square and putting a plastic-wrapped soap on top of each one. She then brought me a cup of luke-warm tea, heavily sugared, and some biscuits. She said, 'How long have you been with the Department?'

I dipped my shortbread and said, 'Since I was seven.'

'Where is your mum?'

I said, 'I don't know.'

Then, 'Have you got a dad?'

'I don't know.'

Even then, I wished I was as interesting as my circumstances. Always, it was, 'What *happened* to the adults in your life, so that you could end up like this?'

Anyway, the owner invited me to stay for 'tea' and I decided I would. Her husband was there. He put a bowl of what looked like puffy pink potato chips in front of me and said, 'Have you had a prawn cracker before?'

I said I had because I thought if I told them I hadn't they might not let me have one.

'I remember the first time I gave them to our kids,' he said, 'I said to them, "Put 'em on your tongue," and you know what happened?'

I didn't know, but I said, 'Yeah, I know. They taste funny.'

He said, 'Yes, but about how they snap you on the tongue?'

Now I was alarmed, but I'd lied myself to the point of no return. I held the foamy pink cracker against my tongue, and felt it gripping.

'Fun, isn't it?'

It was. It definitely was. I ate the bowl of prawn crackers and then all of dinner, too. Afterwards, there were chocolate sweets, called After Dinner Mints, served in slinky envelopes. It would never have occurred to me to leave, until finally the woman said, 'Do you have a bedtime, Lauren?'

A short time later, I moved from the motel. For years I thought it was because the man had given me prawn crackers; perhaps they were for consumption by adults, like alcohol and cigarettes? I can now see that's ridiculous. I don't know why I was moved; I moved a lot, often with no explanation, and while it might seem strange to some people that I ended up in a portable on the Barrett Caravan Park at the age of thirteen, it was no surprise to me or to other foster kids who lived similarly. As long as there were some books – and by now, I had a few of my own – I figured I'd be okay.

The park was as you might imagine. There was a pool, open only in summer and freezing even then; and some playground equipment. Some people had their own kitchens, but most people used the barbecue in the covered forecourt, and washed their tin pans under the tap.

Maybe because I was an older girl, I got a hut of my own. It didn't have a bathroom so I had to shower in the communal lot. The social worker told me, 'Wear rubber thongs in the shower. We can't be responsible if you get a papilloma.' It's a disease of the feet. I had no rubber thongs so I went to the shower in my sneakers and pyjamas. Before I got through the doors, one of the other kids rode by on his BMX and shouted out, 'Watch out for the peephole!'

I put my toiletries down on the tiled floor and searched around the tap holes and the shower head for a hole. I couldn't find one, but still I showered in my knickers and sneakers. After that, I mostly washed in the sink.

I lost my virginity before the month was out. A group of young guys, apprentice chippies and sparkies, came onto the site. They weren't permanent residents; they were working their way up the east coast, where the weather was warm, hoping to get jobs on building sites. I was walking to the showers when one of them called out to me, 'Hey, spunky!'

They'd made a fire in one of the half-drums that were left lying about. I hung by the edges of their campsite, listening as they talked about football, girls, surfing, cars, pretending to be doing something else, until one of them said, 'You want a smoke?'

My guess, on reflection, was that he was eighteen or nineteen. They had P-plates on their cars. He wore jeans and a T-shirt. My Prince Charming!

'Do you live here?' he said, cupping a hand around the flame of his lighter as I bent and inhaled.

'Just for now,' I said.

'Where's your folks?'

'Asleep.'

He said, 'Your mum and your dad, or just your mum?'

I said, 'Just Mum.'

He considered this for a moment, then said, 'Like, near here?'

I said, 'No.'

He thought a moment longer and must have

concluded that I was worth the risk.

'You must be cold,' he said. 'Why don't you come in the tent? I want to talk to you.'

How can I explain how those words sounded to me? He'd said, '*You must be cold*,' and it sounded like, 'I care about you.' He'd said, '*I want to talk to you*,' and it sounded like, 'Nobody else may have noticed this, but you're a person worth having around.'

I went into the tent. Straightaway he started kissing me. I kissed him back. The strength of the muscles in his arms intrigued me; the strength in his tongue surprised me.

I said, 'What's your name, anyway?' and he said, 'Dicko.'

Dicko. Romantic, no?

He took one of my breasts in his hands. I remember feeling ashamed because my breasts were small and I assumed he would be repulsed. He made a move toward the zip on my jeans. I used my hands to push him away. I had a teenage girl's shame about my body. I believed, as all girls do, that I was nowhere near as desirable as I should be; that I wasn't sexy enough for sex.

Also, resisting his advances seemed to be the thing to do. He got frustrated, though, and pushed away from me, saying, 'Hey! You can't do this to a guy.' The change in his tone was immediate, and shocking. He had been affectionate, even loving; now he was angry.

'You're trying to give me blue balls,' he said.

I didn't understand. 'Blue balls, man,' he said, moving rapidly to release his swollen penis from behind his zip. Stroking it, with a pained looked on his face, he said, 'It's an f'en *condition*, man, and it's cock-teasers like you who give it to a guy. You're in here pashing, and you're turning me on, and you won't let me go all the way, and that can make a guy sick.'

Oh, how men can pretend! And who can blame them? He probably did need, more than anything, to ejaculate, right there and then, with me or into the palm of his hand or the flesh of a watermelon; anything would do. How could I know that, though? Desperate not to disappoint, I put my hands over his penis. It was wet – I didn't expect that – and there was a smell I didn't recognise.

'Pull on it, pull on it,' he said. He leaned back against another of the sleeping bags. I got onto my knees, but in doing so, looked up and saw one of his mates at the zipped fly-screen door of the tent, grinning at me. I dropped back and pulled a sleeping bag toward my chest.

'They're looking!' I said.

Dicko had been trying to get his jeans off, but flat on his back with the material tight around his thighs he'd been unable to. He got awkwardly and angrily to his knees and punched the face through the mesh.

'Piss off, will you?' he said, zipping the tent shut.

'They're dickheads,' he said. 'They're jealous. They

wish they were here with you.' His hands were tugging at my jeans, and suddenly, his fingers were inside me. I was startled by the wetness; had not known it was there. He was moaning, 'Oh man, my balls, my balls.' Then, in a different voice altogether, 'You got a franger?' I shook my head. 'You on the pill?' No.

'Suck me off, then,' he said. 'Please, I'm in agony, man.'

It occurred to me that he didn't know my name. I put my mouth over him. I couldn't see but could clearly hear the other guys outside the tent, simulating sex, grunting like pigs and falling against the mesh tent in hysterics.

'Fuck,' said Dicko, ignoring them. 'Fuck, fuck.'

I was frightened of what he was going to do in my mouth. I had learnt about semen in school: it was millions of little tadpoles floating in syrup. How would that feel? But it was fine. I gagged but did not vomit. I slipped my mouth off his sagging penis.

Dicko rolled onto his back and stared at the roof of the tent. His friends were cackling outside. 'Fucking morons,' he said. After an age he added, 'Don'tcha think you better go back to your place, in case, like, your mum comes to check on you?'

One of his mates began fiddling at the zip of the tent, saying, 'Hey, spunky, can you help me out with my blue balls?' There was a cascade of laughter. 'Fuck you,' he said to them.

I heard, 'Cradle snatcher!'

To me, Dicko said, 'Get dressed. Come on, you gotta

go.' I didn't understand his sudden change of mood. I was eager for another of his deep kisses, but when I leaned forward and tried to get one, he shoved me away. He was unzipping the tent, crawling out, not looking behind. I sat back for a minute, confused, then crawled out of the tent, but Dicko wasn't with the guys still sitting around the fire, shoving each other. He was in the distance, his back to me.

'You still up for some?' one of the others said. I felt my face turn crimson. I went back to my demountable. There was a note from the social worker. It said, 'Don't wander off!' I got into bed and spent some time feeling myself, to see what was different. Branches slapped against the tin roof. I heard what I believed to be peals of laughter, although it was probably wind, howling against the windows.

In the morning, I put on my school uniform and some mascara I had squirrelled away from one of the homes where I'd lived, and walked slowly and deliberately by the site where Dicko and his mates had been camped, but they had shot through in the night, worried, I suppose, about the ramifications. I was jail bait, after all. Black coals smouldered in the half-keg. I picked up an empty beer can, one that had been crushed flat underfoot, and put it in my bag. For some years afterwards I kept it, because I thought that it might have Dicko's saliva on it, and that was romantic to me.

I didn't tell anyone that I'd sort of lost my innocence.

Who would I tell? The girls at school? No. There was a code at school regarding sex: the other girls had long ago decided that it was okay to have sex with somebody you were 'going around with' but not with some stranger. I'd be called a slut or a moll, and the only way to avoid it was to stay chaste, or find a boyfriend. And so began a pattern. I would meet a guy and become convinced that he could see something in me that others couldn't. I believed – every time, despite the evidence – that he'd come to rescue me. We'd have sex, and I'd be hurt and surprised when I never saw him again or, if I did, he pretended not to know me.

I never mentioned Jacob to any of the men who slept with me, but of course I knew, in the way you just do, that *rumours* about what had happened in the house on DeCastella Drive were rife on the Barrett Estate. Only once do I recall anybody raising the matter with me directly. The social workers didn't talk about it and neither did the teachers. No, it came up after I'd left Barrett Primary and was in my first year at Barrett High, with many of the same kids who'd been at the primary school with me, but who had only then started to hear and understand the gossip their parents had been trading for years.

I was in the girls' toilet block. It was a classic of the time: there was a stainless-steel trough, six bubblers, one of which squirted water into your eye. The smell was typical, too: urine and diarrhoea, masked with antiseptic. The concrete floor had puddles from the morning hose-out. The ceiling would certainly have been marked by those wads of scrunched wet toilet paper we used to throw up there and leave to dry.

A gaggle of girls was hanging by the troughs, sharing cigarettes. It was the custom in those days to keep your packet in your school bag and then, at recess, hand it around and hope you didn't 'drop' too many, or give too many away. If there was only one or two in the packet, we'd share them between us, passing the butt from lip to lip, trying not to be the one who made it soggy. We talked non-stop and I can't remember any of the things we said.

On this day, one of the girls, a popular girl, Terri, who had already been kept down once and was a year away from her first pregnancy, announced that she had got a bra. She was the first to get one and we – me and the other, flatter girls – were keen to see it. I was still built like a boy, a small boy with nipples that had budded and chafed against my T-shirt. Sometimes there was a mysterious and embarrassing stain in my pants.

Terri was proud of her boobs and her bra but she wasn't going to show it off for nothing.

'I'll show it for a ciggie,' she said. 'You girls get me a ciggie, you can see.'

Somebody had a spare cigarette; it was pulled from the packet and handed to Terri, who put it behind her ear. She was wearing the Barrett uniform – a chequered tunic with buttons down the front – and it had been some time since she could properly close her buttons. Her swelling breasts forced the front of the dress out, and brought up the hem. Make-up was banned but Terri wore it. We all did. Black eyeliner was popular then, drawn around the rim of the eye and along the lower lashes. The teachers would complain, especially when it rained.

'Wipe that off. You look like raccoons,' they'd say.

We thought we looked as good as Prince, maybe better. In her too-short uniform with the gaping buttons and her painted face, Terri would have looked like a girl from a Prince music video.

Terri made a production of her great Bra Reveal. First, she chose the girls who would be allowed to stay in the toilet block. 'Larissa can stay, Lisa can stay, Sharon has to go, and I'm not doing anything while Rebecca is here.'

I wasn't among those supposed to stay and look, but nor was I banished. Terri told me to stand by the door and keep an eye out for teachers. We wouldn't have much time: the girls who had been evicted from the toilets had run into the schoolyard, and were telling the boys, 'Terri's gonna show her bra!' Those who weren't grossed out had formed a group, and were grinning and jostling each other, daring themselves to come closer and get an eyeful.

I kept one eye on the schoolyard. Terri said, 'Is

anyone coming?' and I said, 'Coast is clear.'

Terri unbuttoned her tunic and, with one quick movement, pulled both sides of her dress apart. I caught the briefest glimpse of a bra – an impossibly risqué lace bra with purple satin – and Terri's breasts sitting proud and plump in the cups. It was so lovely, I gasped. What had I expected? A flesh-coloured cloth bra, probably. A bra like those I'd seen hanging on the clothes line at the Christians, with no fancy detail. I'm sure I wasn't the only girl who was impressed, but the group turned to stare at me.

'What are you, a lezzo or something?' said Terri.

I said, 'Rack off.'

She said, 'You're supposed to be watching the door.'

I'd forgotten that. The boys were right outside now, in full holler. 'Show us your tits, Terri! Show us your tits!'

How it spiralled from there into an argument about Jake, I can't tell you, but Terri, flanked by some other girls, started having a go.

'What are you staring at?' she said.

I said, 'Nothing. I was watching the door.'

Terri said, 'You were looking at me like a lezzo.'

Another girl said, 'She's a weirdo,' and another chimed in, 'She's one of those kids from DeCastella Drive.'

'Her brother got killed.'

'Her mum's in prison.'

'*My* mum says that everybody reckons *she* did it.'

'Hey, freak, what happened to your brother? Why don't you tell everyone what happened?'

The girls had formed a hostile circle around me. I felt hot and uncertain and, again, I had that feeling: run, Lauren, *run*, but the boys were yowling like hyenas at the door.

I needed a teacher. I could see from where I was standing that one was on the way, attracted by the noise. I waited for her to break into the circle, but she didn't rush, she meandered, and even when she arrived, all she said was, 'Okay, everybody, show's over. Don't hang around the toilets, it's not clean, it's not hygienic, why would you want to hang in here when it's so lovely outside?'

The boys split. The girls, with Terri out front, strode past me with chins skyward. One of them knocked me with her elbow as she passed.

'You okay, Lauren?' the teacher said.

I was okay. I've always been *okay* . . . just not quite normal and not sure why.

Harley Cashman

Call me old-fashioned, but I'm the kind of guy who likes to read a newspaper. Mum says I started reading *The Sun* – the comics, anyway – when I was about six and I've kept up the habit ever since. Now I live in New South Wales I can't get *The Sun*, so I have to get *The Telegraph*. I don't get the *Herald*. My old man, Tony, tells me I ought to read the *Herald*, but in my opinion, a newspaper has gotta fit against the windscreen, so you can read it while you're sitting in the car.

Anyway, I'm on this job site, north of Sydney, way up north, actually, with the *Telegraph* in the cab of the ute. I always start from the back, since in my view sport is the main news of the day. I'm turning toward the front, when suddenly, there's this picture of a *very* familiar lookin' chick. At first I think, 'Oh, maybe she's one of the ex-girlfriends,' but then I look underneath the picture and the name just jumps out at me: *Lauren Cameron.*

Straightaway I think, 'You can call her what you like, but that's not Lauren Cameron. That's Lauren *Cashman* and that, sir, is my sister.' It had been a while since I'd seen her – twelve years, maybe more – but memory's a powerful thing and I had no doubt: she could call herself Cameron or Kalamazoo, I'd still know it was her.

In the picture, she's walkin' down the steps of Sydney's Coroner's Court, and the story says something like 'Sound of Love'. I didn't quite get what all that was about, but I think, 'Hey, wouldn't it be fun to catch up? Maybe I should give her a call.' Then again, I didn't have her number. You might think the Department would have kept me up-to-date with her contact details, but if you do think that, you've got a skewed view of how the Department works. They probably couldn't tell me their own phone number. So, no, I didn't have her number. But I think, 'How hard can it be to find out? The reporter that wrote the story will surely have it.' I call up Directory Assistance and ask them for the *Telegraph*'s number, and then I ring up and after I get through all the bullshit – 'Do you want to place a classified? Do you want editorial?' – I get to an operator and I say, 'I want to speak to the bird who wrote this story,' and when the reporter comes on the line, I say, 'That photo you've got, Lauren Cameron, that's not the right name, and I know, because that's a picture of my sister. Her name's Lauren Cashman, and I'm Harley Cashman, and I'm her brother, and I've actually lost touch with her and I didn't realise she was in Sydney, because we're from Melbourne, but I want to call her and have you got a number?'

I can tell the reporter's a bit surprised, but I've got a way with women and eventually she says, 'All right, if you're her brother, why don't you turn up at the Coroner's Court because that's where she's gonna be, all week, cos she's givin' evidence at some kind of inquest, and she's gotta be there,' and I think, 'Yeah. Okay. All right. Why don't I do that? Give Lauren the fright of her life.'

So I say to my crew, 'Can you guys finish up the job here? I gotta go to Sydney.' And I'm thinking to myself, 'No, this is gonna be too bloody funny, fronting up at court and saying, "Hi, sis."'

Strange thing is I don't call Mum. I can't say why.

So I spend the rest of the day in the ute, driving down to Sydney and thinkin', 'On one hand, yeah, this is probably not such a good idea after all,' and then, 'Oh, actually, it's a very cool idea,' and, finally, six hours after I leave home, when I'm stuck in peak hour, I'm thinking, 'No, I was right, this is a bad idea.'

But I'm stuck with it now so I park the ute near the Coroner's Court and bunk down for the night. Then, in the morning, I wander on down there. I have to go through a metal detector. I have to ask where the right room is. There are press everywhere, and then I see this girl standing there, this slip of a thing with a mop of white hair, shaking and looking absolutely terrified, and I think, 'Yep, that's my sister.' Couldn't be anyone else. I mean, we're like a couple of snowballs, and the only difference is our size. I'm a big bastard. I take up a lot of space, even in a conversation. I'm the kind of guy, when I'm there you know I'm there, if you know what I mean. And Lauren's not like that. She shrinks back. She's part of the furniture. She's small. Now I know her better, I can tell you everything about her is small. She talks small. She cooks small. She leaves me hungry. She has this dish she makes, where she cuts pork into tiny squares. It's like we're in a recession. When she writes, the letters are all scrunched together. I've got this fantastic signature. People are always telling me: how do you get that on the back of a card? And the first time I saw Lauren sign a bill for something, it was all tight, dark writing and it took her like, forever, to get the thing out.

Anyway, I bowled on up to her and said, 'Mate, it's me,' and she looked at me blankly. That took me back a bit. I thought she'd recognise me. So I go, 'It's me, it's Harley,' and I can see she's thinking, 'Who is this lunatic?'

And then she bursts into tears. And I think, 'Oh man, what's all this about?' She just bursts into tears and kind of falls against me, and that kind of freaks me out. My idea had been, go down there, catch up with my sister – like, how cool is that? We'll have a beer or whatever – and suddenly, she's trying to get in under my jacket or something, and people are looking at us, and she's saying, 'I've got to get out of here. I gotta go, I gotta get home.' And she's off, and out the door, and getting into a cab, and this guy, a reporter, is saying to me, 'Where's she going? She can't go.' But actually, she did just take off and disappear, and I was off my nut about it, thinking, 'Shit, what did they do to her in there? Or, like, was it me that freaked her out?' But then I saw what they were saying about her in the paper and I thought, 'Jesus, I better go get this girl.'

I tracked her down easy enough. She was livin' in a shed out the back of somebody else's house, and when I walked in, I found her curled up like a baby on her bed and she wouldn't move. She was in a panic about photographers. She kept saying she didn't want to be in the paper any more and, given that I'd had time to catch up with what was going on, I thought, 'That's just about inevitable,' but after a while I managed to talk her around. I threw a jumper over her head and we got into the car and then we just drove. I figured, 'I'll head to Mum's.' I mean, I had two choices: take Lauren back to my place, up near the Queensland border where I was sharing with a bunch of building guys, or take her straight to Mum's. It was a no-brainer. We hit the freeway. At first, we didn't talk much, we just listened to some music. I thought, 'This is weird, she's my sister and, like, we've got nothin' to say to each other.' It wasn't really until we stopped at a petrol station, about an hour in, when Lauren got out of the car, with nobody around, that she started to loosen up. I remember this: she bought one of those plastic bags of mixed lollies, with some lolly teeth, and she put 'em over her own teeth and grinned at me with these fake teeth and that's when I thought, 'Well, she's either completely lost it, or actually, it's gonna be fine.' And it was fine.

We got back in the car and continued along, talking crap, mostly – look at that horse by the roadside, look at the kangaroos, and Lauren told me a whole long story about how she met our dad once, and how he was into women and motorbikes, which was kind of interesting – and by the time the night came on I'd even managed to make her laugh a bit. But she was worn out. I could see that, so I thought, best thing to do is get her some sleep, so I said, 'We'll pull in at Gundagai. No point trying to do it in one go.' See, it takes at least twelve hours to drive from Sydney to Melbourne, and Gundagai is as good as halfway. I'd planned to go two-thirds of the way, maybe even as far as Kelly Country – where the bushranger, Ned Kelly, had his last stand before they hung the bastard – but Lauren was weary and I was, too.

She said, 'Only if we can see the dog.'

It took me a sec to figure out what she was on about, but then I got it. The dog on the tuckerbox, that's what she wanted to see. Myself, I'd seen it plenty of times, and I warned her it wasn't much: just a statue, and a poor one, of a dog sitting on a tuckerbox, ears up, alert, exactly five miles from Gundagai – I know, because I've clocked it, and it's just like they say in the song. I took the turn-off, and we pulled up and looked at the statue for about five minutes, and she said, 'Well, okay.' And I said, 'Told you it wasn't much.' And then I said, 'I reckon we better get a motel.' We got back in the car and headed into town. There were four motels, and three had those neon NO signs above the word vacancy, but at the fourth there was no sign, so I went in to check it out and they had one room. I told Lauren we'd have to share, and she said, 'Yeah, let's share,' like it was something I was suggesting.

I said, 'When do you reckon we last slept under the same roof? Must have been twenty years ago?'

She said, 'Probably.' And then she looked at me, with this very strange expression – not panicked, just very strange – and said, 'Do you remember anything about the house in Barrett?'

I said, 'No.'

She didn't say, 'Do you remember Jake?' I figure she thought my first answer covered it. The truth is, I don't remember Jake. How could I remember him? I was, like, three when he died. I know who he is, obviously, but remember him? No, I'd be lying if I said I did. Anyway, she looked for a second like she was going to say something else, but then she lit a cigarette and I thought, 'Okay, whatever. It can wait.'

We checked into the motel and it was soon clear to me that we weren't goin' to be gettin' any sleep. Somehow, we got a second wind, and we sat up, talkin' and eatin' the pizza we had delivered. Like everybody, she wanted to know what happened to my hand and, actually, that felt super weird, lying beside her in the bed talking about it, because how many times had I done that with a chick? Gotten the business over, laid back for the post-coital ciggie, and then been asked, 'What's the story with your hand?'

The story is this: I lost my right arm above the elbow when I was twenty. Technically, that makes me an 'A2J' – an above-the-second-joint, wrist and elbow amputee. Now, most people think that's got to be the worst thing in the world, losing an arm, but I can tell you, it's made precisely one difference to my life, and that is, I pull more chicks these days. No, it's true. The ladies have been good to me since I lost the arm. It gives them something to talk about with me. I size 'em up, and decide what to say. Sometimes, I say I got attacked by a shark, which works better in Sydney than in Melbourne, where, frankly, there aren't that many sharks. Other times, I launch myself into a story, one that's gotten better over the years. I put on this low voice, and I say, 'I was walkin' in the bush when I got trapped in a ditch and a bear was comin' up on me' – you wouldn't believe how many chicks don't question that, since we have no bloody bears in Australia last time I checked – but they just look at you wide-eyed, and then I go on, 'So I'm lying there, in the dark, with these big yellow eyes comin' at me, with branches around me breakin', and I feel this tuggin' . . . on my leg.'

Then I pause, and they say, 'Your *leg*?'

And I say, 'Yeah. It was pullin' my leg. Like I'm pullin' yours!' And of course, right then, they hit me with a pillow, and before long we're off again.

The real story is, I fell under a train. Drunk as a lord I was, like I often am on a Friday night. I'd been in the pub and I'd had a few, and my idea was to walk home since I don't drink and drive. But then I passed the railway station and decided to get the train. And I fell off the platform. That's the unromantic truth. I fell off the platform and the train took the arm off, almost to the shoulder.

The thing the chicks always want to know, when I finally fess up the truth, is, 'Can you remember it?' I always say, 'Mate, it was a top night out. I was legless. And now, of course, I'm armless!'

And once again, that usually gets us back to business.

With Lauren that night, I actually told the truth. 'Yeah, I remember it. The roar, I remember. The arm not being there, I remember that. Looking down and seeing this flesh, all ripped and torn and bloody, and thinking to myself: that skin, it looks like lace. That blood, it looks like wine. I remember that.'

When I woke up after the surgery, I said to the doctor, 'Mate, which arm?' And he said, 'Right,' and that's when I thought, 'Oh okay, cool,' because I'm a south-paw, always have been, so I just went off to sleep, thinking, 'Yeah, that's fine. They can have the right.'

They kept me in an induced coma for eighteen days, and when I came around, I saw that I wasn't near the worst off on the ward. They had blokes who had come off motorbikes, who wouldn't walk again. They had blokes who dived into creeks and hit their heads on rocks, and they wouldn't walk again, either.

What did I have? Mrs Palmer and her five daughters were gone, but like I say, I never made much use of the right, so it was no biggie, really.

I had this cool nurse that helped me. Her name was Angelina, but straightaway, I started to call her Angel. She was just as a nurse should be, all big boobs and as old as me mum, and bustling around me. I actually told Mum, when I was still drowsy, 'Mum, this woman, she's not a nurse, she's an angel. I met her in heaven, and she was wearing a halo, and I brought her back with me.'

Angel was mocking me, saying, 'You're takin' too

much morphine, Harley. I ain't got no halo. That was me hairnet you saw.'

Angel was the one who told me, 'You blokes who have lost a limb, you go one of two ways. Either you start thinking your life is over, or you just carry on like you've dropped a wallet or something. I want you to be the second kind.'

She said, 'Some people, they lose the soul with the limb. You don't want to be one of those guys. When that happens, they don't recover. They might survive, but not for long. They end up hooked on drugs, or wanting to kill themselves.'

She told me, 'If they left your soul on the railway tracks, Harley, things are gonna be bad, but I reckon they got it.' She was quite a spiritual bird, Angel, and I totally understood where she was coming from, because I didn't feel like I'd lost much at all. I felt like I feel after a night on the piss: I was groggy. I couldn't move that well. But I didn't think, 'Oh, my life is over.'

Later on, when I moved from the trauma ward to the rehab, I met blokes who were like Angel said: definitely not all there. I mean, obviously parts of their bodies were missin', but there was something else missin', too, like they'd lost – I dunno about the soul – but like they'd lost the plot.

The other thing I understood from the get-go was there would be women. For a lot of amputees, and also the blokes who end up in wheelchairs, it's like, who is gonna love a freak like me? But girls love the arm. It's not grotesque, it's just kind of missing, and once they see it's not hideous they come flocking. So when the doctor comes around and says to me, 'You may have difficulty relating to people, you may find that people find you some kind of object of fascination,' I'm thinkin', 'You're the one that's lost the plot, mate, if you think that's gonna be a problem.' I'm happy to be an object of fascination. Bring it on.

As for the day-to-day stuff, you do your best. There was pain at the start, fairly constant, and I'd be perspiring, and Mum would say, 'What's happening, Harley?' And I'd say, 'It's my arm. It's aching.' I've heard people say, 'It's like pins and needles,' but excuse me, it's not like pins and needles, it's like a red-hot poker going through your bone. I had a few practical problems: how do you do up a button with one arm? How do you put on a shirt? But that's just practice and also, Mum, she's good with that kind of stuff. She invented me a few things: a steel hook thing that I call the Ruby Button Threader, and a face washer that I can put over the stump, so I can wash the other armpit.

I had to give up working on roofs, obviously, but I didn't mind too much. I kept the business, just hired more blokes to work for me, and the money kept coming in. I had to get the ute remodelled, so the gears were on the steering wheel, and then the rehab people wanted to know, 'Are you gonna go for the claw, or for the prosthetic?' I was pretty keen on the claw but I went for the prosthetic. It's a silicon sleeve with a hand and fingers and, to be honest, I don't wear it that much. I can't see the point. It's bloody heavy, and it's not like you can use it. The thing just hangs there. I do, however, have some fun with it. When I take it off, it looks like something from the Halloween shop. Me and me mates dug it into the ground at the cemetery once, set it up like it was coming out of the ground near one of the graves, and then we sat around drinking, and watching to see the local teenagers come and scream.

The thing wasn't cheap and I suppose I should actually wear it as opposed to piss-fart around with it, but it's not something I can actually hide, the fact that I've got one arm. I mean, people are gonna find out eventually, so why not up-front? Besides that, your arm, whether you know it or not, weighs about five kilos, and although it hangs off your shoulder, it's got its own support. You try hangin' five kilos of silicon off your shoulder, with no support. It's not that comfortable.

So that's the story of my arm. I told Lauren all about it that night in the motel, and the only thing she really said was, 'Did the lady who looked after you freak out when she found out?' And I remember thinking, 'Did who?' Because those words – 'The lady who looked after you' – didn't mean all that much to me. I didn't get that she meant Mum. And that's when I thought,

'Yeah, we don't have the same mum, not any more,' and how weird is that? I find my sister, and then I find we haven't got the same mum. Except we do, obviously. And that got me thinking, 'I better give my mum – I mean, Rubes – a call. I better tell her I'm bringing Lauren.' So I go to Lauren, 'Mate, I'm just gonna pop out and get some ciggies.' And she's like, 'Not for me, mate, I'm giving up.' And I'm like, 'Righto.'

I collected up my keys and my wallet – I could see she was amused, the way I put my wallet in my mouth to open the door – and I was careful to slip my mobile into my pocket. I started up the ute – it stunk of McDonald's and cigarettes, two of my favourite smells – and I drove down to where the Caltex was glowing on the freeway. I stopped out the front, flipped open the phone and thought to myself, 'Come on, Harley. This is no biggie.' I pressed the keys and the phone lit up. If anybody was gonna answer, it was gonna be Mum, and she did.

I said, 'Mum, it's me, and I gotta tell you something and don't freak out.'

She goes, 'It's bad news.'

I go, 'No.'

She goes, 'It's bad news, isn't it, Harley?'

I go, 'It's not, Mum. It's not bad news, it's not good news. It's just news, news.' And she goes, 'Just tell me, Harley,' so I laid it on her. I said, 'I've got Lauren with me, Mum, and we're making our way to Exford.' Then

I said, 'I gotta go. I'll speak to you tomorrow.' Maybe she was speechless because she didn't say much. I closed the phone and sat in the dark cab for a bit.

I wouldn't be exaggerating if I said I've had no more than two or three proper conversations about my birth mum with my proper mum. I always knew my birth mum was in jail. Nobody hid that from me. I remember when I was little, there was a bit of chat about whether Lauren should move from wherever she was living and come and live with us, but it never happened and then, when my birth mum died, I actually saw Lauren, because the social workers said we better have a meeting to talk about it. So we did, and Mum and me, we talked about that, but not much.

Other than that, I can only remember one other time that we talked about my birth mum. It was out on the porch at Exford, and I was sitting with Mum – with Rubes, I mean – and it was about a year or so after I lost the arm, but before I'd moved up to New South Wales. Rubes had simmered a pot of mulled wine, with cloves and cinnamon and orange rind, and we were sitting around the pot-belly on the porch. The frogs were making a regular racket. She was settled into her favourite pozzie on the old Papysan chair, and she had the guitar out, like she does when she's had a few. Maybe because it was all mellow, she said, 'Do you know what I'm thinkin' about, honey?' – sometimes, she calls me honey – and I said, 'No, honey, whatchoo thinkin' about?' She goes, 'I was thinking of the day you came to us, Harley.'

I'm like, 'Musta been the best day of your life.'

And then she goes, 'I always knew you'd meet a beautiful girl and get married and raise a tribe of kids.'

I'm like, 'What choo talkin' about, Mama?' Remember that show, *Diff'rent Strokes,* how the little black kid used to say that? That's what I say to her when she says something totally out of the blue. *What choo talkin' about, Mama?* Because, frankly, marriage and kids? That was some way off. I had no regular lady friend.

But Mum says, 'I thought you might go off the rails a bit, when you had the accident –' which is one hundred per cent false, by the way, she knew perfectly well I was gonna be fine, and if anything, it was her that practically drove the staff on the ward mad, wobbling in with her walking stick, and the incense sticks and the wholegrain muffins that taste like cardboard, and getting her purple robes caught in the door – 'but now I can see it. That accident was the best thing that ever happened to you.'

And I was like, 'Yeah, right on, honey, best thing that ever happened to me, to get hit by a train.'

She said, 'That's right.'

She didn't spell it out any more than that. Look, I don't get too philosophical but, obviously, I know what she meant. She meant that I carried the baggage about

DeCastella Drive all the way to Exford with me, and I was never allowed to set it down, until I lost the arm. At school, I was always the 'foster kid' or else the 'kid that Ruby Porter took in, and wouldn't give back'.

After the accident, well, things are different now. Wherever I go these days, I'm the guy with one arm. That's what people see. It's not: Harley, the kid from the Porter farm. It's Harley, the guy with one arm. This might sound wanky and, like I said, I don't ponder things too deeply, but looking at Lauren, I could see that she still had the baggage. She hadn't been allowed to put it down.

I reckon Mum would have been a bit freaked out about me picking up Lauren. I suppose she would have been thinking, 'How did they find each other? Did he go looking for her?' Which might have got her thinking, 'Why would he go lookin' for her?' In actual fact, I don't believe I've spent so much as one second thinking, 'I must go lookin' for my sisters.' Maybe I had some curiosity about them. Maybe there would have come a day when I did start lookin' for 'em, but I never had the feelin' when I was a kid, or even after, that I needed to track them down and ask them what happened, or whatever.

Anyway, I tried to keep the tyres from crunching in the gravel when I got back to the motel, in case Lauren had gotten off to sleep, but when I got inside I saw that she was just in bed with the sidelight on, pretending to be asleep. I said to her, 'I'll bunk down on the floor,' but she goes, 'Don't be stupid.' And truth be told, there was no room on the floor. There was a double bed and it took up all of the floor space. So I messed around a bit more. There was one of those strips of paper with things you could order for breakfast, and I studied that for a bit. I said to Lauren, 'What do you want to eat in the morning?' But she was so sleepy, I don't think it registered. I went into the bathroom, examined my face in the mirror for a while, expecting her to fall asleep any minute, which would make it easier for me to get into the bed with her, but I could hear her going through the channels with the remote, so I had a shower.

Lauren's eyes were closed when I came out of the bathroom, but she still wasn't asleep. I said, 'Go to sleep.' I closed the pizza box, put it outside the door, relieved myself in the toilet again, burped and brushed my teeth. I came out and stood, waiting. I had a feeling she was listening to me, through her eyelids.

I said, 'Hey, if you wake up in the night and see this, don't get a fright.'

She opened her eyes. I was holding the silicon arm in my good hand. I waved it at her and said, 'Nighty night!' She gave me this sleepy smile, and said, 'Don't let that thing grope me.'

And then, with one swift movement, I got under the covers, pulled them right up to my chin. We tussled over the doona for a bit. I turned off the sidelight, and there was complete darkness in the room. I could feel the weight of her on the mattress beside me.

I said, 'Night,' and then, 'Night, sis,' because I'd never said it before and it felt kinda cool.

She said, 'Night, Jake.'

I wasn't Jake, but I let it go.

Lauren Cashman

In the summer of the year I turned seventeen, I slipped out of my unit on the Barrett Caravan Park to meet up with a guy I'd met somewhere on the Barrett Estate. He'd arranged to pick me up from the carpark outside the railway station. I got into the passenger seat. The guy, whoever he was, waited for me to shut the door, did a U-turn, and started toward the Barrett weir. It was close to midnight and the way was lit only by streetlights, still, I saw a rabbit on the road ahead of us. I turned toward the man behind the steering wheel to share my delight, but he'd already seen it, and swerved toward it. I heard the *whump* as it disappeared under the wheels.

'We got it,' he said, pleased.

We drove until we came off the bitumen, onto grass and mud, stopping, finally, on swampy land near the water's edge. The weir was a popular place for Barrett's kids to park and have sex, but there weren't any other cars with fogged up windows that night. The guy killed the engine, turned off the headlights. He lit a cigarette. He didn't offer me one. 'So, Lauren,' he said, between drags. 'You're from that place on DeCastella Drive, right?'

I said, 'Yep.'

He nodded and said, 'Yeah, right. I thought so.'

He dragged on his cigarette, saying nothing for a minute, then he said, 'So, you know, like, what happened out there?'

I said, 'Where?' and he said, 'You know, in that house. People reckon there was blood all over the walls.'

I hadn't heard that before. I knew it wasn't true, but I said, 'I don't really know.'

He nodded, and stubbed out his cigarette.

He shoved the gear stick into first and, with his other hand, used a lever to collapse my seat and lay me flat. He kissed me and soon he had my pants down around my ankles. His pants were around his ankles, too. I thought to myself, 'So, it's going to be one of those. He's not even going to get undressed.'

He had barely managed to get inside me when he came. He eased himself off and found his way back to his own bucket seat, where he sat with bare buttocks against the vinyl, the hair on his thighs thick and curly. My own nakedness, from the waist down, seemed ridiculous. I crouched over my abdomen, and searched for my jeans on the floor of the car. He popped the glove box, and took out a box of Wet Ones. He wiped over the head of his penis.

'Want one?' he said.

'I'm good,' I said.

He zipped his pants. I zipped up my own. He put the car into reverse, and soon had us back on the road to the railway station. He parked where he'd picked me up.

'You good to get home?' he said.

I said, 'If it's okay, I need a cigarette.' I lit one before he could object. Oh, sure, I could sense that he was done with me, that he wanted me gone, but since I'd started to smoke he lit one of his own. We didn't speak.

Finally, he said, 'You right to go?' And I said, 'No worries.' He didn't move. He was waiting for me to get out of the car. I said, 'Well, thank you.' Only now do I think, 'For what? For not dumping me by the weir when you were done with me, maybe? For having sex with me and making me walk home afterwards, in the dark?'

'No, thank *you*, mate,' he said. 'You're a good root.'

I walked home and went to bed, and the next day I used the red phone in the motel foyer to call the Department. I told them that my caseworker had gone missing the night before – it wasn't entirely untrue, since it was the one who often went missing. A man had tried to break into my room, I said. Nothing frightened the

Department more than the idea that one of the kids might get raped, not because of the trauma they might suffer but because the tabloid TV programs might find out about it, and in so doing find out that hundreds of kids were living practically unsupervised in caravan parks and in motels across the state of Victoria.

They said, 'Stay there and we'll get somebody to you.' When they did, I told them flatly, 'I want to move.' I knew they wouldn't refuse me. I was too old for foster care, and although I was technically too young to be turned onto the streets, it was certainly time for me to transition to some kind of semi-independence. So they set me up in a group house, with other kids who were also almost off the books. All I had to do was prove that I could support myself, which wasn't too difficult. I was still at school but I'd been earning a small income of my own for some time.

I'd taken my first part-time job at fourteen, behind a counter at a lunch place, earning $4.25 an hour. I'd stayed there until I was sixteen, and then, when that place closed down, I got another job in a restaurant, waiting tables after school and at weekends. It was a pretty good job. The boss was Greek. I'd never met a Greek, except for the guy who sold pizzas in Barrett. This guy's name was Alexander, but everybody on staff called him Pop. He seemed, to me, incredibly old, although looking back now I'd guess he was fifty.

On my first day, he'd said, 'I'm going to be watching

you pretty closely,' and then he'd taken a lock of my hair, twirled it round his finger, and said, 'You better keep this up in a net, or something. We don't want it in the food. I don't want the Health Department here.'

I twisted my hair into a bun and then a customer came in and took a seat by the window.

Pop said, 'There you go. Your first customer. What will you do now?'

I said, 'I'll go see what that guy wants?'

'It's not *that guy*,' he said. 'It's *that gentleman* or *that customer*. I don't want anybody called guy here.' And I thought, 'Oh. So it's not only the Childless that talk properly.'

Pop gave me a vinyl menu and said, 'Off you go.' I gave it to the customer and told him I'd be back to take his order.'

'Good,' said Pop, when I came back. 'Now you give him a minute to decide, and then you go back, and see what he needs.'

I went back and said, 'What do you want?' but Pop, who'd been watching, raced over and said, 'She's *new*. She means, *What can I get you*?'

The customer was amused.

'Coffee, Miss New Girl,' he said. 'And eggs with toast.'

I wrote it down on the pad I kept in the pocket in front of my apron, my hands shaking as Pop watched every move. Then he said, 'You have to ask: How would you like your eggs? What kind of toast? Brown, white? Butter?'

The customer must have been a regular. He said, 'She's all right, Pop. Give her time. She's gorgeous. I'll have fried eggs, white toast with butter, thank you *miss*.'

It didn't take long to get into the swing of things, and I must admit that I learnt a lot from Pop. He helped me with my manners: always say please, thank you, you're welcome, may I, ma'am, sir, miss.

We – us waitresses – wrote the orders on a white-board near the kitchen with a black texta that hung on a string. There was a code I had to learn: 'H+C (T)' was 'ham and cheese, toasted' (a T on its own, no bracket, meant tomato) and if you added a 'B' that meant 'brown bread' – which was, by the way, something I'd never seen, let alone eaten. We had WR, too, which meant 'Welsh Rarebit' – and that, too, seemed posh and exotic.

I worked Friday nights after school and all day on Saturdays. Whenever it wasn't busy I was allowed to sit at the staff table and have a coffee and a cigarette while I folded the paper napkins. After the lunch rush, I got thirty minutes to eat a sandwich. I used that time to smoke, too.

When I told the Department that I wanted to move into Independent Living, they asked me whether I intended to make the restaurant job full-time. I didn't. After about a year, Pop had taken to pushing me against the industrial fridge in the kitchen, and groping at my breasts. I'd had enough of it, and enough of restaurants.

The problem was, I had no other skills and had no idea what I could do. Then one day, one of the customers, a girl who was a regular, told me about her job. She was a nurse in a city hospital, and she said they were crying out for aides.

'You could do it,' she told me. 'You don't even need your HSC.'

I asked her what the job involved and she said, 'It's crap. You make beds, empty pans, and chuck out the flowers when people get discharged, but you get holidays and super, which you probably don't get here.'

It sounded all right. I told the Department I wanted to become a nurse's aide and, to their credit, they were excited for me. They found out what I had to do – sit a test, basically – and after I'd passed, they arranged a three-month trial for me, at Melbourne's Royal Hospital. Once I got settled, they moved me to Mernda, a group house with other foster kids who were moving toward Independent Living. Like most of the group houses, it had holes in the walls, the lights were fluorescent and coated in moths, and other kids brought in drugs and ghetto blasters. Nobody mowed the lawn. Nobody emptied the letterbox. Nobody let anybody else get any sleep, regardless of who was working shifts, but still, I was, at last, away from the gossip on the Barrett Estate.

Then, too, for the first time, I was earning what seemed like decent money. I can still remember my first hospital pay. It came in a dark manila envelope, larger than a standard envelope, with stiff notes, never handled, straight from the bank. There was a piece of paper inside. Across the top, it said, 'North West Health Service' and underneath, in smaller letters, 'Name: Lauren Cashman. Employee number: 196875.'

There were other details: taxes paid, union fees deducted, a compulsory contribution to superannuation. There were unexpected additions, too: a laundry allowance, $1.80; and travel allowance, $2.20. Then, in the last column, there was my wage minus tax: $280. It seemed a fortune, and it gave me the feeling that everything would be okay – not immediately, maybe not even soon, but one day, eventually, I'd be on my feet, and everything would be okay.

I guess I'd been at the hospital a few weeks when some of the other aides started talking about having a girls' night. I found myself feeling keen to go. I had never had too much success being friends with people at school, but things were different at the hospital. There was camaraderie among the aides. We were all so far down the pecking order – below the nurses, below the doctors, below even the administrative staff – that we had to stick together.

'No one is gonna drive,' one of the girls said. 'We're gonna get a minibus. It's gonna be ace.'

'Where will we go?' I said.

'You go everywhere!' she said. 'They drive you round to all the discos, the clubs. It's grouse.'

The tearoom was alive with enthusiasm. There would be eight seats on the bus. You could drink all you wanted. It was better to get pre-mixes – UDL cans, they called them – and then you didn't have to carry two bottles.

'You'll come, Lauren?'

I said I would.

Here's what I didn't say, 'This is the first time I've been invited to go out with any girls, anywhere.'

I didn't know what to wear, but one of the other aides said, 'Go to Sportsgirl. They've got great gear,' so when I knocked off on the Thursday – the day before the bus tour – I went late-night shopping. I told the sales girl, 'I've got to go on this minibus. We're going around the discos.'

She said, 'Cool. Everybody's wearing stirrup pants at the moment, and a big shirt.'

I tried them on. The pants had a strap of material that went under the arch of the foot. The shirt had floppy cuffs, and lace across the bodice.

'It's cool,' the girl said. 'Get yourself some heels, you'll be grouse. Cash or Bankcard?'

I didn't have a Bankcard. I said, 'Cash,' and gave her some of the bills that had been folded inside the manila envelope I'd started to use as a purse.

The aides worked late on the Friday. Instead of going home, we got ready in the toilets. One girl, Lisa, said to me, 'Where's your make-up?' I had eyeliner and a small lipstick, a sample that I'd picked up at a foster home. I had an old eye-shadow, with blue chunks, like chalk, falling loose in the case.

Lisa said, 'You can't wear that. Here, let me do your eyes. Look up.'

I turned my eyes toward the ceiling, and let her rest her hands upon my face.

'Up, up!' she said, flicking my eyelashes with a curled rod of mascara, coating my brows, and blushing my cheeks. I hadn't worn so much make-up since Barrett High.

'Mate,' she said, stepping back. 'Look at the difference.'

My eyes were watering. I went to rub them, but Lisa said, 'No! Don't touch. You'll smudge it.' When the pools of water receded I looked in the mirror. The girl looking back at me seemed much older than the one who had been there before.

'Amazing,' said Lisa.

I went into a toilet cubicle to get dressed, using my teeth to snip the tags on my new clothes. My new shoes were tight, but the shop assistant had told me they would give, so I stuffed my aide's uniform in the plastic Sportsgirl bag, toddled out said, 'What can I do with this?'

'Just shove it down behind a seat on the minibus,' said Lisa. 'Nobody will take it.'

We started drinking on the bus, starting with something called Blackberry Nip, and something else called Brandavino. I sat near a window, with a heavy bus curtain knocking against my cheek. I hadn't previously been a drinker, but I'd heard the girls talking all week: 'Make sure you eat something. Make sure you have a glass of milk. It lines the stomach. You won't chuck up.' I'd had a glass of milk from the hospital fridge. The alcohol was sickly sweet. I started to feel loose.

On the bus, Lisa told me that some of the guys from the hospital – young cleaners, mostly, who pushed the buckets around and mopped the floors – would meet us at the club.

She said, 'They've probably already had a few,' and laughed. She looked so pretty and excited.

'Do you know Rick?' she said. She was sitting in the seat in front of me, and had turned around so we could talk. I said, 'Rick?'

'He's the tall guy, the real tall one. You must have noticed him.'

I said, 'Rick? Rick. No, I don't know any Rick.'

'You *do* know,' she insisted. I sensed that she was keen to share something with me. 'Tall guy, really tall. Dark hair. Wears, like, those trainers with the high tops. Wears 'em all the time.'

I could see it was important so I nodded, and said, 'Oh, right. Yeah. Rick.' But I couldn't remember him at all.

Lisa looked relieved. 'Do you like him?' she said. 'Do you think he's good-looking?'

Now what to say?

I said, 'I don't know. What do you think?'

'He's pug ugly,' she said, laughing. The girl who was sitting next to her half-turned in the seat, looked over the rail, and said, 'Bullshit, Lisa. You're so into him.'

'Am not, am not,' she squealed, but the girl in front said, 'Lisa, he's all you ever talk about.'

Lisa denied it, and slapped the other girl's hands. She snatched them away from the handrail, and they both turned, grinning, toward the front of the bus.

In defence of what happened next, I want to say that I didn't fully get what had transpired in that conversation. I didn't know that 'He's pug ugly' could mean 'I think he's a spunk'. I didn't know that 'You're so into him' meant that nobody else could go near him. I wonder, though, whether it would have mattered. The affection of men had for so long been important to me, and the concept of friendship was so alien, that I'm not sure whether I *did* know that Lisa was into Rick, and just didn't care, or whether I didn't realise that it would matter to her that Rick was into *me*.

Lisa turned toward me again, and our foreheads knocked against each other with the movement of the bus.

She said 'Ouch' and rubbed her head. Then she said, 'I don't really like him. I'll point him out to you tonight, and you tell me if you think he's good-looking. But I tell you, he's pug ugly.'

I wondered where she'd heard the phrase. She seemed

to like it. She said it again, '*Pug ugly.*'

Our first stop was a club they called the York Butter Factory. There was a red carpet outside, and a red velvet rope, thick as a serpent, held up by brass rings, to prevent a line of blokes from getting inside.

I went to join the queue, but Lisa said, 'Just come up to the door. They always let in the girls.' A bouncer – a big black man, blacker than any man I'd ever seen – lifted the rope for our group, and we tottered inside. I felt cushioned by the darkness – embraced by the darkness – and yet the lights pulsated, throbbed, at a distance. My ears felt full, too: the music was unbearably loud. We had to shout at each other to be heard, and even then, the words disappeared, so we took to smiling very white teeth at each other. At intervals, an unseen machine spewed smoke, which curled around the limbs of girls on the dance floor, leaving behind an industrial smell.

The bar was full. We stood impatiently, ordering eight Fluffy Ducks, and then eight Tequila Sunrises; eight Slippery Nipples, and then eight Harvey Wallbangers. In the crush, we spilt sticky drinks over the backs of our hands, and as we got drunker, we had to guide the straws into our mouths.

Lisa said something to me. I couldn't hear but it didn't seem to matter. I nodded and smiled as she wandered off onto the dance floor.

'Having fun?'

That was the first thing he said to me.

I had moved into a red vinyl booth, somewhere on the edge of the dance floor. The other girls were dancing. I was by now so drunk that I couldn't focus my eyes. I nodded. My head felt loose and heavy on my shoulders.

'You're cute,' he said.

Did I know it was Rick? How could I have known it was Rick? I didn't know what Rick looked like. He slid into the booth beside me. I felt a strong arm on my shoulder and I was grateful for it: the room was spinning. I felt his lips smear across my face. I turned to meet them. His teeth clashed against mine. I felt a hand in my lap. It took a moment to realise it was not one of the hands that belonged to the man with the lips. I was wedged now, between two men. One was kissing my face; the other was kissing my neck. There seemed to be four, maybe five hands on me. One was inside my ruffled shirt, feeling for my breast; another was in my lap. I moved about in the seat, responding to the hand between my legs and to the tongue in my throat. I felt another hand, a third, reaching under my bra, over my nipples. I was being kissed and caressed and I didn't know who by and I couldn't have cared less, but then I looked up and saw Lisa and another of the girls, each with a drink in their hands, their fingers holding the straw steady, looking at me with something like disgust.

I broke free of the arms around me – it was like

disentangling from an octopus – and stood on unsteady legs. I walked – stumbled, more likely – toward the bar, but Lisa was saying, 'Let's get out of here. This place is a dive. No decent blokes.'

I followed them out to the bus. I knew I'd disgraced myself and was desperately trying to win back their approval.

'Anybody need a smoke?' I said. 'How loud was that music?'

To my horror, I heard the words slurring.

We reboarded the bus. I wanted to get into a seat with one of the other aides, but they were resolutely ignoring me and squeezing in together. I found myself down the back, alone, with my face against the thick curtain. My head was spinning. As soon as the driver started the engine, I vomited.

Lisa said, 'That's so gross!'

The bus trundled through city traffic. The street lights seemed to be galloping. I vomited again and I must have nodded off because, when I came around, it was close to dawn, the bus was parked at some kind of transport interchange. My head was pounding. I had a blister on the back of my heel. The other girls were gone but the driver was sitting up front, drinking coffee from a thermos, reading an early edition of *The Sun*.

Lisa didn't speak to me again and, like Terri at Barrett High, she had a knack of making sure that others didn't either. Still, I heard on the grapevine that she and

Rick had started going out. Apparently, he told her I tried to seduce him.

A few weeks later, at my next meeting with the social worker who was helping to 'transition' me, I asked whether it was possible to get a new start in a new city. They were big on that. They actually had a program then called 'New Beginnings'.

'It'll do you good to get a fresh start,' my caseworker said. 'Where would you like to go?'

I think they expected me to say Ballarat or maybe Geelong, but I had bigger plans. I wanted to move to Sydney. I'd seen the Opera House on a postcard. I'd heard about the Harbour Bridge. It was a fair way from Melbourne – an hour by plane or twelve hours by Greyhound bus. I knew that the Department would pay for the bus ticket, and they'd arrange for me to spend a week at the YMCA. I had some money coming from the Corrections department, money for being a 'victim of crime', and they said I could use that to put down a bond and pay a month's rent in advance.

Oh, and one more thing: if I left Melbourne, I could have my things.

I said, 'My things?' I didn't know I had any things, but my caseworker said, 'There are some things that we have on your file that belong to you.'

They came to me in an envelope, the kind that might hold an A4 report. There were some notes in there from Mrs Islington, and a photograph of me, as a little girl, holding some kind of tea party for dolls. There were some school reports from Barrett Primary, and a copy of a drawing that I made, during group therapy.

There was something else, too: a piece of card, like a birthday card, with a photograph inside. It was a portrait of my family, the family I'd had before Jake died and my mother went to prison. A portrait of four children in blue jeans and white T-shirts, sitting on some kind of table, all smiling for the camera. Except when I looked closer I noticed Jake looked kind of upset.

I looked at that photograph for a very long time. I couldn't remember having seen it before. I stared into the faces of my siblings and tried to feel something, anything, but nothing came. They were like strangers to me.

Still, I took the portrait to Sydney with me. I had it in my briefcase when I went for a new job at the Sydney hospital, and to this day, if I haven't got it with me, I can tell you where it is.

I didn't intend to change my name when I got to Sydney, it just kind of happened. I'd got the Sydney job, and I was filling out some paperwork, and the old lady who was taking it all down and entering it into the computer said to me, 'What does that say? Lauren? Lauren Cameron?' and instead of correcting her, I just said, 'That's right. Lauren Cameron.' Things were different then: you didn't have to have a passport to open a bank account. You didn't need a driver's licence to get a Medicare card. You told your employer what your name was, and they accepted that. If you were going to rent a place, they'd write a letter saying how much you earned. You'd use your lease to get a Bankcard, and so on. It was just much easier to change your name, in a kind of informal way, and I must admit I kind of liked not being one of the Cashman kids.

I told the manager at the Royal in Sydney that I wanted to work all the hours they had, every shift they could give me. She was delighted. She showed me around the hospital: here's the geriatric ward, here's oncology, here's maternity, and here's the chapel. I hadn't previously been inside a church since Jake's funeral. Late that day, I went back there, and sat in a pew with my head in my hands, only to find that I had no idea how to pray. What were you supposed to say?

Please, God, help me?

I tried that but I didn't get anything back. All I could hear was the sound of nurses in rubber-soled shoes, squeaking down the corridor outside. Still, I stayed for a while, imagining what it might be like to have faith, and to really be at peace with the world.

It was a nice idea but, of course, the past is always close behind.

Hayley Cashman

People go to me, 'Must be hard, raising a baby at your age.'

I go, 'I'm doin' a better job than my mum ever did.'

They go, 'Right, where is your mum?'

And I go, 'She's dead and I'm happy about it.'

It spins 'em out, obviously, but I'm fair dinkum. She's dead, and I couldn't give a stuff. Me and Jezeray, we're better off without her. That's my opinion and I'm entitled to it. When I was little, they used to make me go see her in the clink, but then I told 'em I wouldn't go any more, and they couldn't make me.

When Mum first got locked up, I got sent to live with a lady who was supposedly a great-aunt, or somehow related to my old man, a bloke I wouldn't have known if I'd run over him in the street. She was a bitch, that lady. She had heaps of these kids that she reckoned was my cousins, but half of 'em were Abos. We had no shoes and she never bought nappies, and if I pissed on the floor she'd whack me one.

I didn't have a room, I didn't have a bed. There were all these dogs. Once I saw one of the kids drinking from a dog bowl. I don't remember that she sent me to school. I just remember the welfare lady come one day and said, 'Oh, right, this placement hasn't worked out, your great-aunt can't take care of you, and you've got to go to Mrs Mac.'

And I was, like, 'Whatever.' I didn't really care.

Mrs Mac was dead strict, saying, 'Oh, you gotta go to school, and you gotta wear a uniform and you gotta visit with your mum.' That's why I went to the jail, because she said, 'The Department says I got to take you, and you got to go.' It took forever to get out there. It was this really long drive in a bus. But first I had to go to the Department and get ticked off the list, like I was the criminal.

Mrs Mac – that was my foster mum – used to take me there in her car. It was bloody hot and she can't bloody drive. How many times we nearly smashed.

I reckon that Mrs Mac didn't think I should go to the prison, but she goes, 'I gotta do what the Department says.'

It was pretty bad. Mum would be sitting there, outside the prison. Not outside the walls outside, but outside the building, in, like, the garden. It's not like the TV. They don't make 'em wear those jumpsuits. They don't have handcuffs and chains around the ankles. You don't gotta talk to them through the glass with a phone.

So I'd go there, and Mum would be sitting there on a bench or sitting on the grass, or else I'd go sit down and they'd say, 'She'll be here in a sec.' But sometimes, she didn't even bother to come out until the visit was half over, and I'd sit there like a lump, waiting.

When she did come out, she wanted smokes, or else she wanted to whine and carry on.

She'd go, 'It's not my fault I'm here.'

She'd go, 'You know why I'm here.'

I'd go, 'Don't talk about it, Mum.'

She'd go, 'You remember what happened?'

I'd be like, 'Right, I was eighteen months old.' That's about as old as Jezeray and, like, she can't even *talk*.

She'd be like, 'Why didn't you say nothin'?'

I'd be like, 'Say what?' All I know is I had a brother. I had *two* brothers. I had a sister. And then it all went crap and we were dumped like dogs on the welfare state, and shifted from pillar to post. Whatever Mum did or didn't do – and I'm not going into the ins and outs of it – she ended up in prison and that loser boyfriend went with her, and that was it.

I got jack of going to the prison pretty much as soon as I could say I wasn't going no more. I can't say why, it got to the point where she made me want to spew.

249

After that day, when they said, 'Oh, you gotta go visit your mum,' I'd just go, 'No, I'm not going, and you can't make me. If you shove me on the bus, I'll sit in the bus, and if you drag me out of the bus, you'll have to drag me right through the door, and the minute you let me go I'll be out of there.'

They said, 'Oh well, you have to talk to her on the phone,' and I was like, 'You can't make me. Because she'd just scream at me down the phone, saying why don't I visit? She got stuck into Mrs Mac. She'd go, 'That Mrs Mac, she's poisoned your mind against me.'

I'm like, 'No, Mum, you did that.'

Anyway, I stopped speaking to Mum for about a year and then they called me and said, 'Right, you gotta talk to her again, cos she's sick.'

And I go, 'I don't care.'

And they go, 'No, it's serious.'

And I'm like, 'I don't care. You can ring me up and tell me when she's dead and then I'll care.'

And that's actually what happened. They ring up and say, 'She's got cancer. Do you want to visit?' And I'm like, 'No.' And then they ring up and say, 'Oh, she's passed away.' And I go, 'Has she?' And they go, 'Yeah. Do you wanna go to the funeral?' And I go, 'Like, *no*.'

Around that time, they said to me, 'Oh, you can see Lauren. You can see Harley. I'm like, 'I don't even know these people.' They were like, 'Yeah, but we have to get you to see them.' So Mrs Mac drove me into this place in the city and we go in this room and Lauren is in there, and Harley is in there, and it's like, what now? It freaked me out. They're strangers to me and I'm supposed to talk to them and I can't think of anything to say.

I mean, yeah, there was a moment where I did think, 'This is all right, this is kinda cool, she's my sister, he's my brother, and they're not totally dorky, although Harley's a bit odd.' He came in with this fat lady wearing a kaftan thing, who he called Mum, which was a bit weird. It was okay. We did have a bit of a talk about things, and later, I did kind of think, 'Okay, maybe we'll keep in touch,' but it wasn't really up to me, it was up to the Department, and they never mentioned it again, not for ages, except, after Lauren got over eighteen, they rang and said, 'Here, you can have her phone number now, but she lives in Sydney.' And I'm like, 'How come?' And they're like, 'Don't know.' And I thought, 'Yeah, well, I don't blame her.'

There were a couple of times when I wanted to call the number, but I had no credit on my mobile and it would have been a bit strange, anyway, calling this person I didn't know. You're supposed to have feelings toward your sister, but she was basically no more to me than a person on the street. We didn't have anything in common. When we had the visit that time, after Mum died, Lauren told me that she'd never visited Mum, and

I went, 'You're lucky.' So, no, it wasn't like we were gonna talk about Mum.

The truth is, I had one interest, and one interest only when it came to Mum. The social workers had told me, 'Hayley, when you're older you're gonna get this money for being a victim.'

I'm like, 'What?'

And they go, 'If you're a victim of crime, they give you this money, like to make up for it.' And when I told Mrs Mac, she goes, 'Yeah, and when your mum gets out of jail she's gonna try and get that money off you.'

I'm like, 'How much money?' Mrs Mac wouldn't tell me so I asked the social workers and they wouldn't tell me how much, either. They just said the same: I'd get some money when I was older, and I'd find out then how much.

I used to have a guess at it. I'd go, 'Is it a thousand bucks? Is it more than a thousand bucks?' But they never said.

It didn't matter anyway because Mum got the cancer so she'd hardly be coming for the money, would she? And when I got to sixteen, I was up the duff. Mrs Mac got all hysterical about it, saying, 'You're under age,' and all that, but I wasn't worried. I knew I was gonna get the money, and I figured, that'd set me up all right. I just go, 'Mrs Mac, when they give me the money it'll be sweet. I'll set up with some other girls in a flat and study to be a beautician at night, until I get qualified.'

And she goes, 'And who will look after the baby, Hayley?'

And I go, 'It can go into day care.'

Mrs Mac goes, 'They don't have day care at night, Hayley.'

I could see what she was gettin' at. She wanted me to have an abortion. She was like, 'If you have a termination, you can stay here and finish school.' I'm like, 'No way, this is my baby, and nobody is gonna abort it.' And I got in touch with the Department and said, 'I'm up the duff and Mrs Mac says I've gotta move out.' They go, 'We can move you into independent living,' and I go, 'Sweet.' And I moved into this flat, and Mrs Mac came and saw me once and said, 'This is no good.' I was like, 'Mind your business, old lady.'

I was pretty pissed off with Mrs Mac for a while after that, but I did ring her up when I went into labour. Mate, I'm telling you, that was frickin' agony, and I'm like, 'Mrs Mac, you better help me.' She did come to the hospital and all that. She reckoned Jezeray was a cool name. 'Give her a bit of glamour,' I go, and she goes, 'Yeah.' But when I said to her, 'Oh, can you hang onto the baby, I gotta have a ciggie,' she was like, 'The baby's hungry.' And I was thinking, 'Why are you telling me?' And then I remembered, 'Oh, yeah, it's my baby.' That was a wake-up call, I tell you.

I went from the hospital back to the flat, where I was living before Jezeray was born, and basically got screwed, money wise, all over again. The Department said there would be all this support for single mums, but basically I got the Commission flat and Jezeray got to go to the clinic for free, and when she's older she'll go to council day care for free, but that's about it. And the building is full of junkies and pros, and I thought, 'Oh yeah, when I get the money I'll go, but when the money came, they took, like, tax out of it, and it was pretty much gone. I did get a nice bed, but.

Mrs Mac said to me, 'When Jezeray goes to the day care you can get a job,' and I did get a job for a bit, working in this call centre, but it was basically a crap place to work. They give you a desk, and they give you a headset and you basically just ring people up and try to sell 'em stuff they don't want. You aren't allowed to talk to the other girls, and you only get one ciggie break, and all you have all day is people abusing you, so I quit that job. They shouldn't make single mums work, I don't reckon.

I don't deny that I'm still angry at my mum. She left us in the lurch, and I never got an explanation for what happened that day on Barrett. Like, I got an explanation from Mrs Mac and all that, but I wouldn't have minded a bit more, from the Department, or somebody who had a clue. Maybe somebody who was there when Jake got killed, or whatever. I got so desperate once, when I was still a kid, that I tried to ask *Jake*. Like, I shouted up at the sky, '*Jake, are you up there?*' But it's not like I got an answer. And then, that other time, when I had to go see Lauren and Harley after Mum died, I did say to Lauren, 'What happened that day? Do you remember? You know, don't you?'

The weird thing was, she didn't say nothin'. I reckon she knew a whole lot and just wasn't sayin'. And she still isn't sayin', not to me, anyway.

Lauren Cameron

I suppose we were three hours, maybe more, into our journey to Melbourne when Harley told me how much I reminded him of Mum. At first I thought our mum, but no, he meant his own mum, Ruby.

'She's into Cheese and Bacon Balls,' he told me. At the time, I was putting one yellow-stained hand after the other into the jumbo bag between our seats. I'd taken my shoes off and was riding with my toes near the windscreen. We'd long ago lost metropolitan radio and now we were losing the fuzzy stations, too. John Farnham and Cold Chisel and the ditty that Deborah Conway sings about the fellow who leaves pubic hair on her pillow, it was all turning to buzz and static, so I switched it off. I had many things on my mind: the inquest we'd left behind in Sydney, and the stories about me that were surely starting to circulate. I didn't want to think about them, so I said to Harley, 'Do you know we have the same dad?'

He said, 'That's what I'm told.'

I said, 'You don't think so?' And he shrugged and said, 'Mate, from what I gather, Mum had a few blokes around. Who knows who belongs to who.'

I said, 'Well, I can tell you, we've got the same dad. You look just like him.'

I expected him to steer off the road, since I'd done that, metaphorically, when Dad was first mentioned to me, but Harley is steadier than me. All he said was, 'Fair dinkum? Come on, tell me about it.' So I told him. I said, 'I was living with this couple I called the Childless. They had no kids and, from what I could tell, they took me in as some kind of experiment.'

Harley snorted with laughter, and said, 'You're kidding.'

I said, 'I was an experiment to quite a few people. A *failed* experiment.'

He said, 'How many homes did you go to?' I told him the truth: I had no real idea. Four, maybe five? There was Mrs Islington; then came the Childless, and after that, the Christians, and then the motel, and the caravan park, and there was a woman, the one I called 'Dry Foot', because she had some kind of foot disease that made the skin on her heels all red and flaky. She was a weird one. She made it plain that she was in fostering for the money and yet she had no money. All she ever wore was this beige-coloured slip, morning and night, a nylon thing with spaghetti straps, and all she ever did was sit in a floral recliner, one with an ashtray Blu-Tacked to the right armrest. She'd take off her shoes and say, 'I need somebody to do my feet, Lauren.' She kept a pumice stone in a bowl of water – grey water – near the recliner, and she'd get me to slough off the dead skin and rub cold cream between her toes.

I told Harley this, and he said, 'You must have been glad when you got thrown out of *that* home.'

I said, 'I didn't exactly get thrown out of there. By that time, I'd figured out how to get *myself* moved. Most foster kids figure out how to do it, eventually. They get to an age where, if they don't like somebody, they just tell the Department they've been molested. Simple as that. They'll be moved before the sun comes up.'

Harley said, 'You told the Department you got *molested*?'

I shook my head, no.

'I told them that Dry Foot told me to *touch* her, and that was enough for them. If there's one thing the Department doesn't want it's foster parents that touch you, because they can be liable if anything happens. So all I had to say was, "She makes me *touch* her," and they came and picked me up and moved me.'

Harley said, 'But not to Dad's, surely?'

I said, 'No. I was still at the Christians when Dad

came.' See, from time to time, the Department would send my progress reports to Mum, in prison, and to Dad, because they knew who he was from the birth certificate, but apparently the old man never answered. Then one day, out of the blue, he just rang up and said, "I want to see her," and the Department, being all for family reunification, seemed to think this was wonderful. They kept saying, "Your father, Lauren! Wouldn't you like to meet your father?" I had to tell them, "I wouldn't know him from Adam."'

Harley said, 'How old were you?' and I said, 'I don't know. Maybe twelve? They told me he was living with a brother. I didn't even know he had a brother. That meant I had an *uncle,* and maybe cousins. It was a headspin.'

Harley had his eyes on the road. It was hard to tell what he was thinking. He looked happy enough to just be having a chat, but was he wondering what it might be like to suddenly meet his dad – our dad? I didn't know. I wound the window down an inch and let the wind snatch the butt of my cigarette. I said, 'So, anyway, I told them, "Okay, I'll see him." And the Christians were very pleased. Mrs Christian kept saying, "We'll help you get ready!" They wanted me to wear a dress. God knows what they had in mind. Maybe they thought he'd come with a corsage.

I told Harley, 'The Christians wanted me to wait for him in the lounge room, as though we were receiving a guest, or something, but I wasn't able to sit still, so I waited outside on the porch. It was like waiting for Christmas, except Mrs Christian kept coming out and asking me if I was all right, and if I wanted a cup of tea, and if I wanted lunch. I didn't say a word, not all afternoon, and when it was almost dark, she came out and said, "Lauren, do you want to talk about it?" And I said, "No."

'He was four hours late, and then, there he was, behind the wheel of a brown Ford Fairlane.'

Harley said, 'What kind of Fairlane?'

How was I supposed to know? All I could remember, really, was that he'd had some kind of repair job done so one door was grey. He parked up on the nature strip. I thought Mrs Christian would have a heart attack.

I ignored Harley's question and said, 'I remember I looked up and there he was and I just felt triumphant. I thought, "He's *here*. He *came*. My Dad."'

Harley said, 'Well, come on. What did he look like?'

I said, 'Like *you*. He was big. Big, and you know, one of those guys that just looks covered in sandy hair? And there's all freckles under the hair? He looked like that.'

Harley said, 'Fair dinkum?'

I said, 'Yeah, and he had your head. Remember how you used to have this enormous head and me and Jake, we used to call you Moon?'

Harley said, 'I don't remember that.'

I persisted. I said, 'Come on, Harley, how could you forget? Moon Head. You used to go spastic.'

He said, 'I did?' And I assured him, 'You did. You went spastic.'

We drove on for a while, and then Harley said, 'So, go on. He arrives, and he's got this big head . . .'

I said, 'Right. Yeah. His head was the size of a watermelon and he had these huge hands, all calloused from digging ditches or laying asphalt or whatever he did.'

Harley wanted to know how old he might have been. I guessed around thirty-five. I said, 'He told me he was twenty when he met Mum. He was working on Barrett, on some kind of work-for-the-dole program, putting up a wooden walkway. Do you remember that walkway that we used to take to school, me and Jake?'

Harley shook his head, no.

'No. Well, it was a walkway, made of pine planks, and you could use it to get to school, and he built that.'

Harley said, 'Okay. And what did he say when he rolled up?'

I said, 'When he rolled up? I don't know. Probably "Hi". He wasn't a big talker. It was awkward, you know, like when you meet a new foster family and they say, "How old are you?" and "Do you like school?" and you never know what to say. The good thing was, he smoked, and he gave me a smoke there on the porch. Mrs Christian came out and said, "We don't think that's appropriate." I immediately dropped mine into a flower pot, but he took another drag, maybe two, and put it out on the footpath, with his boot heel.

'And then he said, "I'm gonna take Lauren for a drive." There's no way that would have been permitted. There's no way he would have been allowed to be alone with me. But as usual the social worker hadn't turned up, so I followed him out to the car.'

Harley said, 'Mrs Christian just let you go?'

'To be honest,' I told him, 'I don't know whether she did or not. By that stage in my fostering career, I was pretty sure there was nothing she could have done to stop me.'

Harley said, 'So, where'd you go?' And I said, 'To his place.'

I leaned forward, pressed the cigarette lighter, and drew up memories of that day. My father's car had smelled like Harley's car. The vinyl roof was yellow, from cigarettes. There were empty fag packets on the floor and cassette tapes on the dashboard. One of them was broken; all the tape was hanging loose. I asked my father, 'Have you got a pen?' and he took one out of the glove box. It had what appeared to be a woman wearing a black dress on it; when you tipped it forward to write, the dress melted away, so the woman looked naked. I'd used the pen to wind the tape back into the cassette and asked him, 'What's on this?' He'd taken his eyes off the road and said, 'At a guess, Acadaca.' I didn't know who that was. I said, 'Grouse. Should we play it?'

and he said, 'You can't. The tape player eats the tapes. Look in the glove box, you'll find half a dozen if you want to wind 'em up.' So I'd sat with the pen, winding spools of tape, thinking to myself, 'This bloke's my dad' and, 'I'm heading to my father's house.'

He smoked all the way there. Like Harley, he held his cigarette between the two fingers he kept on the steering wheel, but he was right-handed, and every now and then, he'd wind the window down and throw the butt out, and I'd get showered with ash. I don't remember what we talked about, except that he had a lot of complaints to make about the Department. He said things like, 'You wouldn't believe the rigmarole they put me through, to get to see you. I'm on the birth certificate and they treat me like a second-class citizen.' I kept saying the words in my head, *My dad*. Not just Dad, but *my dad*. It sounded totally weird. *My dad. My father. My old man*.

Harley said, 'So, what was his place like?'

I said, 'He was living in a shed, basically, out of the back of his brother's house.'

'Mate!' said Harley. 'So this thing you've got for *sheds* . . . it's genetic!'

But his shed wasn't like mine. I had a granny flat. Dad had a *shed* shed. An old wooden shed. He'd let me open the door with a copper key he kept on a ring the size of a bangle. There was no plaster on the walls, just wall studs, and he had barely any furniture: a mattress on the floor, from memory, and a kitchen, of sorts, with an old stove with four black burners kind of covered over in tin foil. There was a stone sink with an oversized tap, and a particle board, with the outline of tools – a hammer, a wrench, a screwdriver – spray-painted on it, in grey.

There was something else, too. Between the wall-studs, there was pornography. Nothing hard core – there were no people actually having sex, not that I remember, anyway – but every wall was papered with centrefolds that my father had apparently taken from *Penthouse* and *Playboy*. There were pictures of women of the type you never see naked any more: fleshy women with bushy vaginas and fur under their armpits. There were women with big thighs and dimpled bottoms and east-west breasts, women with tan lines (two white triangles over dark nipples and another over their pubic hair), and women lying on transparent inflatable mattresses, with champagne glasses in their hands. It was the most glamorous, the most startling, the most unnerving thing I'd ever seen.

I told Harley, 'There were girls all over his walls. One wall was devoted to black girls. Never in my life had I seen a black girl. I couldn't stop looking at their pubic hair. It was straight and stiff, and the way one of them was standing, with her legs slightly apart, you could see the detail, it was incredible. Now, it's everywhere, but then, Harley, I tell you, this was so, so naughty.'

Harley was wide-eyed and full of mirth. 'So, what did you do?' he said. 'Did you leg it?'

I said, 'That's the thing. Dad didn't even seem to notice. He was just all: 'Do you want something to eat?' And then he was making me an egg, and we were standing amid all this flesh and he was just putting a frypan on the burner, and breaking eggs into those aluminium rings that people used to have. We had it on toast, with these girls looking down at us, like it was the most normal thing in the world.'

Harley was smiling into the distance. He said, 'That's unreal.' And I said, 'Oh, it gets better. Next we went on the motorbike.'

He said, 'Shut up!' He didn't mean, 'Be quiet.' He said it the way people say it on TV; *shut up*, as in, *no way! Really?*

I nodded, smiling, and said, 'We did.'

There was a dirt bike out the back and when Dad asked me whether I wanted a ride, I said, 'Of course,' and he picked me up under the armpits and put me on the back of this thing. I hadn't known where to put my feet and he'd put them in place for me, lifting each foot onto the pedals. He sat down in front, with both hands on the handle grips and said, 'Hang on.' I looped both my arms around his waist. He hadn't given me a helmet. My face was turned sideward, and my cheek was flat was against the back of his shirt. The bike was rumbling through my groin. I could feel his thighs tightening when he used the brake, and I was conscious of my young breasts, pressed against his back. I wonder now if he was conscious of it, too, because he stopped suddenly and said, 'Okay, that's enough, let's walk it back.' And we rolled the bike through the barbed-wire fence and parked it near his shed. I didn't tell Harley this.

Harley said, 'Did you like being on the bike?' and I said, 'I guess it was pretty cool.'

'And, so, what next?' said Harley. 'When did you see him again?'

I took a cigarette packet off the dashboard and waited, in silence, for the lighter to pop. I was in no rush to answer. The truth is, he hadn't come again.

Tony Porter,
Foster Parent

I was in the kitchen when I heard the phone go, and from the kitchen I heard Rubes talking to Harley. I thought, 'He's a good lad. He knows how much Rubes needs him to ring.'

Then she called out to me. I went outside, and there she was in the Papysan, telephone still in her hand.

I said, 'What's up, honey?' and she said, 'That was Harley.'

'I gathered that, honey,' I said, and she said, 'Gather this. He's on his way here.'

'Goodo,' I replied, but in my heart I knew somethin' was goin' on. Rubes looked like she'd seen a ghost. I've known the woman more than twenty years. There's not many of her expressions I haven't seen. Rubes was looking out in the distance. I couldn't quite make out what she was thinking.

She said, 'He's not alone.'

I said, 'No?' and Rubes said, 'No.'

And still, nothing about her expression was familiar to me, which made me think, 'It's a girl. And not just any girl, but a special girl, because that's the only thing that would knock Rubes' socks off.'

Harley's never had any problems with girls, which is quite different from me. When I was a lad, I gave women a very wide berth. Women were confusing to me, but Harley's always seemed to be able to manage. He doesn't scare 'em off, and he doesn't draw 'em in. He told me once, when I asked him whether there was anybody special that was tempting him to move up north, 'Tony, no. My goal is to keep around five.' I said, 'Around five?' and he said, 'I never want less than three, but I like to handle five. You've got to have the skills of a diplomat, but you can do it.'

So, we were used to Harley's girls, and used to the idea that we might see one of them one day, and another the next day, and that would be 'no biggie', as he'd put it. Maybe this was different? Maybe this was something special. Maybe he was even coming to announce an engagement or a pregnancy, or even that unromantic, modern arrangement, 'We're going to live together!'

But Rubes said, 'It's Lauren.'

I'm ashamed to say that the name did not register, not immediately, but I reckon most blokes would react the same. I mean, people come and go, don't they, and after a while, I forget which cousin goes with what wife. Besides, it had been years, probably a decade, more, since I'd given any thought to the fact that Harley wasn't technically my own boy, that he in fact had another family, including siblings. So I said, 'Lauren,' in the way that I hoped wouldn't make it seem like I had some idea what Rubes was going on about.

She wasn't in a mood to help me, though. She just said, 'Lauren.'

I stood there for a bit longer, feeling a goose. I still had a knife in my hand, from when I was in the kitchen, and I don't doubt that I had that expression that Rubes calls 'stunned mullet' on my face. I had no idea who she was talking about, which left me with no other option than to say, 'I'm sorry, Rubes, but who's Lauren?'

She said, 'Lauren is Harley's sister, honey. Lauren is Lauren *Cashman*.'

There was nothing I could do with this information without first putting on my searching face – *Are you okay about this, Rubes?* – and then, when that didn't work, I said, 'You're kidding.'

She said, 'No, honey. Not kidding. She's in the car with him, and they're driving here.'

Rubes had stopped staring off in the distance and was making herself a rollie. I couldn't tell from the way she was busying herself with tobacco and papers how she was feeling about this, so I said, 'Wow. That's amazing.'

Amazing is a perfectly neutral word, isn't it? Depending on how Rubes reacted, I figured I could make it mean 'Amazing good' or 'Amazing, horrible'. I was happy to follow suit with Rubes. I didn't want anything to hurt that woman, not then, not ever. If Rubes was pleased, I'd be pleased. If Rubes was wretched, I'd be wretched with her, and mad with Harley, too.

How did I myself feel? I can't really say. My own opinion is not something I put forward all that much, and mostly I don't have one. My idea is to have a roof over my head and some wood I can whittle, and I let Rubes take care of the office politics, as it were. But Rubes seemed determined to get a response out of me, without letting on what it should be, which was unnerving. She'll do that sometimes: after so many years of marriage, in which she's happily set the tone, she'll suddenly decide she wants to know what *I* think, and honestly, like most of the fellas I know, I've given up thinking anything. She can tell me what we're doing and where we are going, and how we feel about things. It's easier that way, and truly I just don't worry about anything too much either way.

So I did what I do when she gets this particular bee in her bonnet. I said, 'Wow.'

She said, 'Wow? That's all you've got to say? Wow?'

She wasn't angry. She was teasing me, which I must admit came as a great relief, because if she was teasing me, it was obviously all right with her. Emboldened, I said, 'How long have they . . .'

Rubes said, 'Been together?' She was chuckling now. We were talking like Harley had a girlfriend.

'Not been together,' I said. 'I mean, yeah, when did they meet up?'

She didn't know. She said, 'All he told me, Tony, was "I've got Lauren in the car. We ran into each other. I'm bringing her home. Make up the beds."' She was sitting back in her chair now, blowing smoke toward the night sky, looking reasonably pleased with herself.

I said, 'That is so Harley.'

She said, 'Yep,' and she said it in a way that made me think it was okay to plunge in. I hesitated for just a minute, and then I said, 'You okay about this, Rubes?'

She said, 'I think I'm happy.'

Relieved, I said, 'Well, you should be.'

Rubes used to worry about losing Harley to his mother. Part of me was pleased when the mother died just because it put Rubes' mind to rest on the matter. It sounds callous, I know, but as far as I was concerned, Rubes was Harley's real mother, and anything else would have been a complication.

I'd never seen Harley's sisters. There were photographs of them on Harley's file, but it had been a while since I'd seen that. One time, the caseworker made Harley go for what they called a 'contact' visit with Lauren and the other sister at one of the Department's offices in Melbourne, I think after their mother died.

Rubes drove him there; it was probably a condition of having him stay with us. She left him with the case-workers and she told me later she drove around and around and couldn't even tell me where she'd gone, she was just completely out of her mind because she'd heard of cases where the children go into the Department's offices and don't come back.

He did come back, obviously, and probably it was a positive thing, to get the kids together at that point, and perhaps it would have been good if they'd seen each other more often, but the system relied so much on everybody keeping their details up-to-date and being prepared to bring the children into the city office on the right day, and having a caseworker that was up with the latest developments in the family, and I suppose you can guess what happened. There were no more visits. Since Harley never seemed bothered, we settled into our own routine and considered ourselves a family. I guess we forgot, in a way, about the others . . . and now they were on the way to the house, or one of them was, any-way, and we didn't know what we'd be in for.

Rubes said, 'I wonder what she eats?'

I said, 'Food, at a guess,' and Rubes said, 'I suppose she does.'

Now, there's never been a time in our marriage when people were coming to stay and Rubes wasn't planning two days in advance what to feed them, so I said, 'Into the kitchen with you, then,' and she said, 'They're not here till tomorrow.'

I said, 'Don't let that stop you.'

I could see from the look in her eyes that she was still miles away, but she said, 'We should make up the spare bed.'

I knew what that meant, too: *I* should make up the spare bed.

I said, 'They're not here till tomorrow.'

Rubes said, 'Don't let that stop you.' So I went out the back and started yanking at the sofa bed, knowing that no matter how I made it, Rubes would soon be in after me, saying no, let's use these pillows, and no, how about that blanket, but that was fine, so long as she was fine, too.

Lauren Cameron

I took a lover at the hospital. He was a married man. It was every bit as disastrous as you might expect, every bit as wrong, and yet in a sense it brought us – me and Harley – to where we are today, so I suppose I can't say that I completely regret it.

I can't say I hate him – my lover, I mean – because that wouldn't quite be true, either.

I met him at the hospital. Where else would I meet him? I went nowhere else. He was different from the other guys I'd known. He was older, and from another walk of life. He was an obstetrician – a visiting specialist, not one of the regular staff. He kept rooms in a building on Macquarie Street and he brought private patients to the hospital, women who had signed up to give birth in peach-coloured suites in private hospitals, but ended up needing emergency care on the Royal's public wards. They were in their late thirties or even their forties, these women, and yet *primigravida* – pregnant for the first time.

I saw him in a corridor. I was pushing a trolley full of laundry and almost ran into him. It was like one of those scenes in a movie, each of us moving to get out of the other's way. We ended up tangled and laughing, and then just standing there, looking at each other.

He held out his hand finally and said, 'Hello.'

I said, 'Hello.'

I put my hand in his and we kept looking at each other and then, when it occurred to me that I had been standing there too long, I tried to withdraw my hand but he wouldn't let it go. He held it tighter.

I can still remember the softness of his touch. His hand was like a woman's – smooth, gentle – and his gaze was reassuring. As corny as it sounds, I felt the floor slipping beneath me and I couldn't stop thinking, 'He's *here*. Finally, here he is.'

His name was Stephen Bass. He was not a handsome man. He was tall, and too thin for his height, so he stooped when he walked. His hair was combed over a sun-damaged scalp. There was dandruff on the shoulders of his suit jacket. His ears were transparent in sunlight. But the way a man looks has nothing to do with whether they are attractive to you, and he soon became attractive to me.

Our second meeting took place in the hospital cafe-
teria. I was standing in the queue ahead of him, holding
a plastic tray in front of me, waiting to be served. I felt
somebody come up behind me, so close that I could feel
their breath, and somehow I knew, I just knew, it was
him.

'Excuse me,' he said, 'what is that scent? I've been
unable to strike it from my mind since the last time we
met in the corridor.'

I was so startled I didn't say anything.

He continued, 'It's Lauren, isn't it? Lauren, the sweet
cleaning lady, with the oh-so-seductive scent.'

I said, 'I'm not a cleaning lady. I'm an *aide*.'

We paid for our sandwiches and he followed me to
a table. I couldn't think of anything to say, and found
myself wishing that I'd chosen something other than a
curried-egg sandwich that was going to make me smell
bad.

He tried to make up for the mistake he'd made, calling me a cleaner. 'The hospital would not run without
aides,' he said. 'Forget doctors. We turn up, make a
few notes. No, it is the aides that tend to patients. You
should be paid much more than you are.'

His hands were flat against the table, next to his
tray, and that was when I saw the wedding ring. It was
studded across the top with four diamond chips. I guess
we must have both known, even then, where we were
headed, because I didn't try to look away from it. In

fact, I put my hand out, and touched it, softly, with my finger.

He let my finger rest there and said, 'Are you married, Lauren?'

I said, 'No.'

'Too young,' he agreed. 'Take my advice, and don't accept the first proposal you're offered.'

I said, 'You're married.'

He did not say yes, and he did not say no. Instead, after some silence, he said, 'Do you want to talk about that?'

I shook my head.

'No.'

'Okay,' he said.

He took my hands into both of his. I was conscious of people around us – the hospital visitors, the nurses and aides having lunch – but Stephen seemed not to care. I wish I could explain to you what it meant to me that he didn't care, not one way or the other, who saw us together.

Looking back now, I can see the words he'd used – *Do you want to talk about that?* – were deliberately vague. I could read into them anything I wanted and, over time, I did. Alone at night when he was home with his wife, I would sit on the porch constructing stories about his marriage.

They were married, but unhappy.

They were married, but it had gone stale.

They were married, but she neglected him. They had never been in love.

They were married but he'd been lost for a long time. Now he'd found me, he felt as though he was alive again.

They were married, but he wished they weren't. He found it hard to leave his wife after she'd delivered and raised five beautiful children for him. *He would never hurt her.*

It's hard to imagine I believed any of that, but then, I was working from the heart and not the head. Had I worked from the head I would have been thinking something very different: he's a married man and he's happy to cheat on his wife.

The affair started slowly. For a while after that second meeting over the curried-egg sandwich, I allowed him only to kiss the top of my head and to touch my hands. Stephen seemed happy to take it slow. He was old-fashioned. He'd do things like enter the lift last, holding the door open for anybody else who wanted to ride. When we walked together on the street, he'd make a big production of getting on the side closest to the road. He told me it was an old tradition: gentlemen always walked near the gutter, he said, so any horse that came by wouldn't splash a woman's skirt.

'There are no horses in Sydney, Stephen,' I said, putting my hand in the crook of his arm.

'It's my way of saying that wild horses cannot keep me from you,' he replied.

He was wealthy. Once, when I asked him about this, he said, 'Wealthy compared to what? Compared to whom?' I asked whether it was true that he charged $5000 a day for delivering a baby, and he said, 'I charge what's reasonable,' and that alone made me think that he had money in a way that people I grew up with did not. He didn't make a show of his wealth, but you could see it in the cut of his suit and the cuffs of his shirts. He lived in one of those suburbs that Sydney people call 'leafy', when they mean old, established money.

After a while we started to play games that will probably be familiar to cheating couples: we'd see each other in the corridor, avert our eyes, but gently brush past each other, or else I'd get in the lift where he was already a passenger and busy myself with the watch pinned to my uniform, while he would stare straight ahead and then, when we arrived at his floor, touch the back of my hand on his way out.

I wasn't allowed to call him at home, or on his mobile phone, so I paged him pretty much constantly. Sometimes he answered immediately; other times, it would take hours, and then he would be tired, saying, 'Complications,' which I took to mean that the mother, or the infant, had struggled through a birth, although who knows what it really meant.

I asked him once about women and childbirth. I asked whether he understood the pain, and he snorted and said, 'Pain? There's plenty of pain relief available, Lauren, even in the Catholic hospitals.'

There was a clue in that sentence, wasn't there, about Stephen's attitude toward women, and their status in his mind. But I didn't notice it. I was too busy being entranced by his interest in me. For ten years, I'd been the girl on the ward who closed the drapes around patients; who wheeled barrels of laundry down the hallways; who threw out dead flowers. I got on well with the patients, but they were old people and sick people. Nobody on the staff had ever paid me much attention. I had no view of myself as an attractive person, although I knew that my hair was something unusual – maybe even special. I wore it tightly braided at work, with the braids themselves swirled into a bun at the back of my neck. I had to, those were the rules. But then, one night, when I was standing outside the hospital, I saw Stephen getting out of his car across the car park, and I found myself undoing the pins and letting it fall down past my shoulders like a gymnast's ribbon. I wanted him to see it, and I know he did, because the next day, he came over to me at the nurses' station and said, 'I saw you with your hair down last evening, under an umbrella in the gathering rain.'

Then, very slowly, he added, 'And. You. Are. Lovely.'

We didn't talk about sex, not at first. Stephen was, I suppose, trying to decide whether I was the kind of woman who would sleep with a married man, and I was trying to convince him that I definitely wasn't, but might eventually be persuaded.

He seemed to like the idea that it had been a while since I'd last had sex. Pretty early on I told him that it had been ten years. I suppose I told him that because it, too, suited the game I was playing: I wasn't somebody who did this easily, and often.

I put it to him fairly bluntly. I simply said, 'Stephen, I don't know where you think this is going, but I think you should know, I don't have sex.'

'Pardon?' he said.

That was the kind of thing he always said: never 'what', but 'pardon', or perhaps, 'I'm sorry?'

I said, 'I don't sleep with people. I used to, but I gave it up.' And then I explained that I'd had some bitter experiences and that I'd come to the conclusion that there wasn't anything about sex that made me think I'd want to do it again.

He looked absolutely delighted.

'I see,' he said. 'Might I suggest, Lauren, that it wasn't the experience that was lacking, but the man?'

I knew he was right, but still, I let that point – my belief that sex was overrated – become part of the pantomime between us. We'd meet daily for lunch – sometimes at the hospital and sometimes off campus, and we'd flirt and snuggle and even kiss, but whenever things got too heavy, he'd pull away and say, 'Now, Lauren, you mustn't get excited. You know *you don't have sex.*'

I'd say, 'Oh please, come on, kiss me again,' and he'd straighten himself and say, 'No, let's pull ourselves together. Let's talk. Tell me more about you.'

He'd ask me questions about my upbringing. I was wary. I told him about the foster homes, the caravan parks, the motels. He seemed fascinated – I suppose it was so far from his secure upbringing. He asked about my mother. I changed the subject. He didn't push.

Stephen was the first to challenge my view of myself as somebody with nothing at all to recommend me: no education, no skills or profession, nothing solid beneath my feet. He said things like, 'Oh my, you are a sweet and determined girl, overcoming all they threw at you!' He encouraged me to 'own' my past – that was the word he used – saying that my 'gritty circumstances' had been the making of the woman he loved.

He used those words: *the woman he loved.*

I told him about the men I'd slept with, in the tents, and in the front seat of cars. I remembered the boy who slaughtered the rabbit on the Barrett Estate. Stephen held me close and said, 'If you were not a good person, none of this would hurt.'

He wanted to know why I was working as an aide, when I could easily have been . . . I thought he was going to say a 'nurse', but in fact he said a 'medical specialist'. Then he said, 'You'd run rings around the students who come here as interns. Believe me, you could do it.'

I believed it. I believed *him.*

Or did I? I mean, after all, in those weeks and months of courtship, before we became lovers, before his marriage and my secrets collided, I never talked to Stephen Bass about DeCastella Drive. I didn't say to him, 'My mother went to prison. My little brother died.'

I did give some thought to telling him. I knew I would have to tell him, eventually, because I believed that one day I'd win him over and make him mine. I had an idea that I'd show him the photograph of Jake that had been given to me when I'd left Melbourne, and go from there . . . but I never did.

We went to a hotel room in Sydney. That doesn't sound very romantic now, but it seemed so to me at the time. It happened a few weeks after Stephen had said to me, 'You understand, don't you Lauren, that I don't actually want to have sex with you?'

We'd been cuddling together and I'd felt him getting aroused. I thought he was kidding. I said, 'Actually, I think you do.'

He said, 'No, Lauren, what I want is to *make love* to you.'

Something in me shifted at that moment. Mentally, obviously, I gave up all reserve, but physically, too, I felt something give way. We began to talk about when it might happen.

'Immediately,' he said, picking up his tray after lunch one day. 'Enough of this, Lauren. We must begin *immediately* and then continue, frequently.'

How carefully did he choose those words? They were, to me, a silent promise that Stephen Bass was after more than one night's sex. He would be back – frequently – after the first time. This wasn't a fling. It wasn't an affair. It was love.

There was one thing I was still concerned about, though. I was frozen to the point of paralysis at the idea of getting naked with him. It wasn't just that I hadn't been naked with anyone for so long. Stephen worked with pregnant women – and he saw them intimately, in a way that a man in his position must. I kept thinking, 'What if I'm different, and somehow *worse* than other women? Also, when did a man become ambivalent about the female form? Was it when he saw his first, his tenth, his hundredth, or his five-hundredth woman in stirrups?'

I said to Stephen, 'You see so many women; how is it you are interested in seeing one more?'

He looked a bit puzzled and didn't say anything immediately, but later that day, he sent me a note through the internal mail. I picked it up from my pigeon hole, and went into the ladies' loo to open it. On a Botticelli greeting card, depicting the Birth of Venus, he had written the following lines, in his delicate copperplate: *'There ought to be a law against a woman having a pussy as comely as yours.'*

It made no sense; he'd been nowhere near that part of me. With hindsight I can see it was a line he'd maybe used before, but at the time I couldn't stop looking at it. All day I carried the card with me, taking it out of my apron to read it again, feeling the muscles in my abdomen tighten.

I sent a note back.

It was not subtle.

'Take me,' it said.

'I would be honoured,' he replied. 'But this is an auspicious occasion for you, Lauren, an episode of love-making after such a long time. We must make it special. What we need is a special place. With your permission, this is what I shall do. I shall get a room in a hotel. A little old-fashioned, I agree, but let's be a little old-fashioned, shall we?'

We set a date for a Saturday night. I'd have to work the next day, but that would be fine. Stephen spelled out the instructions. He told me to go to the hotel and collect the key and go up to the room, and then call him, for the first time, on his mobile.

'I will have my phone in my top pocket, set to vibrate, near my heart,' he said. 'I will be waiting to hear what room you're in, and I'll come up and ravish you.'

I was pleased with the arrangements because they told me that Stephen understood my fear of being seen as permissive. We would not present ourselves – an unmarried couple – at the reception and request a room. We would be discreet.

And so it was settled. I don't need to tell you how the

day dragged. I worked in the morning and everything seemed to go wrong. I couldn't wait to knock off, but time wouldn't move and then, finally, it was five o'clock. I locked myself in a shower cubicle and used soap and water to shave my legs, nicking myself in my haste.

Hours before it was necessary I went by taxi to the hotel. The man at reception gave me a plastic card and told me it was a room key, and showed me how to use it, but I couldn't get the thing to work, so I had to go back down and get him to go up with me and let me in. The hotel was supposedly posh but the room was nothing much: just a bed against a padded headboard, and a TV in a cabinet. I wasted a bit of time, looking at myself in the mirror, staring this way and that, practising my expressions, and opening and closing the mini-bar. Then, when I couldn't stand it any more, I dialled Stephen's mobile.

He answered first ring.

'Lauren,' he said. 'And how would you be?'

I said, 'I'm fine, Stephen. Oh, Stephen, I'm so *not* fine.'

'You *are* fine,' he said. 'Finer than fine.'

I gave him the room number and sat waiting for him. When the knock came, I opened the door, and there he was, standing in the foyer, an Art Deco lamp on the wall behind him, looking familiar and yet completely out of context, and wearing a terrible pair of shoes, strange lumpen things – sandals – made of rubber that exposed his long toes.

He stepped toward me and we had a clumsy moment – our teeth clicked together as we kissed. He picked me up and carried me, like a child, to the bed. I felt the muscles in my abdomen tighten. For how long had I thought about what this evening might be like? For months now I'd made up every detail, I'd played it out, I'd fantasised. I'd had him kissing my toes through my stockings and stroking the soles of my feet, making me wild with pleasure.

What I didn't expect was that Stephen Bass would suffer the same problem as any randy kid in the back-seat of a car on the Barrett Estate.

I didn't think he'd yank my jeans off from the hem and lie heavily on top of me, so that I could barely breathe.

I didn't think he'd have a penis as white and curled as a witchetty grub and that he'd say, 'Oh, Lauren, oh, Lauren' and come, just like that.

That was how it happened, but I didn't let myself care. I told myself it wasn't important. I put my cheek gently against his abdomen, and lay there, letting him catch his breath, disappointed, obviously, but thinking, 'Well, we've only just begun. It's the first time and we're both nervous and we'll get better at it.'

I was still resting against his abdomen when his pager went. He reached for it. I snuggled up toward the hair under his armpit. I said, 'Are you on the roster?'

He said, '*I'm* not an *aide*, Lauren. I don't have a roster.'

I felt embarrassed. He studied the message in front of him and then said what would be his last words to me: 'You better get dressed. I have to go.'

Barrister for the Royal Hospital, Sydney

(Name withheld for legal reasons)

More than ninety per cent of Australian women have at least one and usually two ultrasound scans during their pregnancy. The aim is not – or, at least, not *only* – to determine the gender of the baby. No, these scans are used to rule out a serious deformity, including Down syndrome and anencephaly (where a foetus has no brain or only a brain stem) and some minor deformities such as clubbed feet.

In more than eighty per cent of cases where a serious deformity is found, a woman will opt to end the pregnancy. In Australia, a woman is entitled to an abortion if continuing the pregnancy would impact upon her wellbeing, or that of the foetus. We can argue from here to eternity about the morality of that decision, but the law is on the woman's side and, in the community, too, late-term abortion in the case of foetal abnormality is widely regarded as a regrettable but understandable decision.

Elizabeth Boyce was different. Her husband was different. When she arrived at the offices of specialist obstetrician Stephen Bass, she was twenty-three weeks pregnant with her second child. Mrs Boyce's first pregnancy had been unremarkable: a healthy boy delivered vaginally at thirty-nine weeks, essentially full-term, with no haemorrhage or perineal tear. This second pregnancy was another matter. The first trimester passed without incident, but, at the twenty-two-week scan, problems were detected. The picture wasn't entirely clear. As good as new technology is, it cannot provide all the answers. The foetus had a curious and seldom-seen combination of problems: an oversized kidney, an enlarged heart, and malformation of the spine.

In the opinion of the Royal's specialists – not only Bass but others he brought in specifically to examine Mrs Boyce's scans – the child's deformities were very likely incompatible with life. If the foetus were able to survive the trauma of birth, it would likely die within a few days. Bass offered Mrs Boyce the opportunity to interrupt the pregnancy then and there, to bring it prematurely to a close: in other words, to abort the foetus before the pregnancy became pronounced. Mrs Boyce declined that option. Bass advised Mrs Boyce there was a significant risk in continuing the pregnancy, both to her own health and that of the child. Nevertheless, Mrs Boyce opted to continue.

Seven weeks later, Mrs Boyce presented herself at the Royal's emergency department, saying that she was in labour. By this stage, she was thirty weeks pregnant. It was a Friday night. Bass ran a series of tests, none of which were reassuring. He told Mrs Boyce that she wasn't in labour, she was having what are known as Braxton Hicks, or false contractions, but he wanted her to stay in hospital under observation in a private room, away from other labouring mothers, in case the onset of labour was imminent and because the outcome was likely to be poor.

Bass did not normally work on a Saturday, which is a privilege accorded the senior staff. He could manage his patients in a way that left Saturday afternoon free. So when Mrs Boyce went into labour on a Saturday, Bass wasn't there. He'd left instructions with nurses on the maternity ward to page him if things got serious – that is, if Mrs Boyce entered the first stage of labour (rupture of the membranes; cervical dilation; contractions less than sixty seconds apart) and so, at around 8 p.m. on Saturday 12 August, 2002, Bass was paged. He arrived at the hospital shortly before 9 p.m., and immediately assumed responsibility for Mrs Boyce. He stayed with her until the child, Baby Boyce, was born at 4 p.m. on the Sunday. As he'd predicted, the outcome was poor. The child did not survive.

Now, stillbirth is a shocking event, particularly in a private hospital in 21st-century Australia. Almost without exception, the parents of a stillborn child seek an answer to what may well be an unanswerable question: why did *my* child die? They bury their child, they channel their anger and grief, and, ultimately, they look for somebody to blame. In the case of Baby Boyce, the obvious target was Stephen Bass.

In the early stages of the formal complaint against the hospital, Mrs Boyce's legal team argued that Bass had disapproved of her decision to continue with a high-risk pregnancy because he knew the child was likely to be born with severe deformities.

They said that Bass had left the hospital on the Friday, knowing that Mrs Boyce was likely to go into labour, and had not returned until it was too late to perform an emergency caesarean, and that he had done so deliberately. Moreover, they said that he had not attempted to revive the baby because he did not want so disabled a baby to live. In short, they said that Bass made a God-like decision to let the baby die.

Now, I've known Stephen Bass for many years. He is an obstetrician of considerable skill. Ambitious? Certainly. I've heard it said that it would not be wise to stand between Bass and a glittering prize. That is a formulation that Bass would likely accept with humour. It has also been said that specialists like Bass will at all costs avoid the birth of a child with serious deformities.

Such cases can and do end up in court, and even those deformities that are apparent on ultrasounds may, in the hands of a jury, be erroneously attributed to labour, and therefore to the negligence of the obstetrician. Huge compensation payments are rare but devastating. It does affect a specialist's insurance.

I do not believe that Bass suggested abortion to Mrs Boyce to protect his numbers, for want of a better term, or because he does not believe that seriously deformed infants should be kept alive. Had there been a way to save Baby Boyce, a severely disabled baby, I'm certain Bass would have taken it.

Nevertheless, Mrs Boyce wanted somebody to blame for her terrible loss. Her legal team asked the State Coroner to look at the case. If the Coroner found that Bass had deliberately let the child die, they intended to take the case to the civil courts, at which point the hospital would likely have stepped in and offered a settlement. In a worst-case scenario, they would also press for criminal charges.

As part of the hospital's preparation for the Coroner's inquest, I had to interview Bass. He told me there were no 'signs of life' as Baby Boyce emerged from the birth canal. In other words, he was of the opinion – that is, of the professional opinion – that Baby Boyce died before she was born, and no amount of intervention would have altered the outcome. There was a fair amount of evidence to back that claim: evidence from

the EFM machine, from the autopsy, from other specialists who had examined the baby, and from the midwife
who had been on duty that evening, and I thought the
combined evidence of these professionals would see the
case resolved in Bass's favour.

I did not expect at that point that Lauren Cashman – or Lauren Cameron, as we knew her then – would
become a star of the inquest. I mean, for Heaven's sake,
she was an *aide* at the Royal. I had her down on my list
of people who had been present at the birth of Baby
Boyce, and therefore as a potential witness, that's all.

But then, when Bass confided in me about his relationship with Lauren, and asked, 'Is it relevant?' I knew
instantly it would be a problem that could potentially
cost the hospital many millions of dollars.

Let me explain: the affair itself had nothing whatsoever to do with the birth and death of Baby Boyce,
but if it became *public* – the obstetrician was in bed
with an aide when his patient had started labouring
with an extremely disabled baby – well, we were sunk.
Oh sure, we could argue that Bass had known Lauren
only briefly, that she had no involvement whatsoever
in the birth process beyond the fact that she was in
the room working as an aide on the Sunday, mop-
ping up blood, and wheeling the empty baby cot out
of the room . . . but let's face it, the detail gets lost in
such cases. The public would be appalled that Bass
had been with his mistress when Mrs Boyce went into

labour, and that public indignation would be enough to sink him.

Was I surprised to learn that Bass had a lover – a very inconvenient lover? No. Nor was I surprised by his choice, in this instance, of mistress. There is something in the psychology of men – of some men – that causes them to seek a girl different in every respect from their wives. Bass's wife, as I understand it, is a specialist in her own field, an utterly brilliant woman who combined motherhood with a career at a time when that would have been a more complex juggle even than today. I understand that she is a generous woman with a lovely wit. There seems little doubt that Bass is either in love, or in awe of his wife. And so, who does he choose for a mistress? A woman who earns $12 an hour.

The instant I saw Lauren for the first time, I knew . . . well, how to put this? I knew there was something of the mongrel about her. She'd come from the wrong side of the tracks. She'd smoothed her rough edges, but there was something not quite right about the way she spoke: occasionally, she'd lapse into a broad Australian accent and then she'd correct herself, and begin speaking like an ABC news reader.

In our first meeting, she'd said to me, 'How is he?' And I understood that to mean that she and Bass hadn't spoken since the birth of Baby Boyce. She asked me whether it was true that Bass couldn't speak to her, because both were to be witnesses at the inquest, and I immediately felt sorry for her because that wasn't true at all, so I told a little fib. I said, 'Well, it's probably for the best that he doesn't speak with you, but perhaps after the inquest, you could give him a call?'

It seemed clear to me that he would never take that call. She was obviously still in love with him, and he was wishing they'd never met. I'd said to him, 'How many people know about this affair?' He'd said he didn't know. I asked Lauren the same question. She said she didn't know, but she suspected there were rumours.

I thought to myself, 'This is a disaster.' But there was nothing to do but prepare for the inquest. It was to be held in the Coroner's Court, on Parramatta Road. The Coroner's Court is a grim building. How could it be otherwise? The Coroner deals with unexpected and suspicious death, with explosions and major fires, with murders and drownings and decapitations. Grief permeates the wall paint.

It's also a busy building. The press likes a Coroner's Court hearing, because the details are usually both fascinating and macabre. The case of Baby Boyce had garnered significant attention even *before* it came before the Coroner, however. Mrs Boyce wanted to acknowledge and honour her daughter, and so she had taken the story to the media long before the inquest, and they gobbled it up. As a story, it had everything the media wants: a wealthy doctor; a child with significant deformities; an attractive, articulate mother prepared to fight for the child's life. We've all seen cases like it: a person who is being kept on life support in a hospital, for example, with parents who refuse for years to turn off the machinery, so the hospital has to take action in court. There was a case like that in the USA; it ended up with even the President himself becoming involved. The right to life is a complex, emotional issue. Columnists love to sound off about it. In almost every case, such matters can be relied upon to spark debate . . . even before you throw in a sex scandal.

In a perfect world, the case would be fought on the facts: we'd argue that Baby Boyce was deceased before she was delivered; they'd argue that Baby Boyce was very much alive; the Coroner would review the case and make a clinical decision, and the matter of Lauren, as I referred to it, either wouldn't come up or would be ruled out of evidence. The world is not perfect, however.

The first hint of the way the inquest would *actually* proceed came to me when I saw Lauren Cameron's name at the top of their witness list. Immediately, I suggested to the Royal and to Bass that we settle, but they would not agree. I told them that the appearance of Lauren's name at the top of the list meant that they very likely knew about the affair, and intended to make an issue of the relationship. They said that they would simply argue as planned that any questions about a relationship between Bass and Lauren be ruled out of testimony, and therefore be kept out of the press.

I thought, 'Good luck,' for it seemed certain to me that somebody, somewhere, had found out about it and blabbed.

Anyway, on we went. The counsel assisting the Coroner was John Bateson. He's a well-respected senior counsel. We'd rowed together at university. I held him in high regard.

He'd opened the hearing by taking testimony from Mrs Boyce and Bass, and then he called Lauren. I got ready to object to just about everything. Bateson started by saying, 'Oath or affirmation?'

Lauren took the Bible and swore to tell the truth.

Bateson said, 'Your name for the inquest?'

Lauren replied, 'Lauren Cashman. Lauren Cameron.'

That was odd. I picked it up, and so did Bateson. He said, 'I'm sorry?'

Lauren said, 'My real name is Cashman, I use the name Cameron. At the hospital, I'm Lauren Cameron.'

I thought, 'Oh great. So now she has an alias, too? She's the lover, and she's a woman of mystery. The press will be *delighted*.'

But Bateson pressed on. He said, 'And you are employed at the Royal Hospital, Sydney, as a nurse's aide?'

Lauren nodded, which prompted Bateson to say, 'You'll need to speak up, for the transcript.'

Lauren had a voice like chimes. She leaned into the microphone, and said, 'Yes.'

Bateson said, 'Very good. And you were present during the birth and death of the child known as Baby Boyce?' Lauren replied, 'Yes.' Bateson said, 'And you understand that this inquest is inquiring into the circumstances of that death?' and again Lauren replied, 'Yes.'

There was a pause as Bateson shuffled through some of the papers on his desk, and then he continued. 'Miss Cameron, you understand that this is not a court of law, don't you? This is a Coroner's inquest. An inquest is an attempt to unravel events leading to an unexplained or unexpected death, and you are here because we would like you to tell us, in your own words, what you witnessed on the day that Baby Boyce was born and died.'

I do love the way we lawyers persist with that fiction: *in your own words*. Not a single witness would take the stand without spending several hours with the hospital's team of lawyers, going over their testimony, time and again. Don't take that the wrong way. We don't encourage the witnesses to lie, but we don't want them to say something stupid, either. We tell them what the questions are likely to be. We go over their answers. The idea is to keep the inquest on the rails.

I listened as Bateson went on. 'I wonder if we might begin with you telling the Coroner what time you started work on Saturday, August 12?'

Lauren said, 'I did not work on August 12.'

Bateson does not like to be corrected. He looked up

at Lauren and said, 'Sorry?'

Lauren said, 'I did not start work until Sunday, August 13.'

Bateson referred to his notes again, screwed up his brow, recovered himself and said, 'Right. Yes. It was Mr *Bass* who started work on August 12.'

There was something about the way he said 'Mr Bass' that made my antennae go up. I thought, 'Here we go.' But I'd got ahead of myself.

Lauren said, '*I* started work on August 13, at noon.'

Bateson was still looking at his notes. He said, 'Yes, you did. And can you tell us, please, what kind of work you were doing?'

Now, that's a perfect example of the coaching, right there. Do you know what you were doing on Sunday 13 August, 2002 – without checking your diary, I mean? Of course you don't. If I told you that you'd been at work, would you know what time you arrived, what tasks you completed that day, what time you finished? No. But the hospital's legal team – me, and others – had gone over this with Lauren, not once but several times. Curiously, she was able to tell me *exactly* what she'd been doing that day. I remember thinking, 'What a remarkable memory,' but then, of course, I didn't know at that point that she'd been with Bass the night before, and girls do tend to remember those things.

Anyway, she went over the details of her shift for Bateson, saying, 'I was on the roster from noon on

Sunday 13 August until around 11 p.m., but I ended up staying longer because of what happened.'

She spoke fairly clearly. There were no signs – not yet – of the distress and humiliation that was headed her way.

Bateson said, 'In the interests of this inquest, Miss Cameron, could you tell us exactly what an aide at a hospital does?'

Lauren said, 'What I normally do, or what I did that day? Because it really depends on the ward. If I'm working with the older patients . . . well, that's different from maternity.'

Bateson nodded, and said, 'I suppose what I'm trying to get you to do, Miss Cameron, is give us a sketch of your normal working day. We can take August 13 as an example. Did you start work on the labour ward?'

Lauren said no. She had started work on the geriatric ward.

Bateson said, 'And what did you do there?' and Lauren, who seemed perplexed, went over some of her duties, saying, 'Well, the geriatrics are the old people. You have to do a lot for them. You have to get them out of bed. I suppose I might have done that. It's not good for patients to lie in bed all day. We move them into a chair, if they are able to sit. It takes two of you, so you normally do that with a nurse.'

Bateson must have understood the difference, but he said, 'And just so we are clear, you're not a nurse?'

Lauren said, 'I'm an *aide*. I've done a ten-week course in being a nurse's aide. I have my aide certificate. You need to do a nurse's course to be a nurse.'

Bateson said, 'And in ten years, you've not attempted the nurse's course?'

Lauren said, 'No,' and Bateson said, 'May I ask why?'

I stood at this point. I said, 'Objection. What's the point of this? Miss Cameron has said she is an aide. She isn't a nurse. We don't need to know why she's not a nurse, surely? Why is she not a doctor? Why is she not a *lawyer*?'

That got a small smile from the Coroner.

'Well then,' said Bateson. 'Please go on, Miss Cameron. What kind of work does an aide do?'

I had warned Lauren that Bateson was likely to ask about her workload. I knew – and they knew – that she'd started work on the geriatric ward, and then been moved to maternity, as the crisis surrounding Baby Boyce unfolded. Probably, they wanted to suggest to the Coroner that she would have been tired, and perhaps confused. That would help their case. I had myself asked her about her duties that day, and we'd gone back through the rosters and the records, to piece together her movements.

Lauren had spent an hour in the hopper, a room with a steel tub and a high-pressure hose, spraying faecal matter out of sheets and gowns before putting them in the laundry. She'd done a full bed change for a patient who had managed to smear faeces over the sheets, blanket, gown and mattress. She had shaved an old man's face, and played bingo with one of the women who could still sit up and concentrate. She had listened to an old war story – one she'd heard 100 times before – and put Pond's cream under the arms and breasts of a woman so deep into dementia that she barely woke any more.

She had mopped a floor. Geriatrics have a tendency to poop all over the place when being lifted from their beds to the wheelchairs, and Lauren's responsibilities included using soft cloths to wipe faeces off the wheelchairs and to shower the patient clean of waste. In her interview with me, Lauren had said that she took these and other tasks seriously. Her responsibility did not extend to healing the patients. That was for doctors, and specialists. She was not required to ease pain, or change dressings. That was for the nurses. Her concern, she said, was with 'the dignity' of patients.

She'd told me, 'I don't try to pretend I'm a friend, and I don't behave like a clown. I am professional, and I treat the patients with dignity. It's not their fault they are incapacitated.' She was appalled by aides who mocked the patients; in particular, one of the male nurses, Jonathon, who called the old ladies 'Ducky'.

'He puffs up their hair with the hairbrush, and says things like, "You look just like a beauty queen, Ducky,"' she'd told me. 'He talks about patients as if they aren't there, saying to other nurses, "This one's like a sack of potatoes!" when he was lifting an old woman, or, "This one's a dead weight, if you get my meaning!"'

Lauren had told me she'd requested a roster change, to stay out of Jonathon's orbit.

'I found myself going around the wards after he'd finished his shift, smoothing down the patient's hair,' she'd said. 'I couldn't leave them sitting there, with their hair all puffed up and ridiculous, and nothing they could do about it.'

I'd almost fallen for her myself, when she told me that, but when Lauren gave testimony at the inquest of Baby Boyce, she kept it neutral. She told Bateson that she would have 'changed some sheets and cleaned the patients, and I would have done some charting'.

Bateson said, 'Charting?'

Lauren said, 'The nurses have to fill out the charts at the foot of the bed: what did they eat, did they pass urine? Did they have a bowel movement, and anything else that might be important, like did they vomit? I don't fill the charts but I make sure a blank chart is there, and a pen.'

Bateson said, 'Is the work tiring, Miss Cameron?'

She said, 'It's finding a pen that's tiring. Good luck finding a pen.'

The Coroner smiled at her.

Bateson said, 'Right. But go on. What else does an aide do?'

She said, 'It was a normal day.'

Actually, it wasn't, not for Lauren. Probably, she spent the whole day thinking about Stephen Bass, and wondering whether he'd call.

Bateson said, 'A normal day? You mean, it was boring?'

Lauren said, 'Not boring, no. I know some people think it must be boring, but it isn't. Often, I am the only person a patient will see in a day. It's sad, when they say, "I want to go home," and there is no home for them to go to, but you learn to just take care of them. I don't feel I'm entitled to feel bored.'

The press was taking a few notes but Bateson was only half-listening. He was looking down at the white binder in front of him, doubtless reading Lauren's written statement that we'd prepared for him, and for her, earlier.

He said, 'It says in your statement you then cleaned up some finger painting. I wonder if you might explain to us the term "finger painting". What does that mean?'

Lauren said, 'It's a reference to the patients sticking their fingers in their own faeces and painting on the walls with it.' Lauren had told me earlier, 'I don't think people understand how often it happens, and, if you don't get to them immediately, they are off, smearing it everywhere. They don't know what they are doing. They are back to being like babies.'

Bateson said, 'And cleaning the finger painting, that

was one of the things you might have done, according to your statement here, before Baby Boyce was born? All these tasks – cleaning faeces, changing beds, lifting patients – you would have been doing all of that for some hours before you were called to the labour ward on the Sunday afternoon?'

Lauren said, 'Yes. I worked on the geriatric ward and then, when I was near the end of my shift, they asked me to go to the labour ward, because something was happening there, and they obviously were short of staff, and so I did.'

Bateson shuffled his papers and said, 'And the labour ward is on the same floor as the geriatric ward?'

Lauren said, 'It's a floor below.'

I was sitting up pretty straight by now. Obviously, we were getting to a critical point, the point where Baby Boyce was born, and died.

Lauren told Bateson there were nine patients – about a normal number – on the maternity ward. Three had already given birth and three were waiting, and three were in labour, to some extent. She told him that she was called into the delivery room C, where Mrs Boyce was labouring. Mr Boyce was there; so, too, was a midwife, several nurses, an anaesthetist . . . and Stephen Bass.

Bateson looked up. He said, 'The obstetrician, Stephen Bass, was there?'

Lauren confirmed this.

I looked over at the press gallery. Journalists were moving around in their chairs, the way they do when they sense something exciting is about to happen.

Bateson said, 'And Mrs Boyce was in labour?'

Just as I'd instructed her, Lauren said, 'I don't think I'm qualified to answer that.'

I thought, 'Good girl.'

But then she went on. 'It was obvious to me that she was delivering the baby. Mrs Boyce was in the stirrups, so I could see . . . um, I could see that she was giving birth, the baby was crowning –'

Bateson interrupted. 'You could see the baby's head?'

Lauren said, 'Yes.'

'And was Mrs Boyce conscious?'

Lauren said, 'Yes. She was in a lot of pain. She was moaning and her husband was saying, "Can't you give her something?"'

Bateson said, 'And what was your job, as you saw it?'

Lauren replied, 'I didn't have anything to do with the birth. I was there to assist the nurse.'

'And what else did you see?' Bateson persisted.

'There was a lot of blood.'

'Blood?'

'Yes,' Lauren said. 'Mr Bass was slipping in the blood on the floor. It was my responsibility to throw down a sheet, to clean the area. But that's normal enough, in a birth. There is blood.'

Bateson said, 'Okay. Now, Miss Cameron, this is important: you understand, don't you, that what is at issue here, at this inquest, is whether or not Baby Boyce was alive when she was delivered?'

Lauren said, 'Yes.'

Bateson added, 'And you understand, do you, that Baby Boyce's parents are saying that their baby *was* alive when delivered?'

Lauren said, 'Yes.'

'And do you further understand that it is the position of the hospital, and of Mr Stephen Bass, that the baby died *before* the birth, and that no amount of intervention would have altered the outcome?'

Lauren repeated, 'Yes.'

Bateson said, 'Very good. Then may I ask you this, Miss Cameron. In your view, was Baby Boyce born alive?'

I got to my feet. I said, 'Objection. I'm not sure how Miss Cameron is going to be able to answer that. She is not qualified to monitor signs of life. As Mr Bateson has already established – indeed, has spent some time establishing – Miss Cameron is not a medical professional, and she has no clinical training.'

The Coroner looked up from the scribbles on his notepad and said to Bateson, 'Try another question.'

Bateson changed tack. 'Okay . . . Miss Cameron, I wonder, can you tell us, once the baby was delivered, did the baby cry?'

Again, I said, 'Objection,' but the Coroner overruled it, saying, 'I think that an aide can answer that.'

Lauren gave an honest answer. She said, 'I'm not sure.'

Bateson tried again. 'Well then, did the baby *move*?'

'Objection,' I said, but the Coroner was with Bateson. He said, 'The witness may answer.'

Lauren paused for a moment and then said, 'I'm going to have to say that I'm not sure.'

Bateson looked doubtful. 'You're not sure whether the baby was moving?'

Lauren said, 'Well, it's difficult for me to be completely sure, because Mr Bass was handling the baby, helping the baby out, so the baby was moving . . .'

Bateson said, 'The baby *was* moving?'

I said, 'Objection,' but it was kind of feeble. I knew that the Coroner was interested in these points. He said, 'Overruled. Go on, Miss Cameron.'

Lauren said, 'The baby might have been *being* moved . . . What I mean is, things were happening pretty fast and there was a fair amount of blood, and I can't be sure whether it was the baby moving its own limbs, or whether it was moving because it was being lifted in the surgeon's hands.'

Bateson jumped on this. He said, 'So the limbs were moving?'

Again, I stood and said, 'Objection. That is not what Miss Cameron said, and not what she meant. She said the baby may well have been *being moved*.'

Bateson rubbed his chin for a second. 'All right,' he said, 'I apologise. I'm sorry. Yes. The limbs were moving, but you can't be sure, Miss Cameron, whether the baby was kicking, the way a baby does upon delivery, or whether it was simply the surgeon moving the baby, from one hand to the other, say, that made it look like the limbs were moving?'

Lauren said, 'That's right. The legs, they were sort of up and down, but I don't know whether that was kicking or whether that was because Mr Bass was moving the baby. Things were happening fast.'

In the public gallery, Mrs Boyce had started to weep. Her husband held one of her hands; her mother held the other. The three of them, all in suits, had been sitting with eyes wide open, so that tears wouldn't fall, but now Mrs Boyce was cracking.

Bateson tried another approach. 'I wonder if we might turn again to what you *heard* as opposed to what you *saw*. Did the baby make a sound?'

Lauren said, 'You mean, did the baby cry?'

The Coroner stepped in and said, 'I don't think that Mr Bateson is asking the witness whether she heard the baby cry. I think he's asking whether the witness heard any sound, is that right, Mr Bateson?'

Bateson said, 'Yes, Your Honour.'

The Coroner said, 'Very well. You may answer, Miss Cameron. I'd like to know that, myself.'

But before Lauren could speak, Bateson said, 'Miss

Cameron, what I am trying to determine is whether you heard any sounds that might indicate *life*? You understand that the hospital contends there were no signs of life. That would mean that there were no *sounds* of life.'

I was going to object, but Lauren interrupted. She said, 'I know what you're asking. There was a lot of noise in the room. Mrs Boyce was in a lot of pain. The father was distressed. There were a lot of sounds.'

Bateson said, 'Yes, but the *baby*, Miss Cameron. You understand that the Boyce family believes that their baby made a sound. What do you say? Did you hear *a baby sound*?'

The room had gone very quiet. Mrs Boyce was looking up, through tears.

Lauren hesitated, and then said, 'There *were* sounds . . . but the sound I heard . . . it was not of *life*. The sound I heard . . . it was more like *love*.'

Bateson said, 'I beg your pardon?'

Lauren said, 'There were sounds. The mother, the father, everybody was so upset. There were sounds, and that's what was in the room, sounds like that. Sounds like hearts breaking. Sounds like love.'

Sounds like *love*.

It was a beautiful way to describe the events of the day, and so it did not surprise me when those words – not Lauren's actual words, but a new and sexier formulation – became the headline in the next day's newspapers.

'Aide Heard the "Sound of Love".' That was how

the *Telegraph* put it. The *Herald* went for a similar line, 'Nurse in Baby Boyce Inquest Heard "Sound of Love".'

After that, of course, journalists began referring to the 'Sound of Love' inquest; the 'Sound of Love' trial; and, finally, the 'Sound of Love' settlement.

Lauren, of course, became the 'Sound of Love' aide. There would be some sniggering about that, but not yet.

Jane Postle,
Reporter

I was one of maybe fifteen reporters assigned to cover the Baby Boyce inquest. Some were from the *Telegraph*, some from the *Australian*, from Nine news and the ABC, plus there were the old hands from AAP and the wire services, guys who have been in the business since my father was a journo.

My dad, Frank Postle, was a reporter on the old Melbourne *Sun*. He was the one who told me, 'Get into the business if you can. You'll travel the world on somebody else's dime; you'll have a front-row seat into history. You're not on the pitch, but by God, you are on the sidelines.'

He didn't get me the job, though. I want to be clear about that. I got the job on my own. I don't work for Dad's old paper, the *Sun*. I'm at the *Herald*, in Sydney.

It's a different stable. Dad wrote me a reference but I had to pass the cadet's test, and I had to get the degree and in the end *I* had to get the job and work my way up from the bottom.

There hasn't been much travelling the world. I've done stock markets. I've done football matches and I've done 'death knocks', where you have to bang on the door of the family of somebody who has died and say, 'How do you feel?' It's not pleasant, but it's what you have to do to get yourself graded, and now I'm graded. I'm a senior reporter. I do courts, and I do inquests. The dirty underbelly of Sydney society, the stuff that happens at the intersection of drugs, money and murder, that's my beat.

The Baby Boyce inquest was obviously a bit different from the stuff we normally see in the Coroner's Court: it was a right-to-life case. It had everybody talking. Should people abort their disabled foetuses? The data shows that almost everybody does, so is the world a less welcoming place these days, for the disabled kids who make it through? That kind of stuff gets people going. You get the right-to-lifers revved up, and then the women's groups jump on, the academics, the churches. It was a case that seemed to interest people. It helped that Mrs Boyce was pretty and sweet; her husband handsome and stalwart; and the doctor, Stephen Bass, so establishment.

I didn't expect to get much out of Lauren Cameron's

testimony. She was listed among the witnesses because she'd been on duty the day the baby had died, but she was an aide, not a doctor, so I couldn't see what she'd have to say. But then, of course, she turned out to be the one who gave the inquest its name. Because of her, we started calling it the 'Sound of Love' inquest. Sound of Love! We didn't realise how funny that was, until later.

So, anyway, I was covering the Baby Boyce inquest for the *Herald* and we'd put a photograph of Lauren in the paper, and that was when Dad called me up, said he had this nagging feeling that he'd seen Lauren some-where before. He said, 'Can you look in the files? I'm sure I've done a story about her.'

I was almost certain he was mistaken. According to her statement, Lauren Cameron was twenty-seven years old, and Dad was claiming to remember her from his days on the *Sun*, so we're talking about a time when Lauren would have been a child.

But there you go. I hate to say it, but Dad was right.

The way the filing system at the *Herald* works is this: every story ever written is stored in a system we call NewsText, and reporters can search the database by using key words, pretty much like Google. If the story was written any time after 1996, you can actually read it on your computer screen and even cut and paste from it. If it pre-dates 1996, the NewsText system will alert you to its existence by giving you the headline and the date it was published, and then, if you want to see more, you can go down to the library in the bowels of the building, and ask the librarians to get out the old, leather-bound newspaper files, and see a copy of the actual page for yourself.

I'd already Googled Lauren and nothing had come up. She had no MySpace page and she wasn't on Facebook, which is unusual these days. Anyway, I typed the words 'Lauren' and 'Cameron' into the NewsText system and I got nothing. Then I remembered that she'd told the inquiry she had two names, 'Lauren Cameron' and 'Lauren Cashman'.

I put in 'Lauren' and 'Cashman' and . . . bingo!

There were quite a few stories with those words. The first one that grabbed me was dated November 1982. The headline was 'MAN BASHES BOY'. There were some other headlines: 'Tiny Jake on Life Support' and 'Jake Outrage: Mother Charged' and 'Little Boy Lost: Funeral for Little Jake', and according to NewsText, Lauren Cashman's name was in all of these stories. I jotted down the dates of the stories and went to the library, which is something I enjoy doing but don't do often enough. Old newspapers have context, they're better than Google. From the ads and the photographs, you can see how people looked and how they lived. You can see how a story was treated, too: did it get splashed all over the front page, or was it buried on page 10? Did they have a cartoon, a photograph, a commentary piece, as well as the news story?

As soon as I found the page with 'MAN BASHES BOY' across the front, I could see why Dad remembered Lauren. She was in the photograph on the front page, sitting with what seemed to be other members of her family – her brothers and sisters – and they all had this pale, haunted look about them. Also, this had been a big story, and Dad was one of the few reporters to actually get it in the paper the day after it happened. He'd stayed with it for a week. It seemed to have got people quite worked up.

I read through the copy: a little boy, Jacob Cashman, aged five, had been beaten to death on a housing estate west of Melbourne. In the first story, Jacob's mother was saying Jacob had been set upon by a man while walking home from the shops, but it turned out she made that up. I was actually surprised that Dad had printed that rubbish. It came out that she and the boyfriend had done it. She went to prison for manslaughter and, from what I could see, she died there, some ten years later. There was no record of what happened to him, and no clue as to what had happened to the other kids. Still, there was no doubt in my mind that the Lauren Cameron I'd seen at the Sound of Love inquest was the same Lauren Cashman in this story. It also seemed obvious to me that people would be interested in the fact that the aide for the 'Sound of Love' inquest had a tragic background of her own.

I looked at the photograph of her, and thought,

'Poor kid.' But, on the other hand, I thought, 'Good story,' and headed to my desk, with photocopies of the original articles under my arm. And then something really strange happened. The telephone rang and it was a guy saying, 'Did you write that story about Lauren Cashman? Because I'm her brother.'

I thought, 'This is too weird.'

He said, 'We've kind of lost touch and I'm looking for her.'

I didn't tell him that I'd already figured out for myself that Lauren had a family. I just thought, 'Well, that all fits. They would have been split up after the mother went to jail.' I didn't let on to the brother, though. Instead, I thought, 'How good is this? If I can get the brother on the scene, if we can get a reunion going, this will be great.'

I told the brother that Lauren was due back in the witness box and if he came down to the Coroner's Court he'd definitely see her there – I'd even point her out if he looked me up, and he promised he would. I took down his mobile phone number and alerted the photographer. 'We may have a bit of a scoop here,' I told him. 'Stick with me at the court today. Something might happen.' Little did I know! I went to court that day, ready to write the reunion story, when the legal team for the Boyce family got up and dropped a bombshell.

Lauren got into the witness stand. This was the day

after the 'Sound of Love' speech, remember, so the press gallery was packed with reporters all interested in what she might say on her second day in the box. The counsel assisting the Coroner, Mr Bateson, stood up and said, 'Miss Cameron, where were you the evening before your shift started?'

I couldn't immediately see the relevance of the question and my first thought was, 'Uh oh, don't tell me she was drunk? Maybe there's going to be a twist in the story.'

Lauren said, 'I was out.'

Bateson said, 'Out where? Out on the town? Where did you spend the evening?'

The hospital's lawyer, whose name I now forget, was going absolutely nuts, saying 'Objection', but it was overruled, and Bateson was allowed to continue. He said, 'Where were you, Miss Cameron?'

Lauren's face went red. She kept looking over at the hospital's barrister. Then she said, 'I was in a city hotel.'

I thought, 'In a city hotel. Not at a city hotel? What's this all this about?'

Bateson said, 'In a hotel . . . you mean a bar?'

A bar! So they were drunk. But Lauren said, 'No.'

Bateson said, 'Well then, where? In a restaurant?'

Again, Lauren said, 'No.'

I was thinking, 'Where are they going with this?'

The hospital's barrister was on his feet again. He knew what was coming. We in the media had no idea.

And then there it was, before us. *She'd been with Bass.* At the very moment that Mrs Boyce was in labour, when he really should have had his high-paid arse on the maternity ward, he'd been in the cot with an aide who later turned up to work alongside him! Excellent! Oh, I can see how it wasn't technically relevant to the inquest, that it probably had nothing to do with whether the baby lived or died, but still, that kind of thing, it just blows a case wide open. Lauren must have known it was coming – I mean, surely she knew it was going to come out? – but still, she looked absolutely horrified.

'You were with Stephen Bass in a hotel room, here in Sydney?' said Bateson. And then, quietly, he added, 'I take it his wife was not present?'

There was pandemonium, obviously. The Coroner had to call a recess. Lauren took off, out of the courtroom. I thought she'd head for the toilets. That's what witnesses normally do. They think they're safe in there but actually, it's always a bonus for us journos if they head to the loo, because once they're in there, there's only one way out, and we're there waiting for them. But she didn't go to the loo. She flew out of the courtroom and into the foyer and stood there, like a stunned mullet, looking this way and that, and then right into the face of a tall guy – a pale, freckly, *white-haired* guy, and I suppose I should have realised at the time it must have been the brother, but I was so caught up in what had just happened inside the court that I'd totally forgotten about Harley Cashman. She quickly took off again, and left him standing there, looking very confused.

The next day, the *Telegraph* had a headline that I won't forget for a while: 'Love Me Do!' They had all the scandalous details: Bass, a fifty-one-year-old married father, had been alone at a city hotel with the twenty-seven-year-old blonde nursing aide, while Elizabeth Boyce was labouring a baby with serious deformities who died in Bass's hands some hours later. It was a perfect story for the tabloids, the kind of thing everybody wants to read. We at the *Herald* wrote it up, too. Naturally, we all sent photographers to Lauren's house – you wouldn't believe how hard she was to find, living on the back of somebody else's property – but soon enough, the nature strip was packed with reporters and photographers. Lauren wouldn't come out, and the lady who lived in the main house kept chasing us off the lawn. My editor kept saying to me, 'We've got to get some quotes from her,' and I was saying, 'What am I supposed to do, break the door down?'

But I was thinking, 'Even if she doesn't come out, I still have the Barrett angle,' something nobody else had. I called my dad, brought him up-to-date, and told him he was quite right, she had been in the newspaper before, and rang off, so I could meet the deadline.

'Love Aide in Family Tragedy.' That was the headline

we put on the story. I wrote:

Lauren Cameron, the nurses' aide who was yester-day revealed to have been in a hotel-room tryst with specialist obstetrician Stephen Bass the night before the birth and death of Baby Boyce, has her own tragic family history.

Lauren's mother, Lisa Cashman, was in 1983 sentenced to 15 years prison for the manslaughter of Lauren's five-year-old brother, Jacob.

Mrs Cashman first told police that her son had been attacked by a man in the local schoolyard, a claim that later unravelled. The case made front-page headlines.

I went through the events that had occurred in the house on DeCastella Drive as best I could. There was a hint in one of the stories that was published at the time that the real details of the case would never be known. The judge had sealed everybody's testimony, so I had a few difficulties putting it all together, but I did manage to make the point that the Lauren who people had been reading about in the 'Sound of Love' inquest was the same Lauren who was on the front page of the *Sun* all those years ago.

Did I think about how Lauren might react to her history being re-told in the newspaper? Not really. The story about Jacob was a matter of public record. It had been reported at the time. We were hardly broadcasting a state secret. True, it was locked in the archives, and yeah, I guess she had changed her name, but she was the one who volunteered to the court that she'd once been somebody else. And anyway, I like to think that my story might have softened her image in the eyes of some people who thought she was just a home-wrecker.

Detective Senior Sergeant Brian Muggeridge

I never forgot the Cashman kids. Lauren, especially, had some kind of hold on me, and don't ask me how, but I knew – I just knew – I'd see her again one day. When I did, I saw her, like everyone did, on the front of the paper, under a headline that said 'Love Aide in Family Tragedy'. They had a photograph of her coming down the court staircase. She still had that hair. I was curious to hear what had happened to her. I knew that her mother had gone to prison, and had died before she could be released. The boyfriend had gone to prison, too, but I had no idea what had happened to him. Paroled, probably, and when that happens, you lose track of them until they commit some other crime. The kids had gone into care and become state wards, and the Department doesn't feel obliged to tell the cops what happens to them after that. You just hope you don't have to turn up ten years later and arrest them because they've gone off the rails.

About a year after Jacob died, a petition went around the Barrett Estate saying the house should be demolished. Nobody had been living there and the place had become an eyesore. There were rumours about bloodstains on the walls. All nonsense, but you can't stop that stuff going around. One group of people, still angry about what happened to Jake, I suppose, wanted to burn the place to the ground. They actually put that up as a proposal; they seriously thought they should be allowed to set fire to the joint, as an act of revenge or some sort of catharsis. The fire brigade said, 'Look, there is just no way we are allowing people to set fire to a house on a suburban street, with neighbours on both sides, so just forget about it.'

That didn't put people off, though. The house mysteriously caught fire one night. Kids had been through the place, ripping out the oven and anything else they thought they could use. The fire fighters put out the fire and boarded up the windows and nailed up the front door, and, boy, did it look like crap then. The house had always slumped, and now it was blackened and the windows were bare, and people really started to complain. It was a prime target for local teenagers, who would dare each other to break in there. Parents didn't help matters much. They used to tell kids that the place was haunted.

After about five years, which is around as long as it takes the Department of Housing in Victoria to do anything these days, they came in and replaced the windows and painted the frames and dragged out the burnt mattresses. They said they were going to put more tenants in there! I could hardly believe it. The first family that arrived were Somali. They came straight from the refugee camp in Kenya to DeCastella Drive! There were nine of them, including six children and a cousin, and it was about four weeks before neighbours got them to understand what happened in that house. They fled. A lot of those refugees are Christian, but some of them have the old black-magic beliefs and they said they couldn't stand it. They heard noises, and they were sure the soul of the child who died had remained in the house.

The place stayed empty for a while after that, but then the Department noticed somebody was tapping into the power grid from there. They sent us to investigate, and when we knocked down the front door we found every room filled with hydroponics and marijuana plants. They were growing in rows of pots in the kitchen, the lounge, even in the bath. We cleaned the place out again, boarded it up once more, and now we keep it on our rounds, which means we drive by occasionally to check on it and make sure nobody moves in there without permission.

I told the kids at the local schools, 'You stay away from that house on DeCastella Drive. It's been set fire to, and it's not safe.' I'm not sure they took any notice. To them, it was haunted, and what kid doesn't want to believe in a haunted house?

Truth be told I've heard the noises in there, too. I go in from time to time. I tell myself it's to make sure squatters haven't moved in, but yeah, I mostly just stand there and look around and maybe remember a few things. The place creaks and moans. Obviously, it's not a ghost. It's the timber in the frame of the house. It stretches and cools, and that makes a noise. There's wagtails in the roof, too. I've seen them twisting on the lawn, and they've got into the eaves and they make a racket. That's what people hear, not ghosts. There's no ghosts, not real ones, anyway.

Lauren Cashman

I woke before dawn, and why wouldn't I? I was in a
strange bed with a strange man beside me. I was diso-
riented. Sitting up in the dark, I thought, 'Where am I
again? Where is this bed? Where is this room, and how
does it fit into my life?'

Then I remembered. I was in a queen-size bed in the
Gundagai Motel on the banks of the Murrumbidgee
River, and the breathing body lying next to mine wasn't
that of a stranger: it was my brother, Harley.

He was stretching his whole body, pointing his big
toes out and putting his arms – or rather his arm, and
the other stumpy thing – over his head and grunting.

My instinct was to nestle down and spoon against
him, but he broke his pose and fished around the floor
for a cigarette.

'Want one?' he asked, and I said, 'I told you, I'm giving up.'

'I noticed that,' he said, handing me the packet, and I took one.

We'd eaten a family-size pizza the night before, but Harley said he was hungry.

'You want breakfast?' he asked, and I said, 'Sure.'

He told me he'd take me to his favourite place, the place he always stopped at on the road to Melbourne, and then we'd go to 'Mum's'.

'She's probably already got the jug on,' he said.

Did he really think this was a good idea? To just bowl up at his mum's place and expect her to be pleased to see me?

He seemed to think it would be fine. He said, 'Mate, we've been expecting you for a while.' He was trying to put me at ease. 'I called her. She's looking forward to meeting you.'

I didn't believe that. I swung my legs over the edge of the bed and went into the bathroom. I must have been nervous because I remember I found it hard to open the plastic packet that the white soap came in. I dropped the face washer by my feet and let water pool around my ankles. I was thinking to myself, 'How is this going to go?'

The café wasn't far from the motel – maybe half a kilometre. Harley drove. He seemed pretty excited.

'Mum and Tony used to take me here when I was a kid,' he said. 'We'd get yabbies from the Murrumbidgee, and come here for milkshakes. And they taught me that song . . .'

He started to sing, 'There's a track winding back, down the old forgotten shack –'

I said, 'It's an old-*fashioned* shack.'

He continued, 'Along the . . . road to . . . Gunda . . . gai!'

The café was called the Niagara . It had curved glass windows, and silver metal lettering – N I A G A R A – above the counter and I remember thinking, 'What is this? Some 50s-style milk bar from *Happy Days*?' It had a vinyl booth and the walls were papered with cuttings from newspapers. The stories were all about an Australian prime minister, John Curtin, who had stopped at the Niagara one night in 1942, in the middle of the Second World War. He had been en route from Canberra to Melbourne and, according to the clippings, he'd knocked on the door. The owner told whoever was knocking to go away, but then he saw Curtin through the glass door and let him in, and made him steak and eggs at a table in the kitchen.

We ordered steak and eggs, too. A waitress brought some coffee.

Harley said, 'You want me to get a newspaper?'

Did I want him to get a newspaper? He and I both knew they'd be filled with stories from the inquest. Did I want to read whatever was now being said about me – the 'Love Aide' – in the newspaper?

No.

But then, Yes.

I couldn't decide, so I didn't say anything. Harley said, 'Okay, look, I'll get one, and if it's real bad, I won't tell you what it says.' The minute he was gone, I found myself thinking, 'Come back.' And then he was back, and sliding into the seat, saying, 'I guess you're not important enough to make the front page any more.' He turned a few pages, then said, 'Here we are.'

There was a photograph of me – upside down from where I was sitting, coming down the steps of the court. There was a photograph of Stephen, too, the one from the hospital's website. The headline said 'Bass Admits Affair'.

Harley said, 'You want me to read it?'

I said. 'Just give me the short version.'

He cleared his throat and began to read. *'Top obstetrician Stephen Bass last night released a statement acknowledging a sexual relationship with the so-called Love Aide, Lauren Cameron.*

Mr Bass, who is married with adult children, said his relationship with Lauren Cameron, also known as Lauren Cashman, was a private matter and he would not comment further.'

To myself, I thought, 'Did he say "relationship", I hope he said "relationship".'

Harley went on, '*Ms Cameron* – that would be you, mate – *has this week been giving evidence at the inquest into the death of Baby Boyce.* And that's it. That's all it says. The rest is just blah, blah, blah, stuff we already know.'

I wanted to ask, 'Do you think it means anything that he says we have a relationship,' but I knew it would sound pathetic. Harley said, 'What a shithead your bloke turned out to be. There's not even an apology to the lady who lost her baby.'

Harley stirred his coffee and studied the picture of Stephen. He said, 'What I really don't get is why you'd want to go with such an *old man*.'

I said, 'Fifty-one is not old.'

He said, 'It's ancient, mate. Seriously, look at this geezer. He's a pensioner. What did you see in him?'

What did I see in him? Solidity. Maturity. Respectability. I wanted him to marry me, and transfer to me some of the stability with which he lived his life. But when I told Harley this, he spluttered into his coffee. 'Mate,' he said, 'if you were looking for a *husband*, probably would have been best to find one that didn't already have a *wife*. All this time you're thinking he's Sir Galahad, does it occur to you that he's *married*? Can you imagine the conversation they're having right now?'

I could imagine it. In Stephen's version of events, I'd be the whore and he'd be the one who'd been *seduced*.

I wanted to think about something else. I asked Harley, 'Have you ever done it with a married woman?'

Harley said, 'Oh yes.'

'Yes?'

Harley said, 'I may *seem* perfect, but it ain't so, Lauren.'

I said, 'Did you feel guilty?'

Harley said, 'No. I felt *afraid*, especially when one of them told me her old man kept guns.

'But seriously,' he said. 'What's the deal with this guy? I just don't get why you'd be hung up on this dude. He's, like, old, married and an arsehole, and you're my sister, but, hell, you're a hottie. I don't mind telling you that. And you're hangin' out with a dude who was born, like, the same year as, I don't know, our *dad*.'

I said, 'Well, maybe I just liked the fact that he seemed to like me.'

Harley said, 'Oh, man, he *liked* you. I bet he jerked off nine nights in ten, liking you. What I want to know is, can this bloke even *do* it, at fifty?'

I was excused from answering because the waitress came and cleared our plates. She said, 'Would you like more coffee?' I looked at her apron, and at the Jiffies on her feet, and thought of myself waiting tables not so many years ago. I said, 'Yes please.'

Waiting for her to return with the coffee pot, I folded one of the napkins into a paper version of the Sydney Opera House, a trick I learnt from Pop. Harley went back to the newspaper.

'There's another story,' he said. 'You want me to read it?'

I shrugged.

He read aloud. 'Love Aide in Family Tragedy.'

I must admit, it didn't immediately occur to me what those words meant. I was thinking about Stephen, not about Jake. Harley was quiet for a moment, then he said, 'It's actually about Jake,' and he started to read out the main points. '*Lauren Cameron is Lauren Cashman, whose brother, Jacob Cashman, died in a house on DeCastella Drive on the Barrett Estate in November 1982.*'

He glanced up at me and must have seen my expression. 'That's all it really says,' he said. 'It's like somebody has joined the dots, and the rest is blah, blah, from the inquest.'

I remembered how close I'd been to talking to Stephen about DeCastella Drive. Had things gone better in the hotel room, had his pager not gone off, had the baby not died, I might have raised it with him. It would have been a mistake. Probably he wouldn't have cared less. But Harley would care. I said, 'How much do you remember about that house, Harley?'

He said, 'Not much. Nothing, actually.'

I said, 'Do you know what happened that night, with Jake?'

He said, 'What do you mean? Of course I know.'

I said, 'Do you know for sure, or do you just know what people told you?'

The way Harley looked at me then, I'll never forget it. He looked right into my eyes and said, 'Is there a difference?'

He went out to the car. I fixed up the bill. Outside, I found him standing with his backside to the ute, grinding a cigarette into the dirt. I said, 'That'll go into the river system, you know.' He said, 'Are you a hippy? You might think you're a hippy, but wait until you meet Mum.'

Not for the first time, I thought, '*Your* mum.'

We got back into the car, and rode in silence for a while. I pulled a cap down over my eyes and dozed in the morning sunshine that was pouring through the windscreen. When I woke, Harley told me that I'd just missed a horse that had the 'biggest donger ever'.

'I should have taken a photograph,' he said.

I said, 'Right. And if you sent something like that to get processed, do you think you might get yourself arrested?'

'Mate,' he said. 'It's a digital camera. I'd email it around. In fact, mate, give me the email address of your boyfriend and I'll send it to him. Tell him you've got a new bloke.'

Was this, I wondered, how siblings spoke to each other? Did they wind each other up like this and then laugh it off? Harley behaved like nothing he ever said could cause me any offence – I wouldn't get angry, or upset – and he was right. But I wasn't so sure I could do the same.

Detective Senior Sergeant Brian Muggeridge

I wasn't surprised – not at all surprised – to hear that Lauren was having it off with an old guy. In my opinion, if you raise a kid without a father figure they'll grow up looking for one. It was unfortunate that it ended up all over the newspapers, but still, Lauren had made something of herself and I was pleased about that. I always got the feeling that Lauren was basically a good kid.

I'd heard rumours that one of the other Cashmans, the baby, Hayley, made a real pig's ear of her life after she left DeCastella Drive. You'd think because she was the youngest, and the least involved, she'd have the fewest problems, but I guess you never can tell how kids will turn out. People on Barrett couldn't stop talking about Lauren after the brother was killed. There was a lot of gossip about her, made worse by the fact that the Department let the house go to ruin. When you've got a house like that in town, falling down, the stories get more absurd as the years go on. I'd heard people saying, 'The kids that lived there were raised in a cult. They all had different fathers and their mother dyed their hair so they'd all look the same.'

I told them they were being ridiculous.

I'd heard people saying, 'There was a girl who lived there who was disturbed. She did something to her brother and the mum took the rap.'

Whenever people told me that, I'd say, 'People who don't know the facts should keep their big mouths shut.'

I do know the facts. I know what happened in that house. I've known it for years. Was Lauren involved? Yes, she was. People were right about that. She was involved, and when she was a kid it made sense to us adults – the cops, the judge, the social workers – to keep that fact to ourselves. You might think that's wrong, but unless you've got all the facts, I don't think you can really comment. It took us enough time to piece it all together. It's not an easy story to tell. The version I've settled on is Lauren's. She was the one who first coughed it up, that long afternoon after Jake died.

Remember when Lauren ran into her mother in the hall of the Barrett cop shop? I could see that something was wrong. She didn't run into her mother's arms. They both took a step back.

So, after Lauren got back to her room I popped in to have a quick chat with her. I knew I couldn't ask her specific questions on the record yet, but I wanted to know what was going through her head, and why she reacted to her mother like that.

The social worker who had taken Lauren into the hall – by that time, we had what seemed like one social worker in every room – was angry and wanted to know how Lauren had been able to run into her mum like that, and why she wasn't told that Lisa was in the same part of the cop shop. I explained to her that it was an accident, but she looked ropeable.

Lauren, on the other hand, didn't look angry at all. When I asked her if she was okay she just nodded, yes, and then said, 'Can I tell you something?' I asked her if it was about Jacob and she nodded again, and I could see she was keen to get out whatever was bugging her. I mean, I've got kids, and I've seen them all churned up when they've got something inside, and they just can't settle until it's out.

The way I've pieced it together, from Lauren's account and then later Lisa and Peter's versions, the day had started much like any other. Jacob had gone off to school in the morning with Lauren. The other two – Hayley and Harley – stayed home. They weren't old enough for school.

The boyfriend, Peter, wasn't working. He stayed in on the couch all day pulling cones. When Jacob and

Lauren came in after school they mucked around a bit. Lisa was trying to fix dinner. Peter was still sitting around getting stoned. The kids started making a racket so Lisa sent the kids down to their rooms, where they banged around.

Then, from what I understand, it went quiet. That probably didn't bother Peter too much, but Lisa started calling out, 'Come and get your bloody tea!' When she got no response she went down the hall and flung open the door to Jake's room. There was Jake with his pants down, waving his little pecker around, and Hayley was stripped out of her nappy. From what I understand, they were having a bit of a look at each other.

Lisa said something like, 'What the hell is going on here?' and Jake said, 'I wasn't doing nothing!', but Harley pointed and said, 'Jake got his pecker out!'

It was at that point that Peter came to see what the fuss was about. When he saw Jake with his pants down and Hayley on the floor with no pants on, he went ballistic. He said to Lisa, 'This isn't the first time he's done this. I've seen this before. I've seen him the other day, playing with his sister in a way that's not right.'

Now, I don't discount the possibility that Jake was having a good look at Hayley. It's entirely possible. You put little kids together, from time to time they might strip down, they might have a look, it's a one-off thing normally, and no harm done. So maybe Jake did have a bit of a squizz at his sister, a bit of: you show me yours, I'll show you mine. But at the end of the day, what does it matter? It's not important. What happened next, that's what's important.

In his statement, Peter said he told Lisa he'd handle it. 'You've got to show him it's wrong,' he said. 'You've got to stop it now or else he'll grow up abusing kids, and don't ask me how I know it, but I know it. You let me take care of it.'

Jacob, remember, was five.

Peter told us he gave Jake a quick kick up the rear and Jake began to cry, so he picked him up and flung him against his bed. He shooed the other kids out and shut Jake in his bedroom. Then he went back to the lounge room, where Lisa was putting a nappy back on Hayley.

Jake kept calling out, 'I didn't do nothing. It weren't me. Why do I gotta stay in here?'

This must have gone on for a while. Lisa told us she got sick of the hollering. She walked down the hall with Peter, and together, they confronted Jake in his room, telling him to shut up and what did he think he was doing, and so on. Alcohol was being consumed. Peter was going back and forward to the kitchen, getting himself beers. Lisa was on the rum and cola, and, of course, they'd been on the cones all day.

I don't know how long the harassment went on, but after a bit Lisa and Peter gave it up and went back to the lounge room to watch TV. Lauren told us that Jake was supposed to stay in his room, but he crept down the hall and popped his head in the lounge, wanting to know if he could come out now.

Lisa said she leapt off the couch and chased him down the hall, but Jacob beat her to the bedroom and shut himself in.

Lauren was a good kid. She put an ear to the door and heard her brother crying. She knocked on the door and said, 'Jake, it's me,' and he opened up for her. He was sitting on the bed, saying, 'It's not fair. I didn't do nothing.' And then he said, 'I hate this house. I'm gonna run away.'

Well, Lauren did what kids will do. She bolted into the lounge room, saying, 'Jacob's going to run away!'

We got two versions of what happened next and, I warn you, neither makes pleasant reading.

Peter told us, 'Lisa loses it. She runs down the hall and she's completely off her nut, just completely out of control. What you gotta remember is I don't know this chick very well, right. I've been in that house, like, six weeks. I mean, shit, mate, she's just out of control with those kids.'

He said, 'She slammed the door. I was stuck on the outside. I couldn't even guess what was goin' on. All I could hear was the bloody shoutin'. I pushed the door open. Jacob was just, like, crouched on the floor.

'Harley and Lauren were up on the bunk. They were, like, crouched together, on the top bunk.'

He said, 'Jake was crawling around. It was like he was blind, or close to it. He was crawlin' around in circles.

'Lisa was near the window. The other kids were shoutin' at Jacob from up the top bunk, just shoutin' and hollerin'. It was like a poltergeist or whatever had got into 'em, and Lisa was eggin' 'em on, saying, *Jump on him, jump on him, jump on him.*

'The next thing I saw, Lauren was coming down off the top bunk, and landing on her brother's skull.'

Now, that wasn't quite how Lisa told it. She coughed up a slightly different story. She told us that she'd had enough of Jake. 'He was sookin' and complainin' and carryin' on, and I couldn't stand it no more, so I went out back to have a ciggie,' she said.

'I come inside, and Peter, that arsehole, has gone back into Jake's room and he's taken the other kids in there with him and the door was shut, and I couldn't see nothin'. I could just hear bangin'.

She was sitting opposite me at the interview table when she told me this. Her face, I'll never forget it, was the face of somebody who felt so hard done by.

'I got the door open and Jake was on the floor,' she said. 'The kids were in there, all the kids, all crowded around Jake, and he was carrying on, saying, 'I didn't want to look!' Peter was growing more enraged. He reached over and stripped the nappy off Hayley – it was one of those Huggies ones – and it was all heavy and foul and stinking, and he started stripping Jake's shorts off and trying to shove him into the dirty nappy. He was shouting, 'You want to act like a baby, you can dress like a baby.'

Jake was protesting, 'I'm not a baby!' Peter replied, 'Then why are you always sooking and crying like a baby?' He forced the nappy onto Jake, saying to the other kids, 'Come and have a look at your new baby brother.'

Lisa told us that *she* ordered the other kids – not Hayley, because she was too small, but Harley and Lauren – to get up onto the top bunk, to get them out of the way. Like Peter, she said Jacob had adopted the foetal position on the floor, and was circling around on his side, like a dog trying to escape a beating.

Lisa told us, 'Peter was out of control. I told the other kids, "Get up on the bunk, get out of the way."'

Lauren remembered it differently. She told us that she'd climbed on to the top bunk, with Harley, of her own accord.

'We wanted to get away,' she said. 'We were scared.'

She told us they'd cowered together, near the ceiling, but the mother looked up and saw them there, and said, 'Jump, Lauren! Jump! Jump on him!'

I've tried to imagine what that must have been like for Lauren. She was six years old. She said she felt her eyes bulging and her head throbbing and all she could hear was the chanting, '*Jump on him, jump down, jump on him, jump down.*'

And she leapt.

Lauren didn't know how long Jake lay on the floor after she leapt. She said he'd stopped moving. He'd stopped trying to find a safe place. He'd stopped crying, and everybody went quiet. Lauren told us that she was praying, 'Come on Jake! Wake up!' and her mum was cursing and Peter was, too. And yes, they tried to bring Jake around by putting him in the bathtub.

It was Peter who told us that. He said, 'I wanted to call an ambulance, but Lisa was freakin' out. She was saying, "They'll take the kids off me!" So I helped her put him in the bath and run the water on him, but he didn't come round.

'I said to Lisa, you're a dumb moll. Look at him, he's out cold. We've got to get help. The kids were just carryin' on so much. We took Jake out of the bath and put him in dry clothes on the lounge-room floor.'

And, of course, we knew that Lisa did call the ambulance. She called triple-O and said, 'My kid's been bashed.'

Now, I gather that Lauren has formed the opinion, in her own mind, that she caused Jake's death by jumping off that bunk. I want to tell you: I'm not so sure about that. Yes, Jake had a dent in the head, but that could just as well have come from one of the adults shoving him in that damn bath. Maybe he took a kick in the head from Peter or even from Lisa, that they aren't owning up to. We don't know. Nobody knows. The point is, Jake died at the hands of his mother and her boyfriend, and I defy anybody to say different. And that's why it made no sense to make the whole thing about Lauren jumping off the bunk public. What would have been the point? She wasn't to blame. The terror she felt that day, I don't want to think about it. So yes, we told the judge the whole story, but not the press, and I'm only guessing that more than a few of the social workers knew about it, because before long, a version of what happened was doing the rounds. But the end result was, Lisa went away for fifteen years; and Peter went away, too.

I would have liked for the parents to have got a bit more punishment, because in my opinion, whichever one of them was telling the story that was closest to the truth, both were monsters, and Lauren was just a kid. Our hope for her – my hope, anyway – was that she'd either forget it or put it behind her. In any case I wanted her to get on with her life, but I see now that's a bit hard to do, when you're carrying stuff like that around.

Lauren Cashman

If Harley had asked me that day in the Niagara what I remembered about what happened to Jake, I would have told him, 'I don't remember much.' Because that's true: I don't remember much.

I remember that Jake had always been a good boy. It was Harley who was a handful. Harley had got into scraps and he liked to carry on. Harley fell out of trees and pulled stuff out of cupboards and drew on the walls. Jake was not like that. When he got smacked it was for no reason and even then, he wouldn't cry out. He'd sulk a bit. He'd object to the injustice of it, but he didn't cry out.

We were pretty close. Sometimes, at night, if we'd been whacked around the head for something or other, he'd sneak down from his bunk and come into my room and we'd tickle each other, on the bottom of the feet. We'd try not to laugh. We knew if we got caught there'd be hell to pay.

We weren't supposed to lie, either, except when Mum told us to, so I think that Jake was telling the truth when he said he hadn't touched Hayley, not that it helped him.

She told me to lie that day. She told me to lie to the police and to lie to the social worker and to lie in court. I used to wonder whether she did that to protect me, but I've got to be realistic. When I finally broke down and told police the truth she didn't go crazy trying to shield me from my own admissions. She went nuts about the fact that I'd dobbed on her. Never once did I hear from anyone that she'd said, 'Look, Lauren had nothing to do with this. Okay, it wasn't a stranger, it was me, or it was him, but it wasn't her.' I thought maybe, before she died, there would be a letter, a note, something, because of course we never said a word to each other after that day with the police on Barrett, but there was nothing.

I've asked myself why I broke down that day, why I blabbed, and I think the closest I can get to an explanation is that I wasn't frightened of telling the truth. That came later, with people I didn't know that well, but there comes a point when you just can't lie any more, not to people you love, and I suppose I reached that point with myself, and in the car with Harley, that day we drove out to his mum's place in Exford.

We were maybe an hour from her door. I took a breath. I said, 'Harley, I've got to tell you something.'

He said, 'You don't have to say anythin'.'

I said, 'I do. I have to tell you this. I jumped, Harley. I jumped off the bunk.'

I waited for him to steer off the road, but he didn't. He just didn't, and I suppose there was a minute there when I thought, 'He hasn't heard me. I'm going to have to say it again,' but he'd heard me. He said, 'I know.'

I said, 'You do?'

He said, 'Yeah.'

I said, 'Do you know everything?'

He said, 'I reckon I do. They went ballistic because Jake was supposedly touching up Hayley, yeah? But I reckon that's not right.'

I said, 'I don't know whether he did or not. I don't think it's right, either.'

Harley said, 'He was what, five?'

I said, 'Five.'

He said, 'So they went nuts and they had us going crazy, too. This isn't news to me.'

I said, 'How do you know?'

He said, 'How do *you* know?'

I said, 'I was older.'

He said, 'Yeah, but we were both just kids.'

It was such a relief to hear those words: *We were both just kids.*

We didn't talk much after that. We smoked cigarettes.

We made small comments about the things we saw out the windows. We listened to the radio. Freeway turned into suburban road, and then into the gravel outside his mum's place. There was a long moment of silence in the car, and then Harley said, 'Well, we're home.'

From my seat behind the dirty windscreen, I could see what Harley couldn't: his mother was standing behind the screen door waiting for us to move. Harley went to open his door. Ruby came out on the porch, leaving the door swinging behind her. She had one hand on a walking stick. She was wearing some kind of robe.

Looking at her, I didn't feel anything. I just thought, 'So that's the woman who raised my brother.' I tried to conjure up some emotion about that, but there was none.

She took a few steps across the porch and said, 'Hey, honey.'

Harley had got out of his side of the car. He said, 'Hey, honey.' This 'honey' business is a joke between them. She calls him honey; he calls her honey; they both called Tony honey.

I looked over the roof of the car.

'You must be Lauren,' she said.

I said, 'Hello, Mrs Porter.'

What was she thinking, at that moment? I didn't know how much she'd read in the newspapers. Harley had told me that she wouldn't give 'a rat's arse' about the affair with Bass but that she'd be terribly concerned about Baby Boyce because she herself lived with a disability. She'd want to know what I thought about whether or not the child would have lived or died.

Harley was two steps ahead of me, on his way up to the porch, but Ruby wasn't looking at him. She was looking at me. I walked toward her. She dropped her cane. I went to shake her hand, but she gathered me into a bosom that smelled of tobacco. I wasn't used to being that close to people. I didn't like it at all. 'Lauren,' she said. 'The long-lost Lauren Cashman.'

We curled like kittens into the Papysan chairs. We talked a bit. We had some kind of lentil dish for tea and we drank Bacardi. It wasn't long before I found that I was no longer sitting upright and trying to be polite. Ruby kicked off her shoes and when Tony came in he gave me a big bear hug and undid the buttons at the centre of his shirt. Harley put his silicon arm on the coffee table, upright, and put a cigarette between the fingers.

At some point, I began to have fun. The evening wore on. I must have been tired and maybe I even nodded off for a moment, because I felt Tony tucking a quilt around my chair. Part of me wanted to feign sleep, so I could hear what they might say about me when they thought I wasn't listening, but sleep came, and apparently it was only when Harley had enough of my snoring that he kicked my ankle and escorted me to my room.

I wanted to sleep in the room that had been his as

a child, but he told me to bugger off and put me in the spare room instead.

I woke to the sound of Ruby in the kitchen, hobbling between the wooden benches.

I said, 'Good morning, Mrs Porter.'

She said, 'For the love of God, Lauren. The three-years-olds at the childcare centre call me Ruby, so I don't see why you don't.'

She is Ruby to me now, of course, and I suppose I'd have to say that she's also . . . well, not family, but one of my dear friends. Harley is my brother. He's also my flatmate. We live together on Sydney's northern beaches. I'm no longer an aide, I'm at nurse's college. Harley lets me live rent-free.

We don't see much of Hayley. There's no animosity between us. It's just that whenever we go to Melbourne she says she can't fit us in, or see us for long. I went through the process of telling her what I remembered about DeCastella Drive, but I'm not sure what any of it means to her. All she said was, 'I don't remember Jake,' and then, 'I don't want to talk about it with Jezeray around.'

As for my relationship with Jacob, well, in the week I spent at Exford I spoke to Ruby about him. She wanted me to do so from the comfort of her expansive lap, with my head buried against her soft bosom, but I kept my distance and hid myself behind a swirl of cigarette smoke. She listened and said things like,

'Everything happens for a reason,' and 'You must have been so afraid.'

I sobbed so hard that I felt I had to apologise to her the next morning, but she dismissed my concerns with a wave of the spatula and went on making pancakes.

After that, I went through a stage where I had to say Jacob's name out loud, to hear how it sounded. I suppose it's part of the process of owning something new, to acknowledge that there was a little boy whose name was Jacob Cashman and, however much I wish it were otherwise, the last contact I had with him was on the floor in his bedroom in DeCastella Drive, with him curled into the foetal position, desperately trying to avoid a blow from above. That's the way it is.

Now, when people ask me whether I've got any siblings, I no longer say no, but nor do I say, 'I had two brothers but one is deceased,' the way some people do. I just say, 'Yes, I do.'

I'm Harley's sister. I'm Jacob's sister too, obviously, but the difference is, Harley's in my life and, I hope, my future; Jacob's in my past, and in my bones.

Would it be right to say that I miss him? Yes, it would. It would also be right to say that there are some things I wish I knew.

Did I try to comfort him, as he lay curled on the floor that day? I don't know.

Did I say anything to him, before the paramedics came to take him away? I don't know.

Did I whisper to him, 'Please, Jacob, don't die?'

I don't know.

Does he know how much I wished he'd lived? I don't know.

I talked to Ruby about whether we should find where Jake is buried. I had this idea that maybe I could talk to him, through the soil, and perhaps ask for his forgiveness, but she said, 'You don't need to visit Jacob's grave to speak to Jacob. If you want to talk to him, Lauren, you just go ahead and speak.'

So I do. Late at night, when I'm alone, I say, 'Jacob, I'm sorry.'

I'm sorry, I'm sorry, I'm sorry, I'm sorry.

I say it with such fervour that sometimes I'm sure that he can hear me. I say it so desperately that sometimes I'm sure that I can will him back to life. But Jacob is gone. He's long been gone. He's also what those of us who are left behind are not, and will never be: he's an innocent soul and he's completely at peace.